See the Fire

Heather Chase FBI Series
Book 5

A.W. Kaylen

Books by A.W. Kaylen:

Heather Chase FBI Series:

Dirt Dealers – Prequel – Free Download
Silent Witness – Book 1
Frozen Justice – Book 2
Chasing Dragons – Book 3
Hunting C-60 – Book 4
See the Fire – Book 5
Invisible Criminals – Book 6
Sleeping Secrets – Book 7 – Coming Soon

Table of Contents

Chapter 1

New York was on fire. Maybe it always had been. Maybe the only difference to this building screaming up in a whirling golden flame was that they couldn't shut their eyes to it anymore. There it was, out in the open, set ablaze in the public eye.

This wasn't your everyday kitchen fire. This was arson, no doubt about it. The fire plunged out from the inside and crawled down the surface of the Federal Records & Accounts building in a long arcing curve. The curve tracing a path from the top to its base, spelling out a giant letter 'C.'

Heather Chase stood there basking in that blaze, mesmerized by its infinite power; she lent her face to the smoldering heat warming her like the rays of a violent and dangerous sun. She knew it had begun again, this fight that threatened to escalate to full-blown war. She didn't waste time fighting the truth, because she knew that nothing from now on would be as obvious or easy as this. Someone had learned to control the fire in this town. The C had. And that made them capable of anything.

The C. That's what they called themselves now, the organization wreaking crime across the city in a series of bizarre and senseless acts. Word on the street was they were the remnant elements of C-60, the terrorist group Chase herself had helped put away; the group that the Bureau and the NYPD had pulled out every stop to take down. That Chase had risked her life for. Yet not long after they'd taken down their leader, the crime wave started all over again.

After more than a month of seemingly random media-related crimes, they'd upped the ante. They'd started writing their name in fire.

As they finally damped down the blaze, Chase approached an exhausted firefighter in a charred yellow fire-retardant jacket sitting on the back of his truck.

"I'm Special Agent Chase, FBI. I need to enter that building."

"Don't bother," the firefighter said, his face eclipsed by a layer of soot. He was breathing heavily and his extreme fatigue shone through his bloodshot eyes. "Nothing was preserved on the floor where the fire was set. They used some kind of petroleum jelly—the sprinklers couldn't put it out."

"I don't understand," Chase said. "Wouldn't such important documents have been kept in fireproof storage units?"

"Right—the thing is, the units themselves malfunctioned."

"They—malfunctioned? Is that normal?"

The firefighter shrugged absently and looked at her with yellowing eyes through a mask of ash. He'd just walked through fire; soon it would be Chase's turn to do the same. But she couldn't feel what lay ahead this time. Her mind felt fuzzy, clouded in the same smoke that wafted up from the broken husk of the Federal Records building. Everything was concealed behind that thick suffocating gauze. She couldn't feel what this firefighter felt, couldn't see what he saw. What she did feel was off her game. And she'd been that way for a while now.

She'd been that way since they went after Bucky, the leader of C-60. Although Bucky is dead now, his demise didn't bring closure or conclusion—all it did was open more mysteries to contend with.

The first mystery was that of Bucky himself: Who was he? Everything had pointed to him being an ex-participant in a series of unethical clinical trials conducted by the now-deceased Professor Sherman of NYU. Except that upon scouring through all available records, there was no trace of Bucky ever having existed in the system. They hadn't been able to get a lock on his prints or dental records. 'Bucky' had clearly been a fake name—short for Buckminster, the inventor of the compound C-60 which Bucky had figured out how to weaponize.

Back again in a circle to C-60. Who were they? In the mad dash to prevent Bucky's plan to cause anarchy, Chase hadn't really stopped to think about it: Who even were the others involved in C-60? How many of them existed? The Bureau had discovered two bases supposedly belonging to them— the abandoned camp of dome structures hidden in Wake Forest, and the single large dome situated outside Poughkeepsie. The domes created in the geodesic shape of the C-60 molecule: Bucky again. It all came back around, all seemed connected, yet nothing connected at all.

The fact of the matter was, there was no trace of anyone besides Bucky being in the 'group' that was C-60. Because Bucky had exploited various delivery services to launch his attacks, there had been no one actually connected to him. And as for the 'evidence' of other people living in his vicinity in the two bases—that could have been faked too. They hadn't arrested a single other person. They hadn't *seen* anyone else. The only other witness they had was a mental patient in Bellevue named Elliot who later was revealed to have a history of confabulation. Elliot himself confessed to having lied about everything.

At the time Chase had been glad for that—she thought if it all began and ended with Bucky then his death would be the end of it. It hadn't been. This new group came out of the woodwork calling themselves *the C*, and they'd already managed to hijack two streaming services and one local TV station and made them play their propaganda message. And now they'd started this game of fire graffiti.

Finding no luck with the tired firefighter, Chase reluctantly hovered by the NYPD. No one she knew was around, which came as a relief. She wasn't in the mood for their chit-chat.

"Agent Chase, FBI," she said, holding her badge. The cops there barely glanced at it, just gave her a sour look.

They were uniforms there to take the basic facts and get out of there. Helping the feds was above their pay grade. Cop think.

"What's the situation?" She asked one of them—a short guy with his holster belt hanging a touch low. A round face and beady cop eyes peered back at her blankly. She elaborated. "Did everyone get out alright?" Blank face. "The building, Officer. Did everyone get out of the building?"

"Evacuation went uh—smoothly. On account of it being so early, not many were around. No serious injuries—we got one or two slight burns, ain't that right Sarge?" He turned around to a flat, pale-faced cop in the back who barely grunted an affirmative.

"That's good," Chase said. "Then no one was in the room that went up either."

"That *blew* up, you mean, agent."

"It didn't blow up—from what I understand, gasoline jelly was used to start the fire."

"Potato, potahto," said the cop. "The dumb scumbags still freakin' ripped the place. A federal building no less. Must have some kinda death wish, eh?"

"You'd think," Chase said.

"What's that supposed to mean?"

"I'm not too clear on their motives, Officer. Not yet."

"Yeah. Course not. They're crazy sons of bitches is why. Just want to burn everything to the freaking ground. I hope you feebs round them all up and lay 'em on the chopping block as an example. Then maybe this town will stop going so gaga."

"I'll keep your suggestion in mind. If you want to expedite our investigation, you could start by telling me something. Did your men find anything in the wreckage?"

"We don't got diddle," 'Sarge' said. "We're canvassing the area now but as far as the building itself," he gestured to the crumbling, smoking husk before them. "Zilcho."

"Security tapes?"

"All fuzzed out," the sarge said. "Some kinda malfunction."

"Seems to be a lot of that going around. What about the C?" Chase said.

"What about them? Sure they probably did it. It's got their name written all over it." The sarge grinned. He was being blasé about the whole affair—to him, it was just a necessary fact, another thing to write down before he went to Dunkin Donuts and ordered a box of a dozen glazed.

"Not the group," Chase said, holding back her frustration. "I mean the letter itself. On the face of the building."

"Ah, that. Yeah. They used a kind of flammable paint. Same MO as the other buildings, right?"

"Same MO," Chase said.

An awkward silence passed between the three of them. Chase felt herself desperately trying to get a read on these cops—she generally didn't have to try so hard to tell what someone was thinking. It wasn't that she'd only just met them—she just felt trapped in thick brain fog. The smoke rushed into her airwaves and she could feel the toxic air enter her bloodstream. A pressure was forming in her head, the beginnings of a real doozy of a headache...

"I heard that the files up there weren't protected properly," Chase heard herself ask.

"Oh yeah," the officer said. "It all went up. Whoosh. There'll be hell to pay to some poor schmuck up the ladder. Probably didn't close the cabinet properly or some such." The cop scratched his face absently. He couldn't give less of a shit if he tried.

"Didn't close the cabinet. Right. What was the nature of those files, any idea?"

"Beats the hell outta me. Some official government crapola. You're gonna have to talk to uh—the guys in charge or whateva... So, are we good here?"

"As you were, Officer."

She pushed down the frustration and tried tapping another officer who seemed a bit more serious. He had a close-cropped crew cut, a dark mustache, and shaded wayfarers on.

"Anything you can tell me about the fire?" She asked him.

"Nothing so far, agent. Uh—we did check the security tapes."

"Did you get anything?"

"You know it's the strangest thing. They've all got this weird static on them."

A flash sparked through Chase then, but instead of starting in her brain it came out in her gut and made her lurch. Screwing with camera equipment was also the C's MO. They had control over the airwaves. They got to decide what was projected.

"So—no leads then?" Chase said, feeling dismal and sick.

"Not a one so far. Ah—but maybe we'll find a way to clean up that security video and..."

They wouldn't. Chase knew that much. Bucky had developed some kind of technology that could replace a video feed—she'd seen him use it in Times Square to replace every screen there with his own twisted hypno-garbage. But if the C had that technology—didn't it just further point to them being legitimate successors of C-60?

The C was the next step. They were something new. Something fluid and fragmented and completely dangerous. She couldn't figure out their motive yet, but she knew they couldn't be ignored. If Bucky had been the initial blast, the C was the fire that followed.

And they'd targeted a federal building this time. It felt like they were picking a fight with the FBI. It almost felt like they were picking a fight with her, personally.

But the problem with bombs is that they tend to erase their own evidence if you make them right. Forensics had barely come up with anything useful. The fire inside had been propagated by gasoline jelly, but they had no clue what was used for the ignition. All they really had to go on was their calling card: At every fire so far they had left a letter C. In the first building, a local cable station, the wall of the lobby had been scorched. In the second building, the Herald News Group, a giant C had been burned into the front lawn. And now, finally, at the Federal Records & Accounts, they'd escalated to burning it into the entire outside of the wall. They'd grown more brazen over time.

They were painting with fire. Sending a burning message—playing God.

But Chase wouldn't fall for their theatrics, not this time. Nor would she get sucked into a meandering trap. It was time to stop playing by their rules. Time to use the full extent of the Bureau's power and get ahead of these punks. This time she would stop the C, and stop them for good.

Chapter 2

The C had been scurrying about town unimpeded for long enough. It was time to see about building a better mousetrap. A gust of air conditioner wind blew through the Data Analysis Team's crusty office, knocking over ramen cups, candy wrappers, and half-eaten subway sandwiches... Chase stood in the doorway looking over a group of six special agents all of whom looked like they hadn't slept in a month.

"Been cracking the whip again, Bookman?" Chase asked her former partner and current SSA of Data Analysis, Bob Fairfax. He didn't seem like he'd had much sleep himself, his wrinkled but usually glossy face looking particularly dull and pale on this visit. He looked like a xeroxed version of himself.

"Good morning to you too, Chase," he said sleepily, draining the cold dregs out of a vending machine coffee cup. If she didn't know any better he seemed almost hung over. "And yes I've been ramping things up around here. If the C really are connected to C-60 then there's no telling what they're capable of. You remember what happened last time, after that pirate video broadcast they orchestrated. Half the city went haywire."

"About that. The more I think about it, Bob, the more I'm convinced that 'C-60' was a hoax. The work of Bucky alone."

He sighed. This wasn't the first time they were having this discussion. "So, we're back to the lone nut theory? I seem to recall you being against that. Now that Bucky's dead and buried you want to bring it back into play?"

"The context is completely different, Bob. All we have of the supposed C-60 now are two empty locations. The findings of the forensic teams we sent out there are inconclusive. There's no real evidence anyone but Bucky himself was ever involved."

Bob smacked his lips and looked around his table in vain for a bottle of water. "Your theory before was—and correct me if I'm wrong on this, Chase—but you seemed to think that the scope of his operation was too big to have been carried out by just one man."

"Certainly. It wasn't carried out by just Bucky."

"Wait, so—what?"

"That still doesn't mean that C-60 was an actual organization. Think about it. How does he send the first bomb to the hotel? Courier, right? Same for the second bomb. And the third too. Each time Bucky went through some kind of service. It was like the gig economy of terrorism with him. Why even use a group? If you can manipulate people, even temporarily—" Bob flashed her a knowing look."—then forming and maintaining a group is just a useless liability. More people to rat you out, more people to turn on you. It makes more sense to go it alone."

"Okay, so Bucky uses gofers for the whole operation," Bob said, hypothesizing. "Uses day laborers he picked up outside of Home Depot to build his big Whack-o-Dome, let's say. Doesn't that still leave a massive paper trail? We've been looking at the data for five or six weeks now—nothing of that sort is out there. If there was, we'd know about it."

"From illegals? Bob, they don't leave a paper trail. They don't even pay taxes. It's the perfect crime."

"Maybe. It doesn't explain how one individual actor was able to wreak so much havoc, however. We only caught him because he got greedy and gave away his location."

"The problem is, we've been looking at Bucky as an everyday citizen," Chase said. "Maybe that's why we're stuck on this. Think about it, Bob—he didn't even exist. You think every day Joe America can live completely off the grid like that? No prints on file, no dental, no DNA. No medical history. Hell, we never even found out his real name."

"Chase—" Bob sat halfway off his seat, leaned in, and whispered. "Surely you aren't implying—you suspect Bucky was a *government agent?*"

Chase just returned the question with a noncommittal shrug. "I don't know what he was. All we can say for sure is that he was no amateur, that he wasn't just some disgruntled loon off the street out for revenge. Our one lead was Elliot, and now he's catatonic. I wouldn't even discount that being intentional either."

"Intentional as in—you think someone got to him? Fried his brain?"

Bob was giving her those eyes—the ones that said in so many words, here's Chase going off the deep end again.

"There's something else," Chase said, almost as a means of diverting his attention. "Something's been gnawing at me lately, something that wakes me up in the middle of the night in a cold sweat."

"What is it?"

"What if the guy we caught in Times Square wasn't even the right guy?"

Bob's face fell off so hard that it nearly hit the floor and went rolling around. His tired eyes hung wide open, his dry mouth. "I don't, I don't understand what you're saying, Chase."

"Think about it—why would Bucky let himself get caught like that? It makes zero sense. He went to all that trouble, kidnapped me, evaded and killed an entire tactical squad, and got away squat free. He could have disappeared right after that and we'd never have caught him. Yet he appears right in the middle of Times Square of all places."

"But that was so he could use that weapon of his. To hijack the screens in the square. Not that we even know what that was all about."

"Exactly, Bob, he used a weapon. But in all prior instances, we know that Bucky utilized third parties as a vector to send out his weapons."

Bob cleared his throat, went over to the next desk, and nabbed another agent's water—the agent looked pretty annoyed about it. Sucking down a mouthful, Bob sat back in his chair, pondering what Chase was saying. "But Chase, if this was just some third party then we'd have figured out who the hell he was."

"I know that. That's why. I don't know. I don't know anymore. Nothing seems to add up."

"Anyway—you were kidnapped by the guy. You should know. You're telling me you can't recognize his face? Bucky wasn't wearing a mask when he nabbed you, was he?"

"No, he wasn't."

"Then you did see his face."

"Sure."

"Then why don't you know if the unsub killed in Times Square was Bucky or not?"

She bit her lip. "It was him. The guy I found in the dome, that is. But if that was Bucky then why is the C still around?"

"Right. That's the question, isn't it?"

"Let's move on," Chase said. "What about the other media crimes this month? Get anything off them?"

"Nothing substantial," said Bob. "The C Channel's hijacking seemed like it would give us something—but we really don't even know what happened. The problem is that whenever something like this happens we get no security footage. They have the ability to—"

"Scramble it out. I know. But someone at the cable station still had to have seen the suspect or suspects."

"You'd think. But all reports on that are negative."

"First Channel 60 then the C Channel. At this rate, any TV outlet with the letter C is going to consider changing their name."

"We had the same kinda idea," the other agent said, the one whose water Bob stole. "We actually set up a trap on the other networks, any station with C. CNN in Midtown, NBC over on Long Island, and uh, what were the other ones?"

"CBS, WABC..." Bob said; then added, "This is Agent Ray Kelly, by the way. He just made GS-8."

Agent Kelly looked to be still in his 20s; he had a stiff brush of black hair atop a hard, flat forehead, long narrow knotted eyebrows that crossed under the brow above the long curve of his nose, a prominent chin, and slits on either side of his mouth that years from now were prime candidates for jowls. His ears poked out sharply on either side like a fox, and his eyes were also fox-like, tear-shaped and glistening, and gunmetal gray.

On his narrow neck, a big blue vein stuck out visibly. There seemed to be a vague hunger in him, but in Chase's muddled state, she couldn't see much more than that.

"Welcome to the big leagues, Agent Kelly," Chase said dryly. "So—by trap you mean?"

"You know, like hidden cameras, additional surveillance, this type of thing."

"And no hits yet?"

"Nothing as of yet, Agent Chase."

Chase sighed. "The problem is that there isn't much of a pattern outside of the pattern they allow us to see. Until we grasp what they're really up to, there's no way to predict where they'll strike next."

"Generally Chase," Bob said, "this is where your uh— intuition kicks in and points us in the right direction."

"I know," Chase said. "But it's telling me nothing this time around. We're just going to have to do things the hard way until we can get something more substantial. Agent Kelly, do you have any ideas?"

"I mean—we were hoping the trap would spring," Kelly said. "The thing is their motives are too unclear. Without catching them in the act, how do you figure out what they're up to? It's a whatchamacallit—a Catch-22."

"He's right," Bob said. "At least back in the Channel 60 hijacking, the video Bucky had them play explained his motive. It let us build a profile of where they were coming from. But the C doesn't do that—when they perform a channel hijack they just play static or random AI-generated images in a meaningless sequence. It feels more like they're aiming for pure chaos than Bucky ever was."

"So, that's that then," Chase said. "A month later we're still at square one."

"Not precisely," Bob said. "We do have one lead to follow up on."

"Which is?"

"Chase, you really aren't on the ball here."

"I suppose not. Are you going to gloat or are you going to tell me?"

"The Federal Records & Accounts management. We still haven't interviewed them. I scheduled a meeting tomorrow at nine."

"Oh," Chase said, feeling her head crushing down a little harder on her brain. "That's good. Good work, Bob."

"Until then, I think you should get some rest."

"He's right, agent," Kelly said. "You look pale, like you could pass out at any second."

"Thanks, I'll keep that in mind." Chase didn't say anymore. She felt so fatigued she couldn't even muster the strength to get annoyed by the comment. And the worst part was she had no idea why.

Chapter 3

"Good morning, gentlemen," Bob said, his smile creasing its impressions into his leathery face. "We're conducting an inquest into what happened at the Records & Accounts building yesterday and would like to get some details straight."

Bob sat down at the head of the table and pointed out the members present in turn.

"You're in charge of security."

"Correct."

"And you're the building administrator."

"Yes."

"And you are in charge of copying and maintaining copies, restricting access, and governing the availability and access to the stored documents."

"Yes, I am."

Bob looked over the three faces again, then folded his hands. "Gentlemen, not one of you saw this kind of thing coming? Not only did you not prevent the files from being destroyed, but I am to understand that none of them have even been backed up."

They looked embarrassed, stunned even. Chase was pretty stunned herself—it wasn't like Bob to go for the jugular like that. Had his relatively new title of SSA gone to his head already?

"We uh... Generally, we'd have a backup of the files in question," the access manager said, a withdrawn, hangdog look crawling over his gaunt, weary face. His short blonde hair came down on one side of his skull where he hadn't combed it back properly.

"Then why wasn't a backup performed?" Bob countered.

"Budget cuts, mainly. It costs on average $0.10 per file, per week to store them here. Imagine doubling that with backups. We store thousands of files here. You can do the math on how much taxpayer money a project like that requires. In fact, we had planned some cost measures next month that would allow us to make a full backup, but unfortunately—it never made it to completion."

"Hold on a second," Chase said. "Was this schedule known by many people?"

"Uh, yes, in fact. An email was sent out to everyone in the building... Why?"

Chase and Bob exchanged a look. Everyone in the building had known about the upcoming backups. It hardly narrowed down the search.

"Why, do you think that this was what incited the arsonist's attack?" the access manager said, a pleading mew to his voice.

"Maybe," Chase said. "It's too soon to say. But tell us about the nature of the records on the eleventh floor. That's where the fire was started and that's where the most damage was done. It's safe to assume that was the target."

"The eleventh floor..." the access manager said. "Right. Yes. Of course. But then—there was the matter of the big display on the front of the building..."

"Let's forget about that," Chase said. "The fact is that whatever was on the eleventh floor was designed to go first. The rest is just theatrics. Quite probably a distraction."

"Alright. The eleventh. Let me think. Uhum yes, that's where some of our more *sensitive* files went, for sure."

"Sensitive how?" Bob asked.

"Things that require certain higher levels of clearance."

"Can you give us some idea of what domain the documents dealt in?" Bob said.

"I'm afraid I—"

"Just a vague idea is fine. I'm not asking you to leak critical information."

"No, no it's not that. You see the documents were eyes only—meaning I myself never got to look at them."

Chase startled a little and shook her head. "You're telling us you governed access to these files and didn't even know what was in them?"

"Exactly. They all worked on a series of codenames. It would be a security risk otherwise. I'm really just a glorified administrator."

"You can say that again," she mumbled.

Bob gave the access manager one of his raisin-wrinkle smiles and said, "Let's look at this differently. Who would have known that the eleventh floor hosted eyes-only-level documents?"

"Ah, yes. Good point." He scratched at the white powder of stubble on his chin and exchanged glances with the others in the room who seemed equally or even more clueless than himself. "That, there would have been fewer who knew about it."

"What about cleaners? Could anyone like that have known the level of clearance needed for those documents?" Chase asked.

"Hmm. Certainly not intentionally. Maybe if they overheard someone talking."

"How likely is it they would have overheard something like that?"

The access manager's face turned sour then, his mouth puckering up and his eyes watering. He thrust his pelvis out and leaned back on the chair in a defensive position: Chase had seen this one a million times, usually by perps who were about to say, "I want my lawyer."

"It's not impossible that something along those lines happened," the manager finally said, diplomatically.

"I need you to do better than that, sir," Chase said. "What kind of access did the cleaner or any other technical staff have to that floor?"

"Yes, well..." He shifted in his seat. He was clearly starting to sweat. Chase smelled blood. She lunged her teeth in.

"If there's been the possibility of a leak we need to ascertain it now before things can get any worse."

He looked up with the eyes of a rabbit facing an oncoming truck: Glassy and still and nearly quivering with horror.

"It's in your best interest too," Bob added.

"Alright, agents. I understand what you mean. You believe that the fire is a decoy, is that what I'm hearing?"

"Yes," Chase said. "I believe that the fire might be a decoy to cover up the fact that certain eyes-only clearance files have been stolen. With all files now destroyed, it is impossible to figure out what the target was."

Bob startled at that. He knew that Chase's bad feelings generally tended to hit the mark. Even though this time Chase really felt like she was guessing more than intuiting.

She went on, "We need to know every staff member that could possibly have had access to that floor, and we need it now."

"Alright," the manager said wearily, looking over the edge of his career at the deep, steep plunge below. "I think—I think I may know of one cleaning lady in particular who was working the building the time the fire broke out."

"A cleaning lady?" Bob asked. He turned to Chase. Chase knew what he was thinking. She was too.

"Let me guess," Chase asked the manager. "She's outsourced from a cleaning agency?"

The manager's glossy eyes opened a notch wider. "What? No, of course not. That would be ridiculous, given the sensitivity of the job."

"Oh." She shuffled in her seat a little.

Bob cut in, picking up the slack. "Then she was under the direct employ of the Federal Records & Accounts building."

"Correct."

"Can we get a name?"

"Lucy. Lucy uh—Child, yes. Lucy Child."

"And her address?"

"Yes, we have that on file."

"Then our best shot will be to go and pay this Miss Child a visit," Bob said, glancing at Chase.

She just nodded and said she agreed, but nothing more. She didn't have the confidence to say much more.

...

Night fell, night released. Bustling about town trying to find a criminal cleaning lady. Human nature lurked in the city, deep in the city. Nature was a wild animal and it hid its teeth and claws under the average Joes walking zombie-like from work, ranting and gossiping and chewing hotdogs at the sidewalk stand. Kelly bought one too. He forgot to eat, it's a real bad habit. He's got his own transport, nothing special, just a Toyota Corolla. It gets the job done. Kelly wanted to get the job done. That's why he entered data analysis, it skips past all the b.s. or at least it's meant to, though in practice it's no panacea.

Kelly remembered his Quantico training like a bright candle that flickered in dark moments, the skills surging through his fingertips. He was sitting there in his Corolla polishing his gun: A standard Smith & Wesson M&P. The latest in law enforcement protection: Its sturdy, reliable steel gave him strength. Better than the old Glocks. Made you feel tougher somehow.

He twisted around the East Village, the mission in his mind. He has a plan to smoke this lady out and it's not exactly kosher, but they have to get ahead of this one. Can't let themselves get led by the nose again, ain't that right? There's still time if they act quick enough—they can prevent some crazy shit going down. All they had to do is find the nexus of the C and dismantle it—it's that simple. As for the rest of it? Mind control and drone bombs and this viral video that people keep talking about? Kelly couldn't give a damn. He wasn't allowed to watch much TV as a kid, had those kinda dipsy religious parents. Didn't grow up with an iPad in his hands. He's young old-school. An anomaly of his peers. But it made him appreciate things differently. Now he's the one behind the computer, he doesn't take it for granted. Now he's the one trying to push boundaries, trying to get a hold on things. He wants to get an advantage over the bad guys.

He headed down East Tenth to a base and broken down red brick dinge-pad on the corner of Avenue C, hidden in the shadow of bigger tenements on the block. He's thinking Death of a Salesman when he heads in there. He's thinking maybe he's not up to snuff. New kid, green kid. Liable to make mistakes, kid. But for some reason, Bob trusted him enough to send him out with this Chase character. Kelly's thinking Bob's real motive lies elsewhere, that maybe the Bookman just wants to buy time to work on his own angle. That's how the Bookman operated. He's an operator. Stick with the Bureau for nearly twenty years, you learn how to operate.

As for Chase—Kelly had heard all the rumors. The Witch of Wall Street, some call her. Rumors that she nearly single-handedly took down a multinational banking crime syndicate. Except no one has any idea how; save that she gets these *ideas*. That she doesn't rely on data so much as read the waves of the universe or whatever. Meeting her hadn't really lived up to the hype, to tell the truth. She seemed muddled, confused. She seemed to lack confidence or drive. Maybe a rumor was just a rumor after all.

The other thing they said about her was that she was impossible to work with. Even worse than most broads on the job. That she didn't take orders and always had to run the show. Kelly was ambivalent about that—he was no stranger to hard-headed folk. Mainly it rested on whether it got the job done or not. If it got the job done, who cared about her personality?

He exited the Corolla and came up on the doorstep of the faded red five-story building. Chase came up behind, swiping her cat's eyes over the street like a big swinging prison light. They hit the buzzer, no one's home of course. They try the others, the old "buzz me in" trick. Doesn't work. They trade a look.

"Fire escape?" Kelly suggests and Chase concurs.

So they turn around the corner to the teal-painted fire escapes leading up from the second floor. Now here's Kelly hunching down under them, his fingers locked tight together like that thing you do with the church and the steeple. Chase pounced off his hands, yoinking down the squeaking ladder. Chase bounded up to the second floor first with Kelly right behind her. She ain't bad looking, Kelly's now noticing. Especially from this angle. What is she, 5'10"? Just above average for a girl. Those tight blue pants accentuated her well-kept form. Her shoulder-length dark reddish hair was tousled behind her in a ponytail. Those penetrating eyes of hers when she looks at you with all that fury and heat. Yeah, Chase is Kelly's type, in fact. Just a shame about her personality. And FBI agents can't date each other anyway, so it's whatever.

They take the fire escape all the way up to the fourth floor where the landlord lives in Room 412. A rap on his window. Two raps. At last, the curtains part to reveal one Josh Guzman, forty-three years old. Major talent besides growing his sideburns out is ripping his mom off for money he can blow on dope—so his rap sheet would indicate anyway. This guy doesn't belong in Alphabet City, he belongs in Greenwich Village... Like sixty years ago. Dude's an artist—or so he believes. Hasn't held a steady job in his life. Shifty mannerisms on his ropy body. Unforgiving light in his milky eyes. A troublemaker.

"The hell is this now?" Grunted Guzman. "What the hell do you think you're doing climbing my fire escape? Has the whole world gone nuts?"

"We're facial hair inspectors," Kelly said. "Have you got a permit for those *burns*?"

"What da? You little shit. Who da hell do you think you are?"

"We're FBI," Chase countered, shooting Kelly an admonishing glance.

"Oh, great," Guzman said. "Now I got the freakin' feds on my door. Scratch that, at my window. Can't you use a freaking buzzer like a normal human being?"

"You weren't answering."

"Oh yeah, blame it on me. Que carajo—is always the fault of poor Senor Guzman! Cabron."

Kelly leaned over to Chase and whispered, "This sack of skin and bones needs an attitude adjustment..."

"Keep it in your pants, Agent," she whispered back. "Save it for the actual suspects."

Kind of intimate, all this whispering. Kelly would be lying if he said it didn't turn him on. But he's a professional and truth be told this Agent Chase has way too much baggage for his tastes. So, he puts the thought out of his head, along with her smooth skin and her delicate smell, her big haunting eyes... Get a grip, Kelly. You got work to do.

Guzman finally lets them into his room—a real treasure trove that place is too. Old computer equipment, TV sets, DVDs, and various kitchen appliances are in a box. Like what did he do, raid a closed-down Radio Shack? The guy even has stacks of magazines tied criss-cross with twine, the whole nine yards. Classic hoarder. The dude probably saves his lint in a jar.

"Alright Mr. Guzman," Chase said. "We're looking for Lucy Child."

"Ayy, mi cabeza. This is one Lucy I do not love, Miss FBI agent. She caused me so much grief I am sincere to say I do not regret her disappearance."

"Disappearance?"

"Si, si. She floated off like a child's balloon at the fair."

"When was this?"

"Couple days ago. Skipped out on her rent too. But no worries—I got her deposit. No one pulls one over on Senor Guzman."

"That much was expected, Chase," Kelly said.

"Right," Chase said. "Mr. Guzman, had Miss Child shown any signs of—how can I put this—acting suspiciously lately?"

"She's been acting weirder lately. Oh at first, sure, she fooled me with that act. Seemed like an ordinary decent citizen. Cleaning lady down on her luck. I say okay you can stay here, no character reference necessary. Then she goes and loses it."

"Can you explain that a little more?"

"Just you know—went all, how you say, morose on me. Don't even talk to me anymore. Oh sure, Guzman is just a rubber dog turd you can sweep under the rug. Don't bother treating me like a human being, huh? I'm just here to fix your pipes when they break, si? To open your door when you too stupid to remember your key. Otherwise, Senor Guzman good for nothing, huh?"

"But you said she was affable at the start—friendly."

"Sure, she was freaking Miss Congeniality at the start, sure. Baked cookies and everything."

"So, can you tell us when the changes started?"

"Ayy, who can say? Couple months maybe. She drops the act entirely. Doesn't speak to me, barely so much as says hello to me when she sees me. That hurts, you know? How much effort it takes to—"

"Alright Guzman," Kelly cut in. "Can you give us a more exact time when she went weird on you?"

"Let's see—ayy. I would say a month and a half. Sure. For three rent payments, she has been this way. But if you ask me—that is the real Lucy, not that fake Lucy with the cookies and the smiling and all that fake garbage. I see right through her."

Chase was biting her lip.

"You got something, Chase?" Kelly asked.

"Six weeks ago—that was when the Channel 60 hijack went down."

"Wait—you think that—"

"Mr. Guzman," Chase said. "You don't happen to have a way of contacting Miss Child, do you?"

Guzman returned the question with a deep belly laugh. "Good one, FBI lady. Good joke. You think people who walk out on their rent stay in touch? Send Christmas cards? No dice."

"What about a phone number?"

"Ayy, no way. Lucy has gone incommunicado. Her phone is dead. And who knows? Maybe even she is."

"Let's hope not," Kelly said. "Otherwise, so is our case."

Chapter 4

"So, show me the video."

The client, one Jeff Franzen, produced the black plastic square with a trembling hand. A Betamax. The spool wound halfway. It hadn't been rewound from its last position. It hadn't been watched all the way through.

The detective dragged out an old TV-Betamax combo he had lying around. Rewound the tape then hit play.

Screen crackling into view, skipping for a while then coming into focus. Camera shot of a white-walled room, crusty paint over a crooked wall. Steel-rusted pipes running the walls. Light comes into the room from somewhere but no windows are visible. The room has a kind of sparse utilitarian feel about it, function over form—like it's a maintenance room or maybe a small warehouse, the detective figures. Low voices coming from off-camera; it's hard to make out what they're saying. Sounds like maybe they're giving directions. Shortly after, a figure stumbles onto the screen. It's a woman: A small egg-shaped face with large eyes, a long nose, and full lips. Long auburn hair parted down the middle that comes down to her shoulders. The face is well-kept but betrays a degree of wear. Probably in her late thirties, or early forties. There's an absent look in those large brown eyes that stare vacantly into the camera, almost like she doesn't realize it's there. Or that she's drugged. Or that she believes she's actually asleep.

"Believes she's asleep?" The client said. "What do you mean by that?"

"Ah, nothing in particular," the detective replied.

On the video, a murmured low voice from off-screen says something inaudible and in response, the woman raises her left hand and puts it on her head. She leaves it there. Another low voice off screen and she removes her left hand and puts it on her lap. Then she sticks her finger in her ear. Back to her lap. This continues, with the voice murmuring and the woman performing simple actions. It would take an idiot not to see what's going on here: She's following orders.

But that's not even the weirdest part.

The weirdest part is how the woman doesn't protest at all.

"She's my fiancée," Franzen explained after the detective had looked at him, puzzled. It didn't explain a thing. "She went missing and then—I just got this tape in the mail."

"To blur out the features, likely," the detective said, more to himself than the client. "So that no clues could be gained from it. So that it wouldn't be easy to copy."

In the video, the low voice is talking to another, closer voice. The closer voice gets picked up: "... Reach you from there. Get in closer."

Sounds of shuffling, the plastic of the camera squeaking and the screen shakes as it gets pointed down. The woman is wearing a skirt that has been pulled halfway up her legs. The man's voice says, "Now, place your hand on your thigh." The other man—whose face can't be seen—does so, his thick hand resting on the woman's upper thigh. The woman cooperates. "Move to the side a little." She slides further toward the center of the shot. "Open your mouth." She does so. "Stick out your tongue." The woman is now sticking out her tongue. "Flick it." She bends a finger and flicks at her own tongue. "Now suck her tongue." The other man leans forward and you can only see the back of his head—but it's clear what he's doing and it's clear the woman isn't struggling at all...

The client gave a small whimper, evading his eyes. His cheeks were already wet.

"Mr. Franzen, I'm not sure I understand," the detective said. "What the hell is going on here?"

"You see," the client pointed with a shivering hand. "The woman in the video is my fiancée, Chloe Bell."

"You said already."

"Well, can't you see? She's being held against her will."

"She is? It's just that it doesn't seem that—"

"Of course, she is, damn you! Don't give me this spiel, I already heard it from the cops!"

"Alright, alright, calm down. I'm just trying to figure out the situation here."

"The SITUATION here is that my fiancée is being—is being—just look at what they're doing to her! She wouldn't—she's not the type of girl to just. I mean look at what's going on here!"

On screen, the woman is bent over the bed and slowly shaking her hips from side to side. "Slowly," the man is telling her.

"Maybe uh—she's at gunpoint?" The detective said. "But she doesn't look like she's scared, is the thing."

"Are you calling me a liar?" The client said.

"I'm not calling you anything. I'm just trying to work this out in my mind."

"She must be at gunpoint or knifepoint or something. They must be threatening her somehow—to go along with this."

"Alright. Now don't take this the wrong way but—has your fiancée always been faithful to you?"

"What the hell? What the hell are you trying to say? That Chloe is just some cheap sleazy whore? My fiancée is not like that! She wouldn't! She would never—I mean what do you take me for?"

"Look, calm down alright? I just had to ask. It changes the uh—it changes how you look at this. How long does this video go on for?"

"I don't know. I couldn't stand to watch. I stopped watching here."

"I get the picture. So, your fiancée goes missing and a few days later this video gets delivered to you. Correct?"

"Yes."

"No contact before that or after that?"

"None. Just the video. And a note saying to wait for the next message."

"When did she go missing?"

"Two—two weeks ago now."

"And when did you receive the video?"

"Eight days ago."

"Two weeks minus eight days. So, they let you sweat the first six. That's odd. They should have known you'd go to the cops."

"Of course I did. They said they—that they'd treat it as a missing person's case at first. After I showed them the tape it had the opposite effect—they actually *closed* the missing persons' case, on account of this proving she's still alive. They said that there's insufficient evidence of wrongdoing on the tape."

"Explains how whoever made the tape had the confidence to let you sweat. That's also kind of particular though."

"What is? Do you—do you have some idea of who they are?"

"Not really—only that they have knowledge of how cops operate. You couldn't pull a stunt like this otherwise. A regular kidnapper would send a note telling you not to go to the cops, and they'd also give you an idea of what they want. But not these guys. They make you wait. Make you suffer. They weaken your psyche first then come in with the hard punch, showing you your fiancée jumping through hoops. Even most pros would stop there—send the tape and a request, tell you to not go to the cops or else. But not these guys— they have the gall to not even mention the cops, to still keep you hanging regarding their request. You don't know what they want, you don't know what's going on so you continue to sweat for days. It drives you crazy. You'd do anything to get her back. I'm betting if they asked you for a hundred grand at this point you'd probably consider paying it."

"Well—I don't have a hundred grand but. I'd look at ways to get it."

"Exactly. It's uh—let's just say we certainly don't seem to be dealing with your common hood here. These are real operators."

"Is my fiancée in danger?"

"I don't know yet." The detective sighed and leaned back on his seat, took a swig of firebrand whisky. One good part about going private was being able to drink on the job. The bad part was how often you needed to.

"No evidence," the detective mumbled. "This woman is clearly being coerced."

"You think so too?" The client's voice was a muddled mix of hope and despair. It was the kind of tone he didn't hear that often outside of this office, but inside it, he heard it all the time.

"So, afterward there's been no note, no calls or anything," the detective said.

"Yes."

"Okay. I'm beginning to get a feel for it."

"Then will you take the case?"

"Hmm. I mean I'll have to watch this video all the way through first—see if there's anything to go on. If I do take the case it'll be $200 a day plus expenses." The detective glanced at the screen again, where the woman just stared blankly into the camera. Clearly, she was on drugs—or something. But it was the something that spooked him. It was the something that made him not say yes straight away. And it was the something that always proved fatal in a case like this.

"Thank you," the client said. "Then I will wait for you to contact me. But now I must leave—I just can't. I can't sit through this. Will you call me when you've made a decision?"

"Sure, why not."

Franzen left him alone and the detective sat there for a while contemplating something before hitting play again on the Betamax. He wasn't sure which was worse—watching to the end of this video or being left to his own devices.

The video starts playing again and Chloe stops making out with the man, who then stands up careful to not show his face to the camera. The woman doesn't seem affected at all. It's as if nothing even happened. It just doesn't register at all. She's breathing, she can move and listen and act. But she doesn't *react*.

The video continues with the man off-screen instructing Chloe to lie down on her back. She's still fully clothed, but somehow that makes the scene appear even more perverse. She is instructed to open her legs and stretch her arms over her head so that they're dangling over the side of the rickety, squeaky bed. A faint sound of a horn outside comes through in the crappy recording. A kind of static intermittently buzzes the screen, similar to the effect an older model of mobile phone or microwave oven has on a television set. The static sound gets more intense as the video continues, and pretty soon that's all the detective can focus on—not what's transpiring on screen, which is really just the other man teasing their captive—touching her in various places but never fondling or rubbing her, just touching her at spots. Again, the oddity of the act just makes the scene all the more perverse. But the buzzing reaches a higher and higher pitch until the narrator's voice can't be heard at all, and it starts to affect the picture too, like maybe it's the tape they used that'd been damaged. Flickering appears across the screen and steadily takes over until there is more noise and signal. And in the last moments of the video, all the detective can make out is two figures rhythmically moving back and forth behind the static—and no matter how hard he focuses on the screen he can't make out what's actually going on. Or maybe he does know what's going on but doesn't want to accept it. But anyway the thing that's coming through the most is that repeating static.

It was then the detective felt himself get hit by something hard and forceful and utterly undesired. It was a realization of sorts: That this video wasn't so novel. That it was something he'd seen before.

And by that point, there was no way he could possibly refuse the case.

Chapter 5

Bob sat up in his chair and smiled broadly. He felt like a whole new Bob. One bursting with enthusiasm and confidence and—to tell the truth, a kind of power. Meetings like this had always used to scare the crap out of him. But what Bob had brought to the table here was no stopgap or makeshift fudge job. He'd brought something of substance. The data had been delivered and he was the delivery boy.

Besides Bob in the room sat ASAC Hogan with his giant jaw and silky black slicked-back hair, a member of Strategy Coordination named Stein who wore a short-sleeved white shirt and specs and looked stiffer than a dead tree, Newman from Technical, a bug-eyed future heart attack patient, and an admin from Finance named Linda something whose pretty blue eyes were wasted staring at computer screens all day.

"Well I don't need to lecture you on the discussions we've had in the past," Bob began, "We at data analysis have gone to great lengths to bolster the power of SET, using various handmade scripts and search parameters to hone it in on adequate forms of data. "

SET was short for Simple Event Tracking. The system was designed to draw relationships between disparate sets of data from a multitude of sources, constructing viable narratives concerning suspects related to a case. In the past, they'd used it to pry out key leads in a number of cases that had hit a wall.

"I won't go into the weeds with you about it," Bob went on, "but suffice to say what we've learned over the decade-plus of working with the system is that SET works best when it's put to work on finding statistically likely patterns—which means habitual behavior. The significance of any event a suspect causes is then determined by comparing it to said patterns. To put it simply, we can not only analyze someone's habitual life pattern, but the anomalies in said pattern. Crime, for most of the population, takes place in the spaces between habitual behavior. Conclusion: Given enough data, we can detect a crime after it happens, or sometimes even while it is ongoing."

ASAC Hogan twirled his finger, telling Bob to fast forward through the preliminaries.

"Right, so what I've been working on recently is to analyze a potential pattern for the C itself. This of course differs from SET's general usage pattern but isn't outside the scope of its power. Ahem. I believe. Uh—"

Crap. Where had his bravado gone? This was Bob in a nutshell: Supremely confident one minute, a sweating mess the next. He could feel the glistening beads collecting on his forehead already...

"So," Bob went on, "to get to the brass tacks of the matter—"

"I wish you would," Stein said snidely. The others gave an inaudible chuckle.

"Right. We took into consideration these facts and, simply put, treated the C as one suspect."

"One suspect?" Newman said. "But the terrorist going by the name Bucky is already dead."

Bob licked his lips, his eyes flashing over the heads. Hadn't they been through this already? Why did he have to explain things to the IT guy?

"I don't necessarily mean that C is one person," Bob said. "Look—so far we've had the three arson jobs, and the TV network jobs, which themselves were modeled on the Channel 60 hostage situation we had last month. These jobs display a level of coordination and execution that suggests more than one person was involved. That's not the issue here."

"But this meeting is about SET, Bob," Hogan reminded him. "We're here to decide on how best to allocate and coordinate the numerous resources at our disposal in an effective manner."

"I'm aware of that, ASAC. I'll try and elucidate the problem more clearly. So, we feed all of this data into SET and attempt to make a generative model in order to predict a group's next crime, and what happens is, it doesn't get anywhere. Why? Because we don't have enough details. It gets hung up on trying to find group activity. But if you scratch that, say okay just treat the C as one suspect, things become a lot clearer."

"Okay," Hogan said, his voice booming through the small conference room. "What you're saying, Bob, is that SET deals with single entities—citizens—so to get it to predict C's actions you've treated C as a single person. Is that a correct understanding?"

"Right. Yes. Exactly." He exhaled deeply and wiped his forehead with a Kleenex.

"Then what has SET been able to predict?"

"When you break it down, the C have been chiefly operating in the entertainment industry. It's what you might call *media crime*." Chase had coined the word, but it had started to catch on throughout the Bureau.

"But it doesn't explain the arson..." ASAC Hogan said.

"Right. It doesn't. Which, looking at it from a SET point of view, is the anomaly in the pattern. Do you catch my drift? The arson is the real crime. It's the significant datum."

"Hold on Bob—" Stein said. "Are you trying to make out like the so-called media crimes were just window dressing to gloss over the arson? That doesn't make sense—why go to the trouble of writing their name on the buildings then."

"He has a point, Bob," Hogan said, staring at him sternly. Bob felt a single drop of sweat land coldly in the arch of his back.

"Actually, that doesn't even matter," Bob said. "Because we're talking about statistics here, not motive. The point is that whatever records were stored in the Federal R&A building must have been highly important for some reason. That's the gist of the conclusion SET came to. The R&A building was the 'true event' if you will, and the rest is just noise for right now."

"If we could figure out the reason for the Federal Records Building arson, it would put us ahead of the C," Linda suggested. To Bob, it felt like someone throwing a lifesaver to him as he padded water in a storm-swept sea.

"Correct," Bob said. "If we focus on that, the rest, I believe, will slot into place naturally."

"Okay, interesting," Hogan said. "And there's no way of figuring that out based on current data?"

"Problem is, the facility stored tens of thousands of records. There's no real way to guess what the target was. And even if there was—we don't have access to what records they were, on account of they all require high-level clearance."

"Hmm," Hogan said, tapping his pen on the desk. "I will talk with the SAC in D.C. and see if there's any leeway we can get on that. But continue Bob, you said you were able to predict the C's next crime?"

"Yes. And excuse me for taking so long in getting to this conclusion but it was important you understood how I derived my—"

"Yes, yes, yes, Bookman," Stein said. "Can we please stop burying the lead here? You're like my dachshund with a turkey bone."

Chuckling spread across the room. Bob took another deep breath. "I believe that the C's next operation will be a business front set up to disguise their ideological pursuits. But making a business from scratch leads to too much exposure. So, the SET thinks they will—that is to say, the SET's model predicts that—the C will target an existing business and take it over. Kind of like the Channel 60 incident, but on a longer timeframe."

The room went stone-cold silent. The silence was so sharp it could have drawn blood.

"You think they're going to *infiltrate* a business?" Newman asked quietly.

"Yes," Bob said.

"What kind of business?"

"We're not sure yet."

"And to what end?"

"That's complicated to explain... But simply put, to further their project."

Stein heaved out a frustrated sigh. "Just what is this nonsense?" He looked around the room. "You think we have so little workload we have time to sit here listening to the Bookman ramble on about fabrications? I mean they're not even good ones. Something this vague and incomplete is completely unactionable. It's a joke. Quite frankly, Bob, I'm amazed they ever made you SSA."

The dead silence rose in the room again, its great giant head crashing up through the floor. Linda made eyes like she wanted to help him but she had no means to do so—she probably didn't know the first thing about what he was talking about. No, Bob would have to drag himself out of the quicksand this time.

"Bob—you seem quite confident in your theory," Hogan said. "Is there some reason for that? We're banking a lot on this being the right course of action. Not only financially—we can't afford to waste time chasing a bad lead."

"Well ASAC, that's why I tried to provide context for the theory before sharing it. See, from your perspective it's completely understandable that you'd brush it off— it's just a vague notion with no specifics, right? Except that you're looking at it through the eyes of a human law enforcement agent. But SET doesn't work that way. Oftentimes—in fact almost always—when the SET catches the vague blurry outline of something, it's only a short step away from resolving it into something very specific and very definite."

"Okay," Hogan said, still using his diplomatic voice that didn't take either side. Hedging his bets in other words. "Let's say you're right—let's say the SET really is onto something here. What would it take to make your prediction more specific? More access to data? More computer power?"

"Well, both," Bob said. "One necessitates the other. It's true that SET could do wonders with more data, but it's also true that when more data is introduced, its computational demands increase polynomially..."

"Okay, I understand," Hogan said. "Next time start with the point, Bob."

"My apologies."

"But if that's the case then it's not a difficult decision at all." Hogan smiled, and Bob caught a strange sensation about it—as if Hogan had been waiting for this all along. But that didn't even make sense. How could Hogan have been waiting for something no one had heard about until a minute ago? ASAC Hogan's poker face didn't reveal a thing. He also needed to get more sleep, that was the problem... Maybe he should cut down on coffee during the day.

"If it's data you need," Hogan said, "then it's data you'll get. I'm going into D.C. This afternoon anyway, so we'll discuss what we can do about that."

"But hold on a minute," Newman said, his brain finally clicking into action. "Excuse my ignorance on the subject, but doesn't the SET already take in every public source of surveillance data out there? And also the NYPD's digital dragnet feeds us data too."

"More or less," Bob admitted.

"Then how are you going to get more data? Where's it all going to come from?"

"You just let me worry about those details," Hogan said. "Bob's job from here on is to try and find this Lucy Child woman. If she knows what the C was trying to steal then we need to find her before they do. Now, do you have any leads on her, while we're here?"

"Just her address, sir. Agent Chase and Agent Kelly have gone down there. Hopefully, they'll find us a lead..."

Chapter 6

Calling in a favor downtown, the detective got forensics to check out the Betamax tape and its envelope but they failed to pull anything off of it. The scumbags behind the kidnapping had been careful. But that didn't mean there were no clues to be had.

He watched it over and over until it clicked: The look of the room, the subtle creaking in the background, the squawk of gulls, and that horn he'd heard. It was pretty probable the video had been taken on a boat. That narrowed it down a little. It narrowed it down a lot. From here on was just pavement pounding. The detective visited the docks for two days straight, harassing any and everyone he could find and showing them pictures of the inside of the boat and photos of Chloe Bell. It was hard work. It was hard on his psyche and his outfit; by the end of the extended canvas, the detective was exhausted from the tip of his head to the broken soles of his shoes.

No one had seen Bell—no one knew anything in this town when it came to people. But as for the boat interior, one enthusiast had a good idea. A boatman calling himself Seadog who ran a rental store on the East River.

"Yeah, yeah," Seadog said. "I knew that looked familiar. It's that total wreck job of Harris'."

"How sure are you?"

"Pretty damn sure. Look at that ugly mother. None of my boats look like that inside the galley, I can tell ya. All that rust—things a damn hazard. Watch if it sinks too, it's gonna poison the well for all of us trying to eke out a living. This day an' age you think anyone wants to ride a boat down the freezing East River? Like hell. They all just wanna sit inside and play their Nintendas or whatever."

"Okay, this is good. Where can I find it?"

"Come with me, I'll show ya. Not like I got any customers."

The Seadog wasn't kidding; the boat he led the detective to was a total rust bucket and it was amazing the thing still even stayed afloat let alone run. It was an old fishing trawler which at one point had been painted white and sky blue, but which had turned the orange silver of scrap.

"Who do I ask to get on this thing?" The detective asked him.

"You wanna get on board that junk heap? I hope you've had swimming lessons, kid."

"Don't worry, I don't intend on going anywhere with it."

"The thing belongs to Cap'n Harris. And I use the term Cap'n very loosely—but it's what he calls himself, understand?"

"What's his number?"

"Written over there on that billboard. But the guy's a lazy bum—if you couldn't already tell from the upkeep of his vessel. Slim chance of him waddling his fat ass down here unless you're willing to put good money on it."

"Even better. Spares me the trouble of asking."

"I like the way you think, my man."

The detective stored Cap'n Harris' number on his phone, then did a sweeping glance at the dock. No one was around. It was March—who the hell wanted to take a walk along the East River in March?

"Screw it," he said and walked down the gangway.

"Hehe that's the spirit," Seadog cried after him. "Stick it to the old bastard."

Taking another look down the empty dock, the detective hopped onto the plank leading up to the boat and climbed in. His every step seemed to jostle the vessel on its dubious moorings and he already started to feel queasy by the time he staggered over to the galley entrance. He tugged at the door but there was little give to it. Taking a step back, he launched his boot right into the flimsy lock, which snapped right off onto the floor with a clang. From down below, the detective heard old Seadog croaking with laughter.

He climbed down the steps into the galley. One glance was enough to tell him this had been the place the video was shot: The way the light came in from the slit windows at the top of the room, the rusty pipes crossing the wall, the lumpy paint, and the warped hunk of scrap with a thin mattress that worked as a makeshift bed.

Okay, so he had the place. But that still left the question of who had used the place and where they were now. With a rust bucket like this, they probably paid cash; there'd be no record of their identity. He could try dusting for prints but he had limited favors to call downtown, which he didn't want to blow all on one case. And besides, the prints would be inconclusive. Who knew how many people had come in and out of here? Homeless bums might be using the joint as a love nest for all he knew. The thought made his stomach roil.

The detective went over to the bed and sat down on it, the image of Chloe Bell washing over him like a cold shower. Her straddling the bed, her vivacious body juxtaposed against a lifeless face. A face free of all fear or worry or even understanding. A shudder ran through him and he had to force himself to get up, his body all pins and needles. He began pacing the room, sorting out the pieces in his head. A lot of questions with no answers. Like a jigsaw puzzle that's all male pieces.

First, there was the client, Jeff Franzen, a total nobody. He worked a regular 9-to-5, a low-level position in advertising. He didn't have much in the way of savings. He didn't have status or access to anything valuable. His fiancée Chloe Bell was just as humdrum, she worked as an office admin at a law firm. They were both leading unremarkable lives in the most unremarkable way. And what did the kidnappers—if indeed this was a kidnapping—even want? To make low-res pornos on Betamax? Franzen was to wait for their instructions. That was a week ago now. What kind of kidnapper waits a whole week before moving? Sure, there is the element that makes the target panic; makes him more pliable and willing to give in to demands. But a week is pushing it. All it does is increase the chances he'll go to the police. Case in point, Franzen had come to the detective for help.

It was at that point the detective started getting paranoid. Started having thoughts that couldn't make sense—like that the kidnappers had *wanted* Franzen to seek out a P.I. but then what was the motive for *that*?

Taking another look around the room for clues, the detective came to the conclusion it was just a common or garden dead end. Nothing special was going on here. It was wrong to give the kidnappers too much credit at this juncture—they could just as easily be screwing up as playing a devious plot. He got Cap'n Harris on the phone and asked for information on the previous renter—their appearance, their phone number, anything. Harris was playing hard to get. And given Harris's profile of not being that scrupulous a character, his silence on the matter suggested the kidnappers had paid extra. But apparently, they didn't even leave a contact number, and Harris only vaguely remembered their appearance—which the detective managed to browbeat out of him with vague threats of getting the boat condemned.

According to Cap'n Harris, there had been two guys, one stocky and the other short. Both Caucasian males or maybe Hispanic. Couldn't remember their eye color and they were wearing baseball caps but maybe one of them had dark hair. Great. So, two guys in baseball caps with dark hair, White or Hispanic. In New York. It was like looking for a lost quarter in a wishing fountain. The dock security cams didn't cover that side, so that was a dead end too. It was starting to seem like these kidnappers were smart after all. They had covered their bases here; but why use a boat at all? And had they taken Chloe Bell somewhere on it? Harris couldn't say. Useless toad.

It was a washout. Without more help on this, it would prove difficult to continue. The best the detective could think of was to maybe try and convince the police to treat this as a kidnapping case after all. But really he wouldn't be able to do that until further instructions came anyway. A day passed, then another. He watched and rewatched the video, trying to find any small clue that might give something away. But no such luck. You didn't get lucky that easily in this job. Not until you'd beaten down every door and shaken down every suspect first. And the worst part was, the more the detective watched the video, the cloudier things got. He found himself slumped over his desk in the middle of the day with a hangover like he'd been heavily drinking—really he'd just been heavily thinking. The sound of the traffic coming through Hell's Kitchen roared through his skull in spite of his double-glazed windows. He wished he could just get his head in order, but lately, it had proven impossible.

So things were looking pretty bleak when a day later the detective got a call from his client.

"Any news?" Franzen asked.

"I'm looking into a few leads..." The detective said vaguely.

"Well, it finally came. The instructions."

"Okay, good. What do they say?"

"They tell me to go to the dock alone."

"On the East River?"

"Yes. Do you know something about it?"

"It's where they shot that video."

"My God. Do you know who they are?"

"I haven't been able to figure that part out yet."

"So, what do we do? I must tell you that I am considering going there, whether or not you advise it. If this is my only shot at getting Chloe back..."

"Okay, okay, calm down. This is a dangerous maneuver. I still think we ought to bring in the cops on this."

"I can't do that. It's too risky."

The detective sighed, trying to weigh the possibilities. "Then if you're gonna go through with this I'm going to have to watch what happens. Make sure they don't try and pull a fast one."

"Yes, that will work."

"But listen, Mr. Franzen—they didn't tell you to bring anything? Money or anything like that?"

"No. They asked me to come alone and that's it."

"Huh."

"What are you thinking?"

"I'm not sure yet. What's the time they expect you there?"

"Three-thirty this afternoon."

"What?! That's only an hour and a half away."

"Something the matter?"

"They're doing this out in broad daylight?"

"That's just what the instructions said."

"Okay then, let's do it. There's a chance you'll be followed so don't come over here. I'll head to the dock myself. Is it lot 11B?"

"Yes, it is. But Detective—how did you know that?"

"It's the same boat. Crud, now I'm really confused. I thought these guys were smart. This is a dumb move." The detective kicked himself for not planting a bug like he originally planned.

"Lot 11B in an hour and a half," Franzen said. "And bring your camera. To film it I mean. Just in case."

"You got it."

...

The sky had cleared some when he got down there, which was just the detective's luck: It made visibility higher, making it easier for him to get seen. But at least it also gave him a better chance to take a photo of these guys. Not that it would do much good if they took off somewhere with his client.

He made a hiding spot for himself outside the entrance to the dock and used his telescopic lens to focus in on Lot 11B. Franzen was already standing there looking sheepishly around. That damn idiot was going to blow it if he didn't act less conspicuous. But here came the other pair now too—dropped off by an Uber whose plate the detective made sure to catch. Next, he zoomed in on the transaction itself—they were having some kind of conversation though he was too far away to hear it. Franzen looked disturbed and suddenly became angry, his face turning pink and his features twisting. He started pointing at them but the pair just stood there calm and collected. In control. Not nervous or anxious at all. They were pros, after all. They said something to Franzen and showed him a phone— whatever was on it made him shut up immediately.

Then, hanging his head, Franzen allowed himself to be led onto Harris' boat. Just before entering the galley, Franzen gave one last longing look out in the detective's general direction. He mouthed the words: "I'm sorry."

In no time at all the boat had started its engines and was sending up a ruckus as the tin can did in fact start out onto the East River on a shaky, jilted course. As soon as it was a good dozen yards out the detective sprinted down the dock to Seadog's place. He was sitting inside reading a paper and drinking from a canteen.

"Seadog, I need to avail of your services."

"Oh?" He said, one eyebrow raised. "By the sound of that floating garbage out there I'm assuming Harris' boat took off?"

"Yeah. And I need you to follow it."

"That's the spirit," he said, getting up off his seat like he weighed nothing. Pretty spritely for an old man, the detective thought. They got onto Seadog's slim fishing boat and the engine started up smooth with a low chugging rumble. Teasing the boat out, Seadog looked out on the horizon at the tin can that had gone ahead of them.

"Where's it headed, any ideas?" The detective asked after they'd been tailing Harris' boat for a while.

"Well, we're headed Southwest," Seadog said, drinking even heavier now since they'd shipped out.

"Which means what exactly?"

"If I didn't know any better, I mean, this just feels like the usual tour route is all."

"So, what does that mean?"

"It means the usual tourist route. See for yourself kid, they just went around Governor's Island and they're heading over to Jersey now."

"What the hell?" The detective said. This was getting complicated—if they got off on the Jersey side he wouldn't be able to give chase as easily. It would mean renting a car, which would take too long.

"Actually, scratch that," Seadog corrected after another few minutes. "They're not headed for New Jersey."

"Then where are they going?"

"Well, if I'm not mistaken, it would appear they're headed for Ellis Island."

Chapter 7

Lucy Child, thirty-five years old, last known location Alphabet City. Slightly large nose and broad forehead, olive-colored skin, and big clumpy hair. She was described by her employees as dedicated, deferent, always on time, and attentive to her job. A model employee. No one had suspected her of being capable of even petty theft, let alone all this.

Her landlord had mentioned that she was well-mannered and sociable too, at least up until six weeks ago...

Ordinarily, she wouldn't be a strong suspect. Not at this juncture. Not until they had something with more meat in it than this circumstantial evidence. But this was no ordinary case. It would stand to reason that they shouldn't rule out any extraordinary avenues. Child had the means and opportunity to pull off the arson theft at the Records & Accounts building. Further damning her case was that she was no longer available at her address and she'd left all her stuff behind in her apartment—from what it seemed, she'd flown the coop.

All they needed was a motive and she would become their key suspect. A new set of facts weighed down on Bob and Chase the more they thought about it.

"Couldn't the same technology that messed with people's minds be in play here?" Bob said.

"I'm not sure," Chase said. "I'm not sure it works like that. We had thought members of C-60 may have been under some kind of control, sure. But now I'm not so sure there even was anyone in C-60 besides Bucky. That weakens the entire control angle. We assumed that the video played during the hijacking of Channel 60 also might have put some kind of subliminal message out there in people's heads. Now I'm not so sure of that either. What if it was all a setup? The more I think back on what happened, the more it all seems like an elaborate prank. Drone bombings, courier bombings. Threats that never transpired. Bucky could have been behind the whole thing, an elaborate scheme to make it look like he had converted *Multimedia Cybernetics* into a weapon. He was using our fear against us and at the time it worked. But now, six weeks later? I'm not sure I buy it anymore. Hell, Bob, we never even *did* figure out if Bucky's bombs were really using Buckminsterfullerene, or whether he just sprinkled it in there as another joke. Our lab techs can't figure out how to make it ignite."

"Chase—I agree with you in part. But you're leaving out something here."

"What am I leaving out, Bob?" She glared at him, daring him to say what she suspected he wanted to say.

"Chase, come on... You can't deny that you lost control over yourself, if however briefly."

"Bob, that was different. I was put into a trance, that was just a kind of hypnosis. Las Vegas stage show fare. Bucky didn't control me to perform a series of complex, convoluted actions. I just blanked out for a while, that's it."

"And Lieutenant Acre?"

"... Let's not talk about that right now, Bob."

"Okay, fine. Even if we leave Acre out of it, you said before—you told me that you believed you were drawn to follow Bucky by something."

"I don't know what I believe now." She curled her lip, folded her arms, and tried to let the words pass her by. She still couldn't believe it. Bucky had claimed he'd led her right to him—that much of the hazy experience she could still remember. And it was certain that she was put into a kind of trance state when she did reach the dome in Poughkeepsie. Given that C-60 could have been one big hoax, then even the entire pretext behind getting Bucky's location—that of Chase volunteering to become part of the group—was also suspect too. If the group was fake, why the whole evaluation process? Why put his location at reach by running that BBS? The whole thing stank. Chase felt like she had walked right into his trap. It was only by a miracle she'd escaped with her life—thinking she'd won. But after the dust had settled, it soon dawned on her that she hadn't won at all. Everything had gone the way Bucky wanted it. He'd gone down in history as one in a long line of famous terrorists, to be listed alongside the greats such as the Mad Bomber and Ted K, and the FBI had only aided in his path to postmortem stardom.

"Chase? Earth to Chase?"

"Look, I have my doubts about the whole thing, Bob. To just what extent does Multimedia Cybernetics really affect the mind? It's still a big fat glaring unknown sitting in the middle of all this. If it's really possible to *hypnotize* people into following commands, then hell, even the little old lady down the street could be a suspect. And if all it takes is playing subliminal messages over the television, why wasn't the Channel 60 broadcast enough to incite total pandemonium? Why did Bucky then later expose himself—ultimately doom himself—to play that video directly on the screens at Times Square? Why didn't Bucky control someone else to pull the Times Square job? Why is the lab at NYU still unable to replicate Bucky's results? Too much about this doesn't make sense."

"Okay, it doesn't add up completely. But Chase—"

"Look Bob, we're not getting anywhere by speculating about past events. Let's just stick to the facts, the data. Isn't that your whole deal?"

"It is," he said, giving her a big cheesy smile. "It is indeed." He turned back around to his computer, where a series of monitors were all blinking away with reams of surveillance footage from all around the city. Bob was the vanguard with regards to using the SET in solving criminal investigations and his techniques had been vital to the Bureau. This had been the key factor in granting Bob his role of Supervisor Special Agent in control of Data Analysis.

"So, Child lives in Alphabet City," Agent Kelly said while the search continued. "She comes to work every day, then poof—disappears after the building is hit. That's suspicious enough to warrant our concern. They say she's diligent, hard-working, yada yada, sure. But then again that's boilerplate. All it means is she kept the place clean. Fact is, everyone was so isolated from one another for security reasons that no one really knew her, not really. They knew she did a good job but that's it. She could have been on the verge of a breakdown or anything."

"Maybe, Agent Kelly," Chase said, "But people don't change suddenly out of the blue—they don't just go nuts for no reason. It's a cliché that someone can be pleasant one day and then snap the next, but in practice, it never happens that way. People like that generally show signs of hostility, strange erratic behavior."

"I'm saying that even if she did show signs no one *would* have seen it. For all we know the stress of everyday life was making her unravel, bit by bit. You think anyone would have noticed? These office zombies with their faces in their laptop screens and lattes? Would they have even known if Child was hopping into the bathroom every hour to snort a line and cry her eyes out in the stall?"

Bob sniffed and tapped on his desk. "Hmm," he said. "So, her behavior *before* the event could be some sort of proof of motive, you're saying? If there was a record of it somewhere. If it was caught on camera for example."

"Exactly. If she was going cuckoo for coco puffs there ought to be some kind of trace."

"That's kind of moot, isn't it?" Chase said, "That building's security footage is a no-go. We don't have clearance. The most we have is a few days of footage, of very specific areas. It'd be impossible to look for signs of errant behavior from that."

"Okay, but what about outside of the office?" Kelly suggested.

The creases came back into Bob's face. "It's not entirely beyond what SET is capable of, in theory..."

"Hold on a second," Chase said. "The way you've explained it to me, SET detects habitual patterns at a macro scale—*Events*. Things like going to work, catching a cab, taking money out of an ATM. Repeatable and obvious actions."

"Uhum," Bob said patiently.

"Don't uh hum me—look, it's not the same thing at all. What Kelly is suggesting is the inference of someone's *mental state* over the course of days or weeks based on barely perceptible changes in their visible demeanor."

"Right, but at a smaller scale, those changes are also events," Kelly said, blowing on his fingertips. He'd just touched his boiling mug of coffee instead of using the handle. "First you get the baseline of their habitual behavior, then detect the anomalies on top of that, right? So just do that on a more detailed level."

"Bob?" Chase looked at him. "SET can't analyze that kind of thing, can it?"

He was still seemingly pondering the problem, his finger tapping the side of his jaw while he looked up and swiveled on his seat.

"Like I said," Bob said. "In theory, SET's systems could be repurposed for something like that. It would require way more power though—and training data."

"Crap," Kelly said.

"Okay," Bob said, "But we have gotten a regular hit, kind of. Two weeks ago we saw her leaving her house here and taking a route South out of Manhattan. We kind of lose her here midway. But SET is highlighting it so it should be a pattern. Look here, one week prior to that, same route. Eight in the evening every, let's see, every Tuesday and Thursday it looks like."

"Can you find where she was going?" Kelly said. "Brooklyn? Queens?"

"Maybe. I'll run a search now." His fingers danced across the keyboard, clattering away as the monitors spun through terabytes of information like a hot knife through butter. Footage appeared from ATM cameras, parking garages, supermarkets, street cameras, restaurants, and traffic cams. The whole city was splayed out and cut open and picked apart for the facts they needed. Hours, days, and weeks of manual investigation compressed into a trivial web search. It almost made all their lives seem insignificant. Just motes of dust on the carpet of the city. At last, the system converged on a particular location.

"What the hell is *that*?" Chase said, peering at a nondescript building in Flushing, Queens with flashing signs out front.

"Let's see," Bob said. "It appears to be... A games parlor of some sort. Here we go: It's called the Keno Lounge."

"The *Keno Lounge*?"

Chapter 8

A light spring shower had started up and the waves churned harder as they approached Ellis Island. The historical landmark rose out of the black bog like a dead lump. In the distance, a tour ferry was skidding on a white thread over the distant water toward it.

"Doesn't add up," the detective said, his voice a murmur under the waves and engine. "Why the hell would they go to Ellis Island?"

"What's that, laddy?" Seadog said. "You'll have to speak up. She's a loud beast, this here Blue Codfish."

"I'm just saying, what is this, some kind of tour they're going on?"

"Ellis has a few secrets to her too I bet."

"I don't follow. Secrets?"

"Think about it. Place is awash with tourists every hour of the day, is she not? And on top of that right out there in the middle of the deep blue. Makes for a pretty decent cover, wouldn't you say?"

"Yes—but with the key disadvantage of being stranded on a frickin' island."

"That's only a disadvantage as long as you believe it to be."

The detective looked at him morosely. With this schooner being tossed about like a crackhead's hacky sack, trying to decode the sailor's riddles was going to prove a tall order. "You're gonna have to explain that one to me, Seadog."

"I mean think about it. Imagine two shady fellows showed up to meet on Ellis for a secret exchange. Neither of them can double-cross the other and run away, can they? And if one of them tries to do the other dirty they'd have difficulty escaping without the body being found first."

"I see. Okay, that makes sense. But this isn't that."

"Isn't it?"

"My client met up with someone, then got on his boat at the dock. Then they ride that rust bucket all the way down here. They go through all that just to do a deal on Ellis Island? Makes no sense to me. No—I don't see it at all."

"Presumably, laddy, there'd be a third party they'd be meeting."

"A third—" Crap. This old Seadog was sharper than he let on. Then again, anyone who could think straight while being tossed about by the cruddy brown foam washing around Manhattan would appear sharp. But it hit the detective then—this was going to be some kind of trade-off. "Chloe Bell is going to be on that island."

"I'd say you're likely right."

"But that makes even less sense. Franzen had nothing to give them. The dude was flat broke. He didn't mention anything about carrying money or anything else today either."

"People have more to offer than just their bank accounts, sonny jim. You've become cynical ahead of your years. This town'll do that to a feller."

"Gee whizz, pops, I'll try to be extra positive in the future." Franzen had a use? What use? He was the most average joe you could find if you tried. A completely nondescript, unassuming character that barely even existed.

...But from another angle, what if that was actually the reason? What if the kidnappers needed someone invisible? Someone they knew was controllable. And who didn't show up on anyone's radar? Someone who, if left to stew for a week in worry, would be willing to do almost anything for you at the drop of a hat.

And what if Franzen wasn't the only one they'd sunken their hooks into? Suddenly, this situation didn't seem so ludicrous anymore.

"Crud," the detective said. But his voice was buried under the drone of the engine, and the Seadog didn't respond.

...

The rustbucket was still docked when Seadog pulled the Blue Codfish into port.

"Alright," the detective said. "It's only 10 hectares. Shouldn't be too hard to find them. Hey, thanks for the ride, Seadog. What do I owe you?"

"Ah, don't worry about it," He said. "Needed to stretch my sea legs anyway."

"Uh—thanks." A free ride? In New York? It was unheard of. The detective gave him another once over—the sailor's red whisky face shined against a gray, bland sky. No doubt he'd show up on the detective's doorstep one of these days expecting a favor or ten. But he'd have to worry about that later. The trail was hot and he wasn't about to let it go cold.

Despite the ever-worsening weather, the island was littered with tourists. He scanned the area with his binoculars but saw no trace of Franzen. Okay, maybe this wouldn't be so easy after all.

"Hey Seadog," he turned back and said.

"Yo-ho."

"Could you do me a—"

"Want me to watch to see if they come back to the rustbucket, eh?"

"Yeah."

"If it means sticking one to old Cap'n Harris, I'd be honored."

"Thanks." Great, now the detective owed him two favors. He disembarked on to the port and ran up to the National Museum first, giving it a quick scan. People everywhere. The more he explored the place the more its utility became apparent. A jostling crowd of Japanese tourists swarmed by with their guide blasting out a million words a minute. Groups of college kids day drinking and lounging around in the garden. Families pushing buggies, families dragging kids. Women eating lunch outside. Old people taking leisurely strolls. The place was more packed than Times Square.

Hurrying through the museum and finding nothing, the detective skipped out and crossed through the cafe section skirting along the line separating New York and New Jersey. His street smarts didn't apply here. He'd only ever come to Ellis Island once on a school trip—he didn't know where any hotspot of criminal activity might be.

He jogged the entire ring around the circular garden and came up empty. Across the river, Manhattan was a blotched smear on the foggy sky, and from the other direction Lady Liberty pointed cautiously upward from the next island over. The detective pulled up a map on his phone and scanned the area. There had to be somewhere fitting; somewhere where they felt comfortable making the trade-off. Then it hit him—a shadow bolted up out of the misty springtime scene—it was the water tower behind the buildings. They wouldn't be here on the outskirts of the island which was tourist hell. The only place to be concealed here was behind the gingerbread-looking house that connected to the museum and ran half the length of the island. Now the problem was how to get behind there.

There had to be access through the house. He explored winding halls with high ceilings and intricate wall moldings, delicate paintings lining the walls, and sturdy wooden floors. The whole area had been freshly cleaned and everything seemed to sparkle. He came out on the other side to yet another park area strewn with tourists of every shape and description. This quaint little island was starting to lose its charm. Back into the house, this time taking the opposite direction. He came to a door leading off the main hall. The detective slowly pushed it open—the inside was dim and the cool shade snuck up his spine. He padded across the stone floor in a less decorated room—part of its furniture stacked and coated in a dust cover. He got the feeling he wasn't meant to come this way. That was good; that meant maybe it's where they took Franzen. Threading his way through the furniture and boxes, the detective came through to another door. This led down a cool, dark corridor in which his every step echoed in the narrow space, the only light given from a small window placed high on the far wall.

Coming to the end, he opened a door and light rushed at him like an oncoming train: He squinted through the brightness to find himself in the courtyard behind the house. An oasis within the island which itself was already an oasis from the noise of the city. The courtyard was surrounded by brick on all sides and the cobblestone path was lined with vibrant plants and shrubbery. Despite the fact this area seemed off-limits, it was still in good upkeep. The air was filled with the fragrance of sweet flowers in bloom and a small fountain trickled away in the center. He traversed the length of this area until he came across a low squat building that seemed worse for ware than the rest of the estate. The brick was in worse shape and the door grubby, and the building just generally seemed more aged than any of the others. As he got closer he realized its windows were formed from stained glass—was it some kind of small chapel? But this wasn't meant for the general public and it was clearly not in use for its original purpose. It may as well have worn a big red swooping light on it and rattled off a klaxon announcing Criminal Dealings Here.

Keeping close to the wall, the detective sidled up to the door and listened inside. Sure enough, he heard voices. Low, secretive voices. He pulled his Beretta 92F Inox, which thanks to his private cop license the city let him carry, and took another step toward the door. No organ music, no sound of a priest giving a sermon. But definite voices. Someone coughing. How many people were in there?

He climbed up to the window and peeped inside and saw the silhouettes of a group of people. Like some kind of dark seminar. Couldn't make out what they were saying. He had to get closer.

Suddenly feeling the presence of something behind him, the detective swung around—to face the barrel of a Taurus 689 Magnum aimed right between his eyes. It was held by a thick-headed man with close-cropped hair wearing a tracksuit. Gave the appearance of a polack or Eastern euro type.

"Easy there feller," the detective said. "You could do some serious damage with that thing."

"Oh yeah? Well turns out that's what it's designed for. What are you doing snooping around here? You a cop?"

"Maybe in another life. Now I'm just private."

"That's a shame, shamus. For you I mean. If you're not a cop then no one's gonna miss ya."

"I beg to differ. Who's going to feed my goldfish?"

"You're in no position to get wise, friend. In case you hadn't noticed, there's four inches of steel stuck in your face."

"Don't worry—I'm sure your girlfriend loves you anyway."

"What—?"

"Listen, buddy," the detective said. "I think we may have gotten off on the wrong foot. I'm only here to find my client, that's it. I couldn't care less about your little reunion for creeps, or whatever the hell this is."

"Sure, sure. But too bad, you stuck your nose in where it didn't need to be and now you gotta come with me until we get things squared away." He shoved the barrel into the detective's forehead.

"Since you asked so nicely."

The goon grabbed him and dragged him along with him right inside the door, finally giving the detective a good look at what lay inside: It was a chapel alright, rows of pews, a long red carpet up the center. The pews were lined with several unfortunate figures. Franzen was among them. They locked eyes for a second, then Franzen quickly looked away. It felt like running into an ex-girlfriend at the bar when she's out with her new boyfriend. The man at the altar had stopped speaking, although the low droning murmur of something coming from the corner speakers still went on unabated.

"Brought us a new friend," the thug said, shoving the detective forward.

"I can see that," said the man at the altar, a tall, clean-cut man with sharp features and piercing shale gray eyes, a thin mustache, and short combed hair. The stiff posture and unperturbed look suggested a military background. "Greetings, new friend. I am Priest."

"And I am Detective."

The thug shoved him. "No, you idiot. We call him Priest."

"Well, they call *me* Detective."

"What's your real name?" Priest said.

"John Jacob Jingleheimer Schmidt."

Priest shook his head like a father scolding a Child and sighed. "Bear in mind that we'll find out who you are anyway, so there's no point in continuing this charade. Plus, given the circumstances, you should be more courteous."

The detective shrugged. "Guess there's no point in hiding it. The name's Acre. I'm a private dick and I'm here to pick up the girl you kidnapped, asshole."

Chapter 9

The Keno Lounge was this two-story joint in Flushing, Queens, a real dumpy, classic New York neighborhood of cramped five-story apartment buildings in various states of disrepair with the lounge itself stuck in the middle. The Keno Lounge itself had a strange exterior of white painted brick with a series of arches set into the side of the wall. In fact, it would be difficult to guess the building's purpose were it not for the large glowing sign advertising its service and the loud exciting music piping out of a speaker onto the street that got your gambling juices flowing. In addition to Keno, half of the floor was given over to a sports bar and they also had an inexplicable novelty shop set just inside the entrance selling slogan-printed t-shirts that said things like "I'm a Pisces—Deal With It," and "New Yorkers Need Lovin' Too!" It was as if the owners couldn't decide what they wanted to do with the place.

The clientele seemed just as fragmented and schizophrenic—the sports bar was dotted with middle-aged to elderly guys, the keno area mostly elderly women, the snack bar was empty, not even staffed in fact, and only a confused tourist was looking inside the novelty store.

"This is so weird," Chase muttered.

"Why? Did you expect Bob to come with?" Kelly said.

"I don't mean that, Kelly. I was talking about this place. Although I'm not sure what I expected from Bob. I guess he doesn't come out into the field anymore. This is just his métier, interfacing with the world from behind a computer..."

"Don't you think his talents are wasted in the field? Besides, he's an SSA now and has a team to direct. Doesn't make sense for him to get down and dirty."

"Even SSAs do field work, Kelly. As a matter of fact, even ASAC Hogan came out in the field with me once."

"What?" Kelly looked like he'd been slapped in the face with a boulder. "The ASAC did? You worked the case, just you and him together?"

"Yeah, once. Only briefly."

"What made him do that?"

"Forget it, Kelly. I was just making a point."

"No, really. I'm interested."

"Look, I don't know. I'm still not sure I've figured that out. At the time I chalked it up to him micromanaging my conduct, or trying to play mentor or something."

"But ASAC Hogan never does that kind of thing—does he?"

"Apparently not."

"Huh. So, what, does that mean he thinks you're special or something? That you have some kind of potential that interests him or whatnot? Do you think it was your legacy from Quantico that caught his interest?"

"My legacy?"

"Come on Chase, you're like a legend over there. The old fart lecturers still mention your name."

"I don't know about that. I just did my best like everyone else. Quantico's full of bright stars, doesn't really mean anything." She shrugged, half-regretting telling him anything about it. Every answer encouraged ten more questions, a telescopic probe that extended inside her and tried to fish out things she didn't want disturbed. She carried on inside and sat down at the keno area, which was currently playing a game. Eighty numbers were displayed on a big screen TV where one by one the numbers were highlighted until twenty of them had been selected. Then the screen dissolved away and it all started again. The grannies and middle-agers were all glued to the screen, making their selections from a little panel embedded into the armrest of the plush chairs facing the screen.

"What kind of case was it?" Kelly whispered to her after a while. "As expected, he just couldn't let it go."

"Nothing that special. It was a murder of this guy, a higher-up in a private company dealing in government documents."

"In Manhattan, this was?"

"Yes."

"Sounds pretty high profile. This was when you were still starting out at the Bureau?"

"I wouldn't say starting out. But I wasn't exactly a veteran either. Anyway, at the time of the murder, some of these documents had gone missing. Government documents. Presumably, the hot point was the fact— hell, I don't even know if I should be discussing this with you."

"Ah come on, just tell me what was so particular about this case. What could it hurt? I'm a special agent just like you?"

No, you're not, Chase thought. You're only a GS-8. But if it would stop him from asking questions about her.

"Well, a senator was involved."

"In the murder?"

"No, not in the murder. There was—other things involved."

"Like what?"

"Like certain, damning materials."

"Damning of the senator?"

"Yes."

"Wait a minute—what? But you said it was a murder— a robbery."

"It was complicated."

"You can say that again."

"Let's just focus on this case," Chase said. "We already have our hands full with that."

"That's true."

"Try and get a feel for this place, maybe something will pop out at us."

The keno area was about what they expected: Wine red carpet with yellow curved lines. Big pleather armchairs, mustard yellow, all sitting in concentric circles around the front screens. The chairs were occupied by a string of mostly ladies and a few men. Mostly old. The humdrum atmosphere became surreal. A palpable tension hung in the room, but Chase couldn't figure out what it was. She scanned around the room but it didn't seem like they were being watched. It sure felt like it though. They watched the current game play out.

"So, this is where a string of arsons has brought us," Kelly said. "Bingo."

"It's not bingo," Chase said without much vigor. "It's keno. They're not the same thing."

"You know I never really understood the difference. My mom used to play bingo though."

Chase's eyes swiveled to the bar where a guy in a white suit sat sipping a cocktail. She wasn't a drinker—couldn't hold her drink at all, in fact. Yet, at this moment she felt like drinking on the job. "Look Kelly, keno is more like a lottery. You select several numbers and the computer calls them out. The more numbers you pick, the more you spend. The more numbers you match, the more you win. That's it. There's no waiting around like in Bingo for the balls to drop out. See—the current game's over already."

"So, you get to play the lottery over and over again. I can see why it'd be popular. Not much thought is required. So, are we thinking that Lucy Child came here to wind down?"

Chase sighed audibly and leaned back in her chair. "I regret getting out of bed today." She poked at the buttons on her armrest. You needed to buy a special card to play, and on the card you bought credits.

"You seem kind of out of sorts, Chase. Even more so than usual. Something got you down?"

"Just this whole case. From the very start, it's been—I don't know. Just not what I'm used to, I guess. I can't feel any momentum. I'm not sure how much field work you have under your belt, Kelly, but cases generally don't stagnate like this."

"Well that's natural, isn't it? We haven't really gotten a solid lead yet. This is our best one by far. You should be glad."

"Okay, but what the hell are we doing? I mean I'm used to chasing ghosts, it's what I do. But keno grandmas? Seriously?"

One of the silver-haired ladies turned back in her seat and shot Chase a steely glare.

"Chase," Kelly said, "I'm not sure I understand—wasn't finding the cleaning lady our best shot?"

"It's our best lead because it's our only lead—and it's a weak one. I mean here is this terrorist group causing havoc all across town and our best shot at finding them is a freaking *keno hall.* Don't you find that ridiculous?"

"I try not to be so self-aware. It gets in the way of the investigation."

Chase turned her eyes on him. He didn't seem to be joking.

"Don't worry though, Chase, Bob has our backs. So, do you want to take the big redhead over there or the curly gray grandma?"

"That's exactly it though—we're secretly depending on Bob to do this all for us. I guess I'm feeling obsolete. If SET has the ability to solve everything for us, what's the point of having field agents at all?"

"Come on now, Chase, don't be like that. The SET system is just a tool."

"Yes, but one that we increasingly depend upon to do our jobs for us. We have this terrorist network out there and we don't have the faintest idea where to start looking for them, bar invading the privacy of every citizen in the city. It's like 9/11 all over again. Except that this time the computer does all the work and without it we're stuck clutching our pieces."

"... Clutching our pieces? That's almost cop talk. Have you been hanging out with the NYPD lately?"

"Anyway, whatever. The game just ended. You go talk to the grandmas, Kelly. They like boyish faces like yours."

"What about you?"

"I'm gonna go talk to that guy over there."

"The lounge lizard in the Elvis suit?"

"I just got a feeling."

"Yeah, so do I. It reads 'total douche.'"

...

The man at the bar was somewhere in his late thirties to early forties, dressed in white jeans, long brown leather cowboy boots, a dark brown leather jacket, and a cowboy hat. And if that wasn't enough he even wore a handlebar mustache to complete the ensemble. He was sitting at the bar all alone sipping on an unknown ruddy drink that Chase thought if she asked what it was he'd probably answer 'sarsaparilla.'

"Hey thur, purty eyes," The man said in an expected southern drawl. "What's a girl like you doing in a place like this?"

"What's a girl like me doing here?" Chase said. "What's a cowboy doing at a keno club sports bar... In *Queens*?"

"Well I'll be darned. You have me thur. So, can I buy you a drink?"

"No thanks, cowboy. I just need to ask you a few questions."

"Oh brother. You a cop or somethin'?"

"Somethin'," Chase said.

"Jus my luck. Now here I was thinkin' I'd finally struck gold and it turns out—ah shucks, what the hell. Go ahead n stick me like a pig, purty eyes. I won't put up no fight. Can ah at least buy ya a drink?"

"I don't drink on the job," Chase said. Usually, she thought. "Did you ever see this woman come around here?" She slipped him the face photo of Lucy Child from the employee records of the R&A building.

"Hmm. Why sure, that's Lucky Lucy."

"Lucky Lucy?"

"Uh huh—just a little pet name you understand. On account of she won so darned often."

"Won at what? Keno?"

"Yis ma'am. Why that girl is the most divined creature I ever saw walk this earth. One time I saw her get five out of five twice in one day. You know the odds of that? Ain't damn high, I cun tell ya. I tol' the old girl she should invest her luck into somethin' more profitable, but no, she said. Only intrusted in the keno."

"Did you two speak together often?"

"Sure. Often enough. Good old Lucy was here twice a week."

"What did you tend to talk about?"

"Ah you know, usual types a thing. Life, love, work. How bad the Knicks suck," He gestured to the big screen at the front of the bar which was showing MSNBC Sports.

"She talked about her work with you?"

The cowboy shot her a wily eye and poked at the rim of his hat with a stiff finger. "More or less. What was there to talk about? The lady cleaned floors, as far as I come to understand it..."

"When's the last time you spoke?"

"Well now, lessee. Going on more than a week now." He finally turned to her, dropping the southern charm in place of a flash of horror in his eyes. "Ain't nothin'... *Happened* to her, is there?"

"I'm afraid she's gone missing."

The cowboy's eyes looked her over anew. "Say now. This is gettin' a mighty toasty. If you're thinkin' that I had anything—"

"I don't suspect you, relax cowboy. I just need to find Miss Child in relation to a—crime that was committed, at her place of work."

"I see. I see." He breathed hard, down the rest of his drink, and signaled to the bartender for another.

"Aside from small talk, did Miss Child ever mention anything about her personal life? Money issues, maybe a family member in trouble, this type of thing?"

"Well now. Let me think. Can't say she ever mentioned money trouble. Hell, this is Lucky Lucy here. If she wanted money all she had to do was go bet on some horses, I reckon. Probably woulda cleaned up and everything."

"Okay. Just one more question, did she seem—off? In the previous weeks, that is."

"Hmm. Now that you mention it, I did get a bit of what you might call a cold breeze these days. Why—you saying she had somethin' going on?"

"It would appear so."

"I mean I'm sorry to hear it if anything bad's happenin' to poor ol Lucy, but I have to say I find it a mighty relief."

"Why's that?"

"Well hell girl, it means I haven't done lost my mojo after all!"

Chapter 10

Acre was hauled into yet another backroom behind the chapel with his hands zip-tied behind his back like a hog. Trapped in a backroom behind a hidden meeting place, in a closed-off courtyard of a mansion on Ellis Island. "Geez, you guys think this is enough secrecy?" Acre said to the thug. "Maybe you can dig a secret tunnel too."

"Keep talking and we'll dig one alright—and you'll be lying in it."

This was getting ridiculous. It felt like falling asleep in a dream. Or maybe that was the nausea talking—he couldn't get out of this daze he'd been in, in fact, it was only growing worse. Something about the inside of the chapel had done a number on him and all his strength had been sapped.

"You stay here now until the Priest is finished," the thug said, leaving Acre here in this dark, dank room, the only sound a low background drone. Pretty soon he was feeling sleepy. He needed to snap out of it. This mental bind he was in—that was how they got you. Made you think you were powerless, unable to fight back. They beat you in spirit even before your body broke. So, this tool had him at gunpoint, so what? By the look of him, he was a total amateur—one swift sidestep and that Magnum would be in Acre's own hands. Except why was it he couldn't bring himself to move? Why did he let himself get shoved into this back room, and why didn't he do anything when this prick stole his prize Beretta Inox?

He felt like this whole thing was some kind of joke about his existence. Here he was trying to put his best foot forward and save the damsel in distress and now he was the one captured. Where was the justice in that? But these thugs didn't need justice. They had the force of cold steel and the power of their convictions. Maybe that's what Acre was missing—ever since leaving the force he didn't believe in much of anything anymore besides making his next paycheck.

Ever since that night when he'd lost control of himself, he'd lost his mojo. His very essence had been put in question.

It proved to be the inflection point of his career. Up until that point, he was Lieutenant Henry Acre, NYPD hotshot. Fast track to a Captain's seat, maybe even Chief of Police or Mayor someday. Acre always got his man. Quickly rising to detective in Hell's Kitchen, he had made more collars than the rest of his department combined. Within eighteen months he was Head Detective and cleaning up the streets like Hell's Kitchen's own floor scrubber. No one fell through the cracks on his watch.

But maybe that was his major weakness too—that he couldn't bear to fail. That's what had made Acre so recklessly pursue C-60's original leader Bucky. It was what made him walk right into the trap, following him without backup through the crowd in Times Square. If only he had waited for Chase and the other tacticals, maybe what transpired that night wouldn't have happened.

Maybe he wouldn't have popped that terrorist bastard in the head with his Beretta.

At the hearing, he had no real defense. He'd shot a suspect in cold blood right in front of a crowd of witnesses and it had all been caught on surveillance footage. Ironic that a tool of the law would be the ax that fell on Acre himself.

Due to getting a decent lawyer, he wasn't convicted of murder on account of the threat Bucky posed with an unknown weapon. That was something at least. But in the end, the NYPD still had to cover their asses, and the bad publicity the whole event had summoned rained hell down on the department. While much of the public lauded Acre for "taking out that scumbag," there was still a whole other demographic who felt the exact opposite—that what Acre had done constituted a violation of basic human rights. That he had executed a criminal before he could be brought to trial. He had played judge, jury, and executioner, ignoring the legal system entirely. Therefore, he had no right being a police officer. Such voices didn't blow over, either— they only got louder as time went on. And while Acre thought the whole movement against him stunk worse than an Astoria fish market, the situation was thoroughly out of his hands by then. Eventually, the Chief of Police intervened and that was that. Acre was thrown out on his ass. No more badge, no more gun. No more career. He wouldn't even have gotten his hands on a private license had he not held dirt on the right people.

Acre yawned in the dark, locked room, trying not to doze off. He got up off the chair and started pacing the place. With time on his hands and a boiling rage in his gut, Acre refused to drop the thought. Something about the whole setup leading to his departure from New York's Finest had just stuck in his craw. The public outcry felt orchestrated—certainly motivated more by bad press coverage than anything. And if there was one thing that the last case had taught him, it was not to trust the media. Who wasn't to say that the whole press had been controlled by remnants of C-60? After all, they'd only caught Bucky and no one else. Plus, C-60 had already shown their ability in being able to influence people via the media; hell, this technology of theirs was the marketer's wet dream. Even Acre himself had momentarily fallen under its spell. So, was it really that far out there to assume that they had co-opted the media and turned the public against him? That they had conspired to take Acre out of service and thus make him no longer a threat?

It was exactly like something they'd do. But try telling that to the stone-headed chief of police.

So he dropped the whole thing and went private.

And without the crutch of the NYPD to depend on, Acre's entire repertoire had to change overnight. He learned to become agile and nimble. He learned to get to leads fast—zip straight to them the way a certain broad at the FBI had done, wring the information out of them before the trail went cold.

His whole attitude up until that point had been about protecting and serving—putting a dent in crime. Doing what they could. But the moment he went solo that all changed. He realized that it wasn't enough to just do your best. Up close and personal with the gripes of real-life clients, he realized how much his actions affected their lives. That it wasn't about putting a 'dent' in anything. You had to stop the bastards out there from making people's lives hell, end of story.

After completing a few cases this way, Acre had gotten his confidence back. On downtime between cases, he began to scratch the itch that had never left the back of his mind: Finding out what happened to C-60.

It was made easy for him when various media crimes began happening over the city. So, they were calling themselves 'the C' now. Whatever they called themselves, it was still the same handiwork. Still the same technological angle. And still that same sadistic tendency to inflict fear on the populace. And he even thought he'd grasped their tail at last, a pattern in the recent arsons.

But that was when he'd gotten the job from Franzen. And he'd temporarily had to put the investigation on hold.

Yet sitting here, rendered completely helpless by just one Magnum-wielding thug, Acre began to question his own ability again. If he couldn't even get a hostage back, how could he possibly stop the C?

The door opened then, and Priest sauntered in with his lackey in toe.

"Okay, Acre. Henry Acre," the overgrown altar boy was saying. "Looks like you had your five minutes of fame already. So, you're the one who shot Bucky."

Acre stirred inside. "You know Bucky?"

The altar boy shrugged. "Of course. He's a pop icon at this point. Perhaps even our generation's Ted Kaczynski. But no one can tell you the name of the poor FBI sap who wasted decades of his life to capture Ted. That tells you something, doesn't it?"

"Yeah, that this country prefers its villains to its heroes. Anyway, who cares? I'm not exactly trying to get my face on the cover of Time."

"Not only did you not get credit for your efforts, Lieutenant—or, sorry, ex-Lieutenant, but you even got kicked off the force. Tut tut. Should have handled the situation with more tact."

"Oh yeah? Well if you saw a known bomb terrorist carrying a suspicious box into Times Square, what would you do?"

"Tut tut again. All the reports say Bucky activated the box *before* you shot him. In fact, you killed him in cold blood. Wasn't that the issue you had with New York's Finest fascists?"

"This isn't about me. I came here looking for Chloe Bell. I couldn't give a damn about Bucky."

"You don't seem to understand what position you're in, Mr. Acre. It's not one where you can make any demands. But—if it will set your mind at ease, Miss Bell has already been reunited with Mr. Franzen."

"She has?"

"Oh yes. You didn't see her just now?"

Acre thought back. As a matter of fact, Franzen had been sitting next to a broad. How had he not caught that? Well, he had a gun to his head, that's why.

"Ah, shucks," Acre said. "That's that then. Case closed."

"It's too late for that, Mr. Acre. So, you see you really should have kept your nose out of our business. But now that you've seen our—gathering—we must decide what to do with you."

"Frankly, I could care less what weird cult crap you get up to in here. Go ahead, drink goat's blood, summon Mammut or Xenu, or whatever you like. My job was to get the girl back. The girl's back. Therefore, no more job. No more Acre. Just give me my rod back and I'll be out of your hair."

"I'm afraid it's really not so simple."

"Sure it is. Now be a good altar boy and get this goon here to stop pointing my own steel at me, before I ram it so far up his ass he'll have to brush his teeth with WD-40."

Priest sighed deeply. "You really seem to have trouble accepting authority, don't you Mr. Acre? It's no surprise you were kicked off the force—in fact, it seems to me it would have happened sooner or later."

"I sorta came to the same conclusion myself on that."

"Then perhaps you should use that same ability for reflection to meditate on what this situation bodes for you."

"You're not gonna off me, come the hell on. This is Ellis Island, for Christ's sake, not some rusty warehouse by the docks. How would you even get rid of the body?"

The Priest cracked a smile. "Too smart for your own good—that's your problem, Mr. Acre. And indeed our problem too. No, it would be unwise to kill you here. Not when we have such a good thing going. The only thing is to have you forget this ever happened."

"Consider it forgotten," Acre said. "Now this zip tie is really starting to chafe, so—"

Priest gestured to the goon, who set a portable television down on the desk. "We'll let you go soon," he said. "But first it's important you watch something."

The television began playing a series of incomprehensible fragmented images superimposed on static as the men walked out. The throbbing sound that had been plaguing Acre ever since walking into the chapel now increased in volume until he could feel the blood inside his skull washing over him in a red wave.

"Oh crud," he groaned, feeling the room spinning around him. "Not this shit again."

Chapter 11

They were back at the field office. Bob was sitting there with his coffee between two hands like a little boy about to listen to his bedtime story as Chase relayed their findings from the lounge.

"So, this Lucy Child character is in deep with some shady people and needs money fast. Makes her an easy target for manipulation."

"Wait a minute, Chase." Bob swiveled around on his seat, his mouth gaping like a goldfish. "Are you trying to tell me that Lucy Child was sinking in *keno debt*?"

"What? No. Bob—the keno is just a decoy."

"The keno isn't the point, Bob," Kelly added.

"Okay, go on..." Bob said.

"The connection is—ah screw it. Kelly, you tell him." Chase went back into the break room and slipped back two aspirin.

"What's gotten into her?" Bob said.

"Who knows?" Said Kelly. "You know her temperament better than me."

"I wish I could say that I do," Bob said, shooting a worried glance back toward his ex-partner.

"So, about this amusement hall, it's not a real casino, right?" Kelly said, taking the baton. "Because gambling is illegal in this state outside of Indian reservations. The New York Constitution says you can only bet on horses or play bingo or lottery games."

"Right," Bob said.

"And keno is almost sorta like bingo. Kinda. So, it's not considered illegal gambling."

"Right."

Chase groaned, sitting down at her desk and resting her head in her hands.

"Hey there," Bob said. "Are you okay Chase?"

"I'm fine Bob, just super duper. Don't let me stop you. Keep going, Kelly."

"The Keno Lounge is a front, Bob," Kelly said. "It's being used as a front for the illegal stuff."

"Oh come on, you're telling me they're running an illegal gambling operation right there in the open? In Queens, no less."

"It's not that uncommon, Bob," Chase said. "We've seen it before."

"Yeah—buried deep in the recesses of Chinatown," Bob said. "Not in the middle of a residential district. What kind of illegal gambling are you talking about?"

"Bookmaking," Kelly said. "What else?"

"Bookmaking?" Bob said, tapping at his computer. "But sports betting is legal now, I thought." He typed some more. "Yeah—says here the State Gaming Commission allows it at four different places."

"Okay, now check where those four places are," Chase said in a throaty, strained voice. "All the way out in nowheresville. And New York law makes it so you have to be there in person to bet. Hell one of them's even up by Binghamton for Christ's sake. You're gonna take two, three hours out of your day to place a bet on the Knicks? It's not happening, Bob."

"Okay," Bob says. "I see your point. So, the premise is they're doing illegal bookmaking. How do they get away with it?"

"It's actually kinda elegant," Kelly said, grinning. "We stayed there for hours until we figured it out. The way it works is, certain keno numbers on certain rounds represent certain bets. When those in the know pick those numbers, they're actually making a bet on a team."

Bob looked at him, dumbfounded. "That's—completely—"

"Genius?"

"I was going to say ridiculous. Okay, what about the size of the bet? They surely don't use the keno bet amount itself, it would be too small. There's a limit to how much you can bet on keno, right?"

"There's a multiplier," Chase said, head still buried in her arms. "It's determined by a secondary number on the board. Say you make a bet of $5 and choose the 10x multiplier, that's a bet of $50."

"Remarkable," Bob said. "But then wouldn't other players make bets by accident?"

"Nope," Kelly said. "We figure the way it works is it only counts as a bet if they're like a member or whatnot."

"Hmm. How would they even do that?"

"There's a card you have to use to play the game," Chase grumbled. "You could just give the members of the real gambling circle a special card."

"Okay," Bob said. "Okay. This is—yes, I could see this working."

Kelly leaned forward, his face scrunching up with excitement, the joy of pursuit. "Only those privy get to play, and you'd have no way of proving what's going on. Likely all the players have the codes memorized and don't even carry a crib sheet or nothing."

"Okay, sure. But then how do they collect their winnings?"

"What do you think, Bob?" Chase said. "Keno."

"Keno?" Bob blinked a couple of times. "I'm not sure I follow."

"The game is rigged to let someone win their bet through a game of keno," Kelly said.

"You're shitting me," Bob said.

"Shit, you, I do not."

"Okay—" Bob said, "maybe I can, maybe I can get in touch with the State Gaming Commission and get a backlog of all their past keno games. We might be able to find the pattern then."

"Wait—" Kelly said. "You can do that?"

"Of course. They have to record the outcome of each game to prove they're not using faulty odds to con their customers. Alright, cool, I've sent an email through channels for the data. But so here's the ass-kicker: Say these guys have this elaborate setup to place sports bets in plain sight. The question is—who's behind it?"

"That's the part that's going to make you flip," A deep voice said from the door. Standing there in the frame was a large, well-built man with a square jaw, curly slick hair, and impeccable taste: OrgCrime Section Chief, Tony Montana.

"Section Chief Montana..." Bob said. "Don't tell me this is what I think..."

"Yup. The good old mob up to their old tricks. We've been trying to nail this gambling racket for months but could never figure out how they were pulling it off. Until now, that is. Come with me, I'll explain it all to you."

...

The Organized Crime floor was decked out in leather seats, floral engraved sidings, and walls in elegant color tones of creamy whites, deep browns, and ruddy burgundy. It had style, it had class. It didn't look like the Bureau at all. Chase could scarcely believe Montana had gotten the leeway from ASAC Hogan to remodel the place like this. It looked like a freaking resort.

On one side, a space had been given over to a giant whiteboard on which was drawn the crime network they'd pieced together so far. Photos of different men, places, and captions detailing various past crimes connected to one another by string. Montana was gesturing to it with a telescopic pointer while his team milled around in the background half-paying attention to the score they already knew by heart.

"See this big void around here," Montana told Chase and the others. "This is what came out of us busting Vigotti. But as you can see from the scattered entities around here," he said, pointing to various photos and bios pinned to the wall. "It didn't stay a void for long." Chase scanned the wall and found mostly Italian mafia types.

"Wait a second," Chase said. "Didn't the *Dragons* move in on that space?"

"They were in the process of doing so until you took out Uncle Bing," Montana said. "After that, they've kind of gone underground."

"Isn't this whole map the underground?" Kelly asked.

"That's cute, son," Montana said. "But there's underground—and then there's *underground*."

Kelly looked at his two cohorts for help, but they didn't say anything. It didn't necessarily mean anything. It was just Montana showboating as usual.

"So, anyway," Montana said, pointing back to the few 'entities' in the void. "Here you can see our two major players here." He pointed to a balding slim man about 5'10" in a flashy-looking gray suit with a smug grin that made you want to punch him. "This one is Saul Sparks. Career con man. Got busted several times in the 2000s for various scams and since then has stepped up his game and become less visible. We're thinking he's the mastermind behind the keno front. Then on the right here," he said, pointing to a man of indeterminable age due to cosmetic work—he vaguely looked to be in his forties but with a full thick head of hair and no wrinkles and was dressed in casual but expensive wear in dark colors. Botoxed eyes stared out from a stiff face that once probably was a real looker. "This one is Brady Mayo. Also a grifter, but is more of an ex-gigolo and middleman than a straight-up conman like Sparks. He used to be a front for jewel thieves in Midtown, back when you could still pull off a stunt like that without getting crucified."

"The two of these slimeballs are working together on this?" Bob asked. "Gambling doesn't seem like it would be their thing."

"We have no direct evidence yet, but peripheral evidence would seem to suggest that yes, they are in a conglomerate of some kind."

"*Sparks? Mayo?*" Chase said. "They don't sound very Italian, Section Chief Montana."

Montana shrugged, his overdeveloped shoulders almost splitting his pinstripe suit when he did. "The mob has changed. They've become more open to working with the local scum."

"I don't get it," Chase said. "How is it even the mob then? The mob is a family, it's organized. What you're showing us just seems like a loose, fragmented bunch of career criminals."

"They're connected, just not in ways that are immediately visible."

"Jesus," Chase said. "You sound just like Bob."

"Nothing works straightforwardly anymore," Bob chimed in. Except he didn't seem too upset by that, in fact, he was beaming out the creases on his golden face, much like Kelly, who was practically jumping up and down at the prospect of going after the legendary mafia.

"How do you know they're connected if you haven't been able to bust the keno front?" Chase said.

"Good question, agent," Montana said. "That's the hard-nosed attitude we look for in the Bureau."

Chase made a gesture of semi-acceptance; really she was just annoyed at Montana's usual smoke-blowing. He went on, "See, a couple years back, Sparks and Mayo were both prime suspects in a local pyramid scheme. Reports indicated the scheme had earned upwards of three million dollars from here in Manhattan and Long Island."

"That's a lotta dough," Kelly muttered. "They shook down grandmas for all that?"

"It wasn't just vulnerable old people—they also fleeced many somewhat reputable financial folks. Call it a testament to the sophistication of these two sharks."

"But you never caught them," Chase said.

"Right. We could never make it stick. The pair had switched from working directly with the marks to obscuring their moves behind an outsourced team— even though the grift was local, it was executed through an international proxy."

"But if that's the case then why'd they switch to something they could be way more easily caught for?" Chase said. "And if they made millions of dollars why even—never mind, I know the answer to that one. Greed."

"There's that hard nose again," Montana said, grinning. "Well, what we're thinking is that the international grift cost them too much in terms of labor and management.

Ended up cutting into their bottom line. So, they had to change tack here—how do you retain anonymity while still making a large cut of the profits? Well, the Italians had a few good ideas on how to do that—after all, they'd been doing it for a hundred-plus years in this country..."

Bob said, "You use a legitimate front to hide your real operations—choose a place that deals in a lot of money."

"Very good, Bookman," Montana said. "That way it makes it too hard to see anything cockeyed is going on. The real doozy is that all the money they handle through keno is legal, so it's pre-laundered. No IRS problems after the fact when you start buying Mazerattis and yachts. And what could be a better front than gambling? As far as anyone on the outside is concerned, it's all random—and no one can prove otherwise."

"The Commission didn't find anything wrong with their results," Bob said. "I'm figuring the lounge must have some kind of method in place for evening out the odds—makes it harder to win for others in the process. Means they not only win the usual house cut but also recover partial losses by screwing over the real keno players. A double grift."

"A picture is starting to form here," Chase said. "So, Lucy Child gets in deep with these gambling sharks, maybe runs up a bad debt. She's in trouble. But she also has an immediate way to make money fast—selling top-secret documents. Maybe these pseudo-mob characters even offer to fence the documents themselves, given

Mayo's background. Child doesn't have much choice but to comply—but at the same time, she knows the Records & Accounts building is locked down tight—if anything goes missing she'll be a number one suspect. She catches this C hysteria on the news and decides to capitalize on it—it's the perfect patsy. Not only does burning that building pin the blame on the C, but it also destroys the evidence that anything was taken."

"So, you're thinking it wasn't the C after all," Kelly said.

"It also explains why the flammable material used was something as every day as gasoline jelly," Chase added.

"But how do we prove it?"

"Simple," Chase said. "We catch these keno sharks. And then we catch Lucy Child."

"It's not quite that simple," Montana said. "Like I said, we've been going after these two punks for months."

"In that case," Bob said, "I think I might have a way to help you expedite that."

"Here we go again," Montana said, wearing a troubled smile. "You and your damn computers."

Chapter 12

Acre woke up with an orchestra in his head playing hard percussion. It was like someone had thrown a jar of jumping bugs into the drum of his mind. Stumbling around his blurry apartment he ransacked shelves and drawers for an aspirin.

How much did he have to drink last night? He could barely remember. He must have ordered gin. He told himself he was going to stop ordering gin. Gin always resulted in a day of regret afterward. And what the hell, getting loaded wasn't going to solve this case. The case, the case, the case. What was it again? He could barely gather half the details from his mind, knocking back five aspirin and downing it with milk from the fridge, then spurting a thick white spray across his kitchen. The five aspirin clattered uselessly to the tiled floor and his head still pounded. He checked the milk carton: Three days expired. What in the hell? Another bad omen. Washing his mouth out, he downed five new aspirin and waited for them to kick in before mopping up the spill. Then, because he couldn't find his lighter, lit the gas on his oven top to light his cigarette. When the blue flame wolfed around the ring it hit him: What he'd found. Smoke meandered across the kitchen as he recollected the facts.

There was this character named Saul Sparks, a two-bit hood from a one-bit neighborhood. One of the New Mafia, what they lacked in organizational support was made up for in pure slippery cunning. Which is why Acre hadn't been able to get a lock on the exact particulars of his operation so far. He remembered getting close to something when he started drinking, and everything after that was blacked out. Acre was meant to track down a set of documents Sparks was holding onto. That was the case. Seemed simple enough when he took it. But this mafia crap was proving a hard sell.

No matter. A mobster like this was his bread and butter. Sneaky or not, Sparks was the kind of guy if you pounded enough pavement he'd eventually jump out of the cracks. Twisting out his cigarette in the sink, Acre downed another three aspirin, teased back his lengthening dark hair, equipped his Beretta 92FS Inox, and slipped on his black leather coat.

The only problem with pounding pavement was that his brain was already pounding. Luckily, there was an expedient method to both getting ahead on the case and shutting up the rave currently going on under his skull. The spring afternoon rain rushed down at him as he slipped into the bar in Queens. A known hood joint, its denizens eyed him with a cool detachment. In his hung-over state, Acre wore a kind of gauze of inequity that made him look more like fellow scuzz than a cop.

"Gimme a jack and coke, landlord," Acre spat. "And make it dry. I'm wet enough as it is."

"That'll be nine bucks—and lose the attitude, unless you want to take another shower."

The bartender was a hard ass and drove an even harder bargain. Nine freaking bucks. Acre swallowed the drink in a few gulps then switched to beer—at nine smackers a pop, whiskey was a luxury. Especially when he was no longer getting paid expenses. In fact, he wouldn't get paid unless he found the documents. Oh yeah. That little niggling detail was something he still couldn't work out. Why the hell had he agreed to those terms? Was he just trying to punish himself at this point? Questions poured down harder than the rain in Queens, while answers were about as forthcoming as a smile in Queens.

"Know a guy by the name of Sparks?" Acre asked the bartender, slipping him a twenty. If he was going to burn greenbacks in here it might as well be on information.

The bartender shot him a cold look. He shot Andrew Jackson an even colder one. Acre's wallet ached as he pulled out another. Now Jackson had a twin. The bartender's gaze elevated in temperature by half a degree. Enough to melt the ice a fraction.

"Saul Sparks?" He grunted. "Sure, everyone knows him."

"Knows what about him?"

"That he runs the Keno Lounge a few blocks from here," the bartender said, smirking as he slipped the two notes. Okay, so maybe a smile in Queens wasn't so rare after all. Only problem was, the only time you saw one was after getting screwed. Acre slammed his hand down on the notes, garnering him some attention from the dark characters across the room.

"Whoa there, jack," Acre drawled. "I didn't pay forty smackers for the contents of a Google search."

"Oh yeah?" The bartender growled back, leaning over the bar. "Well, I don't put my business in jeopardy for the price of four jack and cokes."

"Then maybe you should charge less for them, you rip-off artist."

"What I charge for drinks in here is my business. Until that's your name on the sign out there I suggest you keep your advice to yourself. Not that it's anything to you—but the rent around here ain't so damn cheap."

"The rent, sure. I'll bet. The rent to pay your gambling debts, you mean."

The bartender's eyes widened a fraction. That was a bingo.

"So, that's it huh?" Acre said, returning the Queen's smile. "Sparks is leaning on you. How much you in for?"

"I don't know what the hell you're talking about," the bartender said. "And frankly, I think you better beat it before you upset the other customers..." He gestured to the corner where the patrons had switched from skulking to eyeing him down. Anything could trigger a beatdown now. But screw that—Acre's head was still baking like a fruit cake on Christmas and after all of this trouble he was going to get his money's worth or else.

"Know what I think?" Acre said. "I think you're in big. I think half your little rinky dink overpriced-jack-and-coke-selling bar here is under Sparks' thumb. And I bet he can put the screws on you if he finds out you talked. But guess what, you apron-wearing ape? If I talk, he's gonna think you talked anyway. So, if you don't want me to talk, you better talk. Capiche?"

The bartender rolled the conditions around in his head like dice in a cup. Eventually, he seemed to grasp the stakes involved. Acre had made a big enough disturbance to give the impression of a nuisance; he was using that to his advantage.

"Lousy good-for-nothing snitch," the bartender said, taking a more defeated tone. "You keep on making threats like that and one of these days you're gonna find yourself sitting in a bathtub full of ice and missing a vital organ or two."

"Yeah, yeah, yeah. The future is the future. I wanna know about the present."

"You already guessed it. Gambling."

"Fine. It's gambling. Big deal. A two-bit mobster like that, what else can he do? Extortion is too messy and loud. And he's probably too much of a pussy to run guns. Plus, rumor has it Sparks started off in horses. But I know he's given up that line because the whole thing's run by the guys in Jersey now. So, what's he got going on? And don't give me none of this keno crap either 'cause I ain't buying it. What is it? Greyhounds? Cock fights? Some little back room run by illegals?"

"It ain't cock fights. This is New York, pal. Not bumfuck Tennessee. What do you think makes the most moolah, huh?"

Acre paused for a moment and his eyes flickered around the dive bar—he caught the patrons no longer looking at him but now glued to a small TV hooked up to the wall which was showing a basketball game. The Bucks were playing the Celtics. They were glued to this crap. Why? No one down in Queens gave a hot diggity damn about the Celtics. Not unless it was for one reason in particular. The pieces started fitting together: A bar familiar with Sparks, in bed with him maybe. And all its denizens hooked to the boob tube, glued to a crappy basketball game between teams they could care less about.

"Jesus Chrimler," Acre spat. "He's a goddamn sports bookie."

"Well look who graduated middle school," the bartender said. "Congratu-fricking-lations. Now can you kindly get the hell out of my bar? All this standing around of yours is giving me indigestion." He went to swipe up the forty dollars again.

"Not so fast," Acre said.

"Ah, geez, what the hell do you want now? You finally rubbed those two neurons of yours together and came up with half an answer. Put the rest together yourself. I

ain't changing your diapers. I don't have anything more
for you."

"Sure you do. First of all, I wanna know how you make
the bets. And then I want another jack and coke. This
time on the house." The bartender started twitching
and Acre felt the blood rushing to his brain. This was
what he needed. This got his veins to open, got his
lungs working. His legs fired up and his eyes stopped
stinging. No better way to start the day than shaking
down punks like this. This bartender was just a big fish
in a small pond, and Acre was the neighborhood cat.

When the bartender made his move he telegraphed it
like an airport marshaller landing a jumbo jet. Before
he'd even reached his beefy hand halfway under the bar
to the double-barreled sawn-off shotgun beneath, Acre
already had his silver inox in hand and pointed, from
under his jacket, right at the bartender's sweating pink
head.

"Now," Acre said, suddenly feeling his headache
subside. "About that drink."

Chapter 13

At least now they were on the hunt and not spinning their wheels in myth and hearsay. The C's media crimes had only gotten worse—their viral messages were starting to crop up hidden in the broadcasts of random TV shows and news programs and even on some streaming services and no one seemed capable of figuring out how they were doing it.

In the old days, it was possible—with a powerful enough transmitter and in-depth knowledge of the technology—to interrupt an ongoing TV or radio broadcast and insert a pirate broadcast over it momentarily. That was in the analog days, however. Since everything had gone digital, that kind of airwave piracy was nigh-on impossible due to the signals being encrypted over the air. The modern alternative would be to hack into the station's computer network, which would be incredibly difficult to pull off repeatedly without getting caught. Another, more plausible way, would simply be to place an inside man in the TV station who could insert the frames into the transmission for you. But after an investigation of the stations by both the FBI and NYPD, no such tamperer could be identified. Was it really just a hugely sophisticated hacker group behind all of this?

The answer seemed too simple to Chase. It didn't seem like the C at all; and especially not like their progenitor, C-60, who had almost blown up an entire building just to get their video on the airwaves. Their M.O.s couldn't be more distinct. Was the C a natural evolution of what Bucky had started?

Chase thought herself around in circles about it but no answer popped out. The only rational way forward, she figured, was to approach things differently and tackle the other crimes supposedly pulled off by the C: The arsons. And even though Lucy Child was by all appearances a copycat arson, something about it made Chase believe that solving the Child case would put them a step closer to figuring out the truth behind the C. Maybe it was the fact of the sensitive documents involved, or maybe not even something explicit as that, but just the vague sense of impenetrability of the case that felt so much like them. In any case, they had to get to the bottom of this. And if SET was the way to do that then so be it.

While Chase was reluctant to go back to relying on SET again if Montana's story was anything to go on, basic pavement pounding wasn't going to solve this one. Sparks and Mayo were tricky characters who weren't going to slip up so easily. They weren't your usual amateur criminal who lived the straight life until circumstances tempted them to step out of line— making a host of mistakes in the process. The career criminal was a different breed: It took away the advantage of law enforcement because they knew the rules of the game just as well. They knew how not to get caught. If anything, this whole keno setup wasn't a badge of ignorance but a mark of their supreme confidence.

The best way to approach this, Bob posited and Chase concurred, was to forget the two players for now and instead try to find the weak link in their organization.

It took a few days of data wrangling, but eventually, Bob found an in...

"Eighth and Forty-Eighth? As in the Minnesota Strip?" Chase said, hands on hips and standing there in front of an impossible conclusion. SET had come up with a pattern linking the keno operation to the red light district of Hell's Kitchen. But the computer had to be wrong, didn't it?

"It makes sense if you consider the keno front doesn't have high enough of a payment bandwidth," Bob explained.

"High bandwidth? Bob, what in the hell are you talking about?"

"Okay, so imagine this, Chase. They start out doing it all through keno, I'm sure. But the more successful their operation becomes, the less the lounge can be used to directly pay out. Think about it. It would be too suspicious if they kept giving people big payouts—too detectable. Your cowboy friend even said something along those lines, right? That's why they called her Lucky Lucy just for getting two fives in a row. Okay. So, assume she got that due to a hidden bet she made. But what if someone's secret bet wins even bigger than that? They'd have to pay out with an even more outrageous win. I have the Keno Lounge's payout table here—say someone bets on an underdog team with odds of 100 to 1. You'd have to win a seven-out-of-seven in keno for that. Now in sports betting you might get lucky and hit that a couple of times. But what are the chances of getting a keno seven-out-of-seven twice in a short time period? Astronomical. At least, it's rare enough that if it happened, the regulars at the Lounge would get mighty suspicious mighty fast. And then Sparks has to contend with the possibility of snitches."

"Okay Bob, I see your point. And due to the maximum bet size, they can't fudge it with a different keno outcome either."

"All I'm hearing here is that Keno was a bad choice for their front," Kelly butted in, lumbering into the room carrying a box of bear claws and chewing on one himself. "It's too limited."

"What else were they going to do, Kelly?" Bob said. "Bingo has the same limitations with the added problem of being too slow—the payment bandwidth is even smaller. And the lottery can only be run by the State. Keno was the only way to do something like this out in the open, not on a reservation, and not in some casino out in the sticks. And that people would come to play even in some rathole neighborhood at all hours of the day."

"Fine," Kelly said. "So, they try it for a while, it becomes too successful and they find themselves looking for other methods of payout..."

"Right," Bob said. "So, I'm thinking maybe Keno works fine for maybe ninety, ninety-five percent of the time. But if you can't pay the big winners and word gets out—that puts you in a bad spot."

"They're liable to rat on you."

"Exactly. Need to keep the whales happy—that's the number one rule of making money in a gambling operation."

"So—can we get back to why SET thinks it's the red light district?" Chase said.

"I mean, it's a shady as hell place to make a payoff, sure," Bob said. "But SET has got Sparks' henchmen heading up there on a regular basis."

"Sloppy," Kelly said, his mouth full. "Careful guy like that leaving a trail so easy."

"They have plausible deniability," Bob replied. "They could argue they were just indulging in their more—base needs."

"That would be the conclusion most people would draw," Chase said. "Without SET."

"Bingo," Bob said.

"Not bingo, keno," Kelly said.

"What also makes it so perfect," Chase said, ignoring Kelly's idiotic joke, "is that up in the Minnesota Strip, people know to keep their mouths shut. So, it's just another couple of perves heading into a sleaze pit motel for a quick one, right? Who cares? No one."

"What if they really are just perves though?" Kelly said, sucking down his donut with a large mouthful of coffee. "You can't rule that out."

"Oh, they're going up there for more than nightly company," Bob said. "And this is how I know..."

He brought up a graph showing correlations between Sparks' henchmen's visits to the red light district, the distribution of payouts at the Keno Lounge, and statistical anomalies in various sports game events—in particular, a recent match of a win of the 76ers against the Knicks coincided with a trip to the strip. It had been a particular anomaly in odds due to the fact the 76ers' MVP Joel Embiid was injured and didn't play that match. The payout had been forty-two-to-one. Big money.

Chase just stood there, completely stunned. Not at the result, but at the way they'd found it. So, this was what crime fighting was going to look like from now on? It was just so completely unlike what they'd done up to now. All she could do was look at her former partner with awe. Behind that mild-mannered demeanor and creasy face, there were the makings of genius. He'd unlocked the power of SET in a way no one in the Bureau had thought to. Everyone in the FBI had always treated this tool as a useless appendage, just an annoyance that didn't give enough return on your time investment. But slowly, over the course of a decade, Bob had reinforced the interface to the system and made its hidden power more accessible.

While OrgCrime Division had been chasing the keno sharks for months, now, in a matter of days, they had their most solid lead yet for taking them down.

"This is incredible," Kelly spluttered. "We have them by the balls."

"Yeah, but don't squeeze yet," Bob said. "We still have to catch them in the act or all of this is just circumstantial evidence."

"How are we going to do that?"

"I have a few ideas there," Bob said. "I've already coordinated with NYPD Vice to make sure they have no ongoing sting operations. They gave us the green light for the red light, if you will."

"What are we talking about here Bob?" Chase said. "The green light for what? You're requesting someone from NYPD Vice go undercover on a sting operation for us?"

"Yes to the undercover part, no to Vice," Bob said.

Chase peered at him, confused. "Then who is going undercover?"

He and Kelly both stared back at her. Then the unspoken shoe dropped.

"Oh, no way," Chase said. "No freaking way."

"Come on Agent Chase," Kelly said. "You were the one who was itching to get back in the field."

"I wanted to get back in the field with my SIG Sauer, not with a mini skirt and pumps. Forget it."

"Alright," Bob said, raising his hands in defeat. "I guess we'll just get another agent." He turned to Kelly and asked, "what do you think of Gonzales?"

"From Violent Crimes? Hachi machi. She'll do the trick. Or there's Magdalena from Financial—she puts the pep in your step if you know what I mean."

"Yeah," Bob said, "doubt she'd be up for this job though."

"True. Oh hey, what about that Jones chick with the big—"

"Oh my God," Chase groaned. "You guys are doing this on purpose. Fine, I'll do it, alright? I'll go dangle myself out there like a worm on a hook."

"Well," Bob said innocently, "if you're sure you're comfortable with it."

"Screw you, Bob. Just shut up and tell me what the plan is so I can go grab these goons. And I just hope to god that all he pulls out of his pants is a payout."

Chapter 14

In Hell's Kitchen, the spring rain was falling in big soaking clumps that shone gold under the streetlights and Chase had to hide under the awning of a restaurant so as not to get drenched. She shivered as the backsplash off the sidewalk sprinkled her body and gave her goosebumps. A catcall from a passing beat-up Ford jolted her—made her remember where she was and what she was doing. She felt like ripping the guy's nose off and feeding it to him. Except not really his nose.

Evening on the Minnesota Strip, and here's Chase in a leather jacket and black tube top, miniskirt over black stockings. An attempt at fitting in but not standing out too much. Bob had spotted an anomaly in a recent game: The Pittsburgh Pirates of all teams had totally creamed the Mets, winning four runs against two. No one could have seen it coming and the odds had been twenty-to-one against the Pirates. If anyone had bet on that game, the payoff would absolutely have to go down outside of the Lounge.

The tips of Chase's hair had turned soggy and limply hung over her shoulders. It gave her an extra worn down, ratty look that at least helped fit the part. She shivered under the awning next to another girl; Lyla she called herself, a big blonde with high hair and cherry red lipstick, long lashes, tight-fitting clothes, and pockmarked greasy skin. They chatted a while but Lyla didn't seem to know much. Probably leery of Chase, whose presence meant more competition. Plus she was a strange face. The girls all knew each other down here. Chase was beginning to think it was a bad idea coming down here herself. She was leery of everyone and everything. All she could carry was a .25 Colt Vest Pocket. She hadn't felt this vulnerable in a while. She hadn't felt like this since Bucky had captured her in Poughkeepsie.

The scene came back to her in pounding echoes, usually at night. The darkened room where surround speakers infiltrated her mind with invasive noise, a beat that wouldn't end, that liquefied her reason and locked her body against her. The flashing TV screen made her thoughts swim with images, words, and concepts that weren't her own. The sheer terror of losing control of herself—and worse—not even having the freedom to be afraid. Because the fear only came after the fact. Because at that moment Chase hadn't been Chase.

In some ways, she hadn't been herself ever since.

"You shoulda brought a better coat," Lyla's voice broke through the memory, and Chase snapped to and found herself violently shivering under the awning. "This unpredictable spring weather can be a killer. Catches you off guard."

"Yeah," Chase replied, her voice cracked. "I see what you mean."

"So, where you from?" Lyla said, an animal curiosity and vague fear behind her big dark eyes ringed by mascara. "I ain't seen you around here before or nothing."

"I'm from... Ithaca," Chase said.

"Old Finger Lakes, huh? I got an aunt who lives up there. Why'd you come down to this hole?"

Chase shrugged. "Same reason as anyone I guess. Unrealistic dreams. I'm trying to make it."

"Oh yeah. As what?"

"Well, I'm not sure yet."

Chase shot the proz an awkward, hangdog look—which she didn't have to fake really, given her present mental state. Lyla burst into a screeching laugh that almost tore through the awning.

"Ah—I'm sorry," she said through tears of laughter. "It's just—gawd. It's such a sad old tale, ain't it? You have all these dreams, these ideals. Then you come down here and realize that people only want you for your—"

"Hey baby, looking good!" A man cried from a car crawling by with the window down. A thick head with beady eyes and receding hairline Chase suddenly felt grateful for the rain—it put a natural barrier in between them. Eventually, he stopped trying to get Chase's attention, but Lyla couldn't hook him instead. She seemed not so happy about that. Great. There went the rapport they were building.

Chase could feel Lyla's contempt burning into her, but it was also mixed with a kind of gratitude that she wasn't standing here alone. All of these things flashed on Chase in an instant because she was standing here with her, seeing into those shifty green eyes and watching the breath flood out of her mouth in soft white clouds, watching her hug herself and stamp the ground when the chill came in on the wind. They weren't data, they weren't statistics. In fact, all of these things would be called anecdotal by the data guys and written off as meaningless. Yet to Chase this was all the meaning there was. For a moment everything else about the case—all its complexities and bends and turns—its connections to terrorist activity, larceny, arson, media crime, gambling—it all passed up in that same white vapor cloud and lifted on out into the New York sky.

"The truth is," Chase said. "I had a friend who got in trouble up here." She sniffed, making the most of her frozen state to affect an air of humanity or non-copishness.

"Oh yeah? What's her name, maybe I know her."

"Lucy."

"Hmm. Can't say I know her. She hooks around here?"

"Kind of. Anyway, she was meeting with this guy here and—"

"In here? Like right in the Motel M?"

"Yeah."

"And they did something to your friend?"

"Money was involved. I—I just," Chase played it coy. Didn't want to give away or make up too many details. That made it easier to get caught in the lie.

Then she felt something. Something about that next car, the way it crawled up to the curb. The guy inside was not watching the girls, not interested. Some kind of determination there. Curly mop of hair, flattened nose as if it'd been beaten in, eyes black as tar. A thin mouth on a weak chin. When he exited the car he looked up and down the street—so far could be the usual shifty john behavior scanning for cops. Except there was more to it than that. He just wasn't looking at the girls, not even when Lyla purposefully bent over and revealed her cleavage or the girl further down the way raised her skirt a little and put some leg on display. The guy just wasn't into it. He was holding a briefcase when he came out of the car and his body language was defensive. Too defensive. And defensive in particular about that briefcase.

Chase turned away from the man so her mouth was hidden and said, "We got a possible."

"What was that?" Lyla said to her.

"Oh, I just said maybe I'll take him."

"Wow, you have some strange taste, sister. But by all means—I sure as hell don't want to go with him. I hate that guy, he reminds me of a weasel."

"He's been here before then?"

"Oh sure. Delilah hooked him a couple times but she ain't around."

"Where'd she go?"

Lyla shrugged. "How should I know? I ain't her keeper. Anyway, girls in this business have a short shelf life, know what I mean?"

"Sure."

The men approached them gingerly. Chase wanted to grab more details from Lyla but time was up. It had to be him—she could feel the waves of guilt swelling off him. He may as well have been a kid stealing his first candy bar, how shady he was acting.

"Want some company?" Chase asked him. His eyes flickered back and forth up the street.

"Delilah ain't here hun," Lyla helpfully added.

"Oh. Okay. I guess..." The man gave Chase the once-over. She felt violated just having those black beady eyes scan her like that, running all down her body. She had to hold back the shiver. Her stomach churned. Something was way off about this guy. It wasn't just that he radiated waves of guilt—something else. Something sinister. It made her body close its doors and batten the hatches. All her internal alarms rang out in a red whooping alarm. *This guy was dangerous.*

They headed together up the musty stairs of the roach motel. The Bureau had bugged her clothes, though she couldn't hear them because wearing an earwig would be too obvious. The man kept the briefcase on the opposite side of him to Chase, she noticed.

"So, what's your name, honey?" Chase asked, pushing down the disgust deep inside.

He shot her a greasy look that made her want to gag. "Vance."

Vance. She didn't know any Vance in the outfit at all. This wasn't how it was supposed to go down. One of Saul Sparks's men was meant to come in person—she would recognize them and give the Bureau a sign by saying the code 'Domino' out loud. But this wasn't right. She started to doubt herself. Was that briefcase really the payoff for the Pirates game? Or was it just a coincidence? Crap. If this went any further and it turned out this Vance character was just another john, she'd have to refuse the guy his 'service.' Chase was a dedicated agent, willing to put her life on the line for the job. But putting that on the line was just one step too far. The corridor was dim, two of the bulbs were broken. The floorboards creaked. Chase's heart began to thump louder and faster as they approached the door to their room.

"Alright, I gotta wait for someone," Vance said, and a wave of relief washed over Chase, making her weak at the knees.

"Someone else is joining us?" She said, adding an extra whine to her voice. "You know that cost extra, right?"

"Relax. They're not here for that. Just gotta do a little *trans-ack-shee-on*, you feel me?"

"Hey now, I'm not getting busted for no dope deal," Chase said, pretending to get antsy.

"Cool your panties, sweet cheeks. Ain't nothing like that, I promise. Hey—stick around and there's an extra twenty in it for you."

"You got yourself a deal, monsieur," Chase said, pushing down the urge to vomit.

Vance snuck his hand into his inner jacket pocket and Chase instantly dropped her hand to pull the .22 from under her skirt—but it turned out he was just taking out a small flask of whiskey. He knocked a mouthful back and offered the flask to Chase. "Care for a taste?"

"I'm good, thanks."

His phone went off then. "You here? Good. Room 311." Then he turned to Chase and said. "Get yourself ready, honey. Papa will be with you in a short while."

She was getting herself ready alright. She checked her phone while Vance was preoccupied and typed a message to Bob. "Possible DOMINO in five."

A knock came on the door. The guy Vance was meeting was a plodding elderly man in a fatigue jacket with a sneaky glint in his eye.

"That it?" The man said, alternating his eye over Vance and Chase's bodies.

"Yeah, it's all you," Vance said. Still not confirming what was in it.

"Alrighty then," the man said, taking the briefcase. Crap. This was no good. She needed to see inside that thing.

"You just gonna trust him?" Chase said snidely, making it sound like she was half-joking. "You ain't gonna take a look inside first?"

The man stopped and thought about it, scratching his chin. "Girly here's got a point. Where are my brains today?"

Vance shot Chase a dirty look as the man lugged the briefcase over to the bed and set it down. "Better safe than sorry," he said.

At this point, Vance was acting shifty. Chase had kept her eyes on the briefcase but could see him in the corner of her eye pacing. She wasn't meant to see what was in that briefcase. The old man opened it and whistled.

"What you got there, pops?" Chase said, nearing the bed with a casual gait. "Is it your birthday present?"

She looked down at the inside of the case: Sure enough, stacked in neat piles sat several thousand dollars in one-hundred and twenty dollar bills.

"Wow," Chase said, feigning awe. "Someone's rich. How's about giving your girl a tip—"

Just then Chase heard Vance make for the door. He was bolting! She reached down and pulled the .22— Vance saw her, turned, and fired off two shots into the room as he leaped out the door. Chase hit the ground in time but the gambler man got clipped.

"DOMINO! DOMINO!" Chase yelled into her wire. "We got a runner!"

She pounced to the door and lay flat against the wall. Turned around into the corridor—Bam, another shot blew a cloud of splinters out. Waiting for Vance's footsteps to fade out she took pursuit at a distance. No need to get too close. She made her way down to the first floor just as Vance was fleeing out the main doors—to find himself surrounded by the FBI tacticals.

"FBI! Put down your weapon and get on your knees NOW!"

The rain was coming down in bucketfuls. Vance knelt there on the sidewalk with his hands raised into the pouring sky, the streetlight a yellow halo on his soggy head.

"You bitch," he said, looking back at Chase who had her .22 trained on him. "I knew you were much too pretty to be a hooah."

Chapter 15

The Keno Lounge of all places. So, that's how the bastard was pulling it off. It was a ridiculous idea, but Acre had to admit it had balls. Even at eight at night, the place was stocked by pretty much the silver-haired clientele he expected—it looked like a Golden Girls convention in there.

Acre scanned the joint: Cheesy decor and lighting, frayed reclining seats, thin faded green carpet that looked like a holdover from the 1970s, complete with five decades worth of drink stains and cigarette burns. A whole veneer of cheap sleaze coated the place. Half the chairs didn't match the tables and looked scavenged from Good Will then repurposed, each one with a little console on the airplane-style armrest where the players inserted their cards and picked their numbers. The fixtures were cheap and outdated, and the fluorescent lighting gave the place a harsh, clinical glow. But despite its shabby appearance, the keno lounge was packed with people all clutching their armrests and eagerly waiting for the next set of numbers to be called. One look told him it was the only source of excitement in their lives.

Stepping inside was like walking into a wall of cigarette smoke—they obviously didn't respect New York's indoor smoking rules too much. He didn't mind—in fact, he lit up one of his own Camel death sticks. Acre had to squint to make out the keno board on the far wall, which rattled off number after number, highlighting them on a big grid while dusty old folk half-asleep in their chairs continued to feed their quasi-addiction.

The sports bar set on the other side of the room is what stood out to him most—inside, multiple TV screens displayed the Kings playing the Suns and a few of the customers were watching, a few others were blathering to one another. None seemed that invested though—they didn't have that gambler's fire in their eyes, the damp patches under their arms from having real money on it.

The air in the sports bar was thick with the smell of stale beer, sweat, and more cigarettes. The dimly lit room was lined with worn-out booths and sticky tables, and the only source of light came from a flickering neon Budweiser sign that hung above the bar. The walls were adorned with faded posters of long-forgotten teams and players, and the floor was littered with peanut shells and discarded napkins.

The patrons were a motley crew of die-hard sports fans and locals looking for a cheap drink. They huddled around the bar, cheering and jeering at the flickering television screens, their voices drowning out the blaring sound of the game. The bartenders were gruff and unkempt, their faces weathered by years of hard living and late nights. Yet there was something strangely comforting about the dingy bar, a sense of camaraderie and shared experience that was hard to find anywhere else in this lonely town of wandering souls.

Acre walked in and ordered a jack and coke—seven bucks—then sat down at the corner of the bar keeping a lookout for anyone reacting strongly. No dice. The game went on and fizzled out.

Next up was the last game of the night—if something didn't happen with this he'd just have to head home and rethink his approach. But this time it was the Washington Wizards vs. the Portland Trail Blazers. The Vegas odds were stacked high on this game since the Trail Blazers were no match for the Wizards. But in the past, the Blazers had shown that they could sometimes pull a surprise win out of nowhere. It was precisely this kind of match-up that was like crack for a gambler. He should know. He'd busted enough of them in his time.

The game turned out to be a nail-biter from start to finish. As the clock ticked down in the fourth quarter, the score was tied at 120-120, with both teams playing their lungs out and drenching the floor in sweat. The crowd was all on their feet, screaming and cheering as the tension in the arena grew to a fever pitch. Inside the bar, a similar tension was arising, but Acre had his eye for certain characters in particular—not the one/s on their feet hollering, but the ones gripped to their seat and frozen solid.

With just a minute left on the clock, the tension was so tight that Acre could hear the buzz of TV static in his ears. He took his eyes off the game and scanned the room again: There. Right there. The guy with salt and pepper hair and a mustache wearing a light blue polo shirt. His face was wet as a newborn baby and the thick vein on his neck was visible from all the way across the room. He clutched his glass until he was white-knuckled and Acre was afraid the glass would shatter in his hand.

The Wizards' power forward Kyle Kuzma drove to the basket, faking out two Blazers defenders and sinking a layup to put the Wizards up by two. Acre used the opportunity to switch seats and sit down beside the man.

"Shit—where's their damn defense?" Acre growled, pretending to be equally engrossed in the game. "I got money on this shit."

"Shh!" It was clear the man did too. A crumpled square of paper lying on the bar next to the man's glass had the following:

Lakes agnst Warriors

Jazz agnst Thunder

Mavericks agnst Spurs

Blazers agnst Wizards

The first three were crossed out. He'd just lost the past three games and everything was riding on this one. On this one final minute.

The Wizards tried to finish the job, but Bradley Beal's three-point attempt missed the mark, bouncing off the rim and into the hands of the Blazers' Trendon Watford. Watford sprinted down the court and launched a desperation shot as the buzzer sounded, the ball soaring through the air in a parabolic arc and swishing through the net just as the final horn sounded. The Blazers won by one point.

The bar cheered and the man beside Acre leaped up into a frenzy, screaming at the top of his lungs. "YEAHHHHHHHHHHHHHH! HELL YEAH!!!! I KNEW THE BLAZERS COULD DO IT! EAT IT, YOU WIZARD SLEEVE BASTARDS!!"

Many of the customers got up and left with a hangdog expression but one or two stayed in their seats, sipping their drinks with a suspicious look. As if they were waiting on something. One by one they left, but to Acre, it seemed like they were making sure not to all leave at once. They all had that winner's glow too.

Something was going on here. He couldn't be more sure of it. But when the man next to him finished his third victory beer and staggered out of the bar, Acre was met not by an answer, just another question.

He stood there gaping at the other end of the room. There in the filthy lounge seats, all four men from the sports bar were sitting down. Playing keno.

Three grown men, sports nuts, drunk off their heads. And playing keno at ten in the evening.

Acre casually walked over and sat down. On the way, one of the four spotted him and shot him a knowing smile. A conspiratorial smile.

This was it, Acre thought. This was the setup. Somehow—and he had no idea how but—the payoff was going down here. He sat through the first game.

Then realized that he was getting some odd looks. Because he wasn't playing and his screen wasn't turned on. Dammit—he shuffled out between games pretending to hit the john then came back and on the way bought a game card, then joined in. He just hit random numbers—six of them. He'd never played keno in his life and had no clue how it worked, but it didn't take long to pick up. He won money for the numbers he matched right, and the other numbers he got wrong just drained the amount he betted. Thus, the goal was to match enough numbers to earn more than what you bet. Game after game of this went on, winning some, losing some, pointless. Until around the twentieth or so game when suddenly fireworks sparked out of the main game board on the wall and a message appeared on the screen.

Congratulations: Mike Newman. Five in a row! $700.

At this, Mike gave out a short hoot and the others politely clapped. Then he picked up all his stuff and walked straight to the counter and collected his winnings.

Was this normal behavior? Like hell. After getting a winning high like that the natural tendency is to keep playing, to take full advantage of the hot streak. Acre had been to Vegas before and he'd never once seen someone win and then immediately bail. This was no win. This was a payout.

After another thirty games playing just one or two numbers idly, it happened again.

Congratulations: Francis Barber. Four in a row! $450.

Okay, now it was really starting to stink. Even a total blockhead could see this wasn't right. If keno had these odds it would break the house within a week of opening.

In addition to the old folks who kept playing in a half-nap daze while drinking tea from plastic cups, there were still the two remaining guys from the sports bar, one of which was the guy who had been sitting next to Acre and whose plays he'd caught. He decided to try something. He got up and pretended to hit the john again, then came back and sat in a seat a few seats behind the man from the bar. Now he started copying his picks in each game. Every game the same picks: 11, 2, 3, 5, 22, 42. He lost $10. He lost $20... Acre was beginning to sweat. His wallet wasn't so fat, especially after hitting that joint earlier with the expensive jack and cokes and the tight-lipped bartender. His loss climbed to $30... $40... This guy was betting the same numbers over and over and in the same non-numerical order. He seemed to become irritated, glancing around him rather than at the screen when the board revealed the winning numbers. Then something clicked in Acre's lightly throbbing head. Instead of picking all the same numbers, he tried changing a few of them.

And on the next game, as if by magic—the guy from the bar's numbers all hit: 2, 3, 5, 11, 22, 42. Six in a row.

Congratulations: Randall Gray. Six in a row! $1,500!

Congratulations: Henry Ackroyd. Three in a row! $100!

Due to the size of his bets, Acre didn't make out as hot. At least he broke even. But more importantly, he had Sparks' whole operation pegged.

This sly piece of work was using the Keno Lounge as a front. Ejecting his card, Acre walked casually to the exchange booth alongside Randall Gray. But Randall wasn't smiling at him this time. In fact, he made a point of not looking at him.

Crud. Had he figured out that Acre was the one blocking him from winning? He'd made Gray lose a good hundred bucks doing that. Rethinking his strategy, he slowed down and let Gray take his winnings first. Once he'd disappeared, Acre then approached the booth.

"$100 on your first try," the girl said, smiling her practiced, stiff flight-attendant smile. "You must be a lucky man, Mr. Ackroyd."

"I guess I'll know that by the end of the night."

She smiled again, this time a slight confusion on her face. She had a symmetrical face with high cheekbones, a delicate nose, and full lips that curved into a gentle smile. Her eyes were large and expressive, a warm brown color that sparkled with feigned curiosity and interest. Her hair was thick and shiny, falling in soft waves around her shoulders, and her skin was smooth and flawless—probably used to being hit on. She was definitely out of her league at this joint.

"What's your name, honey?" Acre said, playing his expected role of drunken sleaze.

"It's Amy."

"That's cute. It suits you. Say, what are you doing later?"

"Oh, heading straight home..." She flashed him another cold, professional smile that made him feel icicles inside. Just as Acre took his bills and snugly placed them inside his wallet, his brief good feeling was split by a bolt of lightning as he felt a hand on his shoulder. Reaching for his gun, his right arm was then yanked back. Hard. He felt a cold lizard breath on his neck and a shiver ran down his spine.

Turning to the beefy enforcer who'd arm-locked him, Acre shot back a tired grin. "I don't know who the hell you are, pal, but I really think you should change your brand of toothpaste."

"Keep on like that and you're not gonna have any teeth left to brush, Ackroyd."

"What's the big idea grabbing me?" Acre said. "I don't bend that way—and my elbow don't neither."

"Just come with me. Our manager would like a word with you."

"Oh yeah? Well, maybe I don't want a word with him."

"Too bad. If you want your elbow to stay connected to your arm you won't cause a scene."

"Yeah. Right." Acre turned to the girl and smiled meekly. "Sorry Amy, I guess I'll have to take a rain check on our date."

The enforcer yanked him sideways. "The only date you have tonight is with destiny, jerkoff."

Acre groaned. "Jesus dude, you should spend less time in the gym and more time working on your clichés. That was terrible."

"Shut yer yap."

Chapter 16

In the center of the room sat a battered wooden desk cluttered with papers and liquor-soaked tumblers. The gruff would-be manager of the lounge sat behind it, eyeing Acre with suspicion as he was shoved inside. It was a place where shady deals were made, secrets were kept, and fortunes were won and lost in the blink of an eye. But the manager wasn't Sparks—Acre had already seen his picture. This was someone else.

"Henry Ackroyd," the man drawled.

"Yes. And you are?" Acre said.

"The tooth fairy," he said unhelpfully.

"I'm guessing you're the manager—well, I'm not sure what the problem is," Acre said, feigning ignorance in an attempt to make them drop their guard. As soon as he saw an opening he was going to high-tail it right on out of there like a comet on fire.

"The problem is, you take us for suckers, that's what the problem is."

"How can I take you for a sucker, when I don't even know you?" Acre countered. It seemed to do the trick. The man behind the desk begrudgingly introduced himself.

"Fine, you wanna play that game? I'm Mayo."

"Mayo. As in tuna?"

The enforcer gripped the nerve in Acre's shoulder; meanwhile, the manager went beet-faced. This clearly wasn't the time for such levity, but Acre couldn't help himself. This man looked so disheveled and slack that it inspired vague disgust. Even his hair seemed not to want to cling to his head—it just kind of lazily sprawled on top of it.

"Alright," Mayo said, "I tried giving you a chance and you wanna play silly-ass with me. Well, I'm a busy man and I got no time for such games. So, how about we do things the hard way after all? Crunch—you hold him there while I prepare."

Prepare? That didn't sound too good. Acre needed to think of a way out of this. And fast. Else he was well on the way to losing some precious function of his body.

"Okay, fine, you pass," Acre said.

"What's that now?" Mayo said distractedly, fumbling with a padlock on a suspicious steel locker in the corner of the room.

"I said you pass. Sparks sent me down here to see how you'd handle it if someone got wise to the keno setup."

Mayo stopped mid-action and turned, an eyebrow raised on his fat greasy head.

"Yeah," Acre said. "Surprise! Also—where did you get that locker? You raid the local high school or what?"

Mayo turned fully to Acre, who was still being pinned down like a mug shot to a corkboard. "Say I choose to believe this story," Mayo said. "You know I can just phone Sparksie to find out. And if he says you're spouting dung then you know that's going to result in some very bad things..."

The threat was useless—Acre was already facing very bad things. How much worse could things get? No, he had to bank on this. See it through to the end. Besides, if phoning 'Sparksie' was an option, Mayo would have just phoned. He wouldn't have stood there guffing.

"Listen Mayo," Acre said, "let's cut the egg salad here—" Another pinch of his shoulder courtesy of Crunch. "Alright, alright, alright, look," Acre said. "If Sparksie was available to take your every nagging call, he wouldn't leave things to you to begin with. And if he could trust you, he wouldn't even have to send me down here. You starting to get the picture? This is seeing whether *you* have the moxy to handle situations for yourself. It's up to you whether or not to make use of this opportunity. How long are you gonna suck on Sparksie's teat, you big baby?"

"Alright that's it," the enforcer said, grabbing Acre by his shirt collar and dragging him up.

"Cool it, Captain Crunch," Acre said. "Can't you see your boss is thinking?"

Crunch turned to find Mayo thinking it over. This greasy-headed goon had probably seen every con and grift in the book—in almost any situation he would have told Acre to shove his opportunity and done the right thing—called his partner. But every mobster, every dirtbag, every sleaze ball in the city had that one weakness, their Achilles heel. And if you could find it and twist the knife in it, all of their knowledge and experience just went out the window. It was like they reverted back to childhood or something. Acre had used the technique countless times out there on the street, he knew how effective it was. And if he was going to get laid out, it wasn't going to be by a two-bit lapdog like this. Coming here while Sparks wasn't around had been a boon.

"Fine," Mayo said. "Let's say I believe you. I can't just let you walk outta here."

"Of course not," Acre said. "That would be too easy on me."

"Give me back the hundred," Mayo said. "In fact, make it two."

Acre's wallet shrunk in horror as he wiggled out of Crunch's grasp and pulled it out, saying sayonara to lunch for the rest of the week. Sliding the bills across Mayo's desk, he accidentally knocked over the half-filled highball, sending a flood of spiced rum and ice over the surface and wetting several of the notes strewn there.

"Oh man I'm sorry," Acre said, dabbing at the spill with his sleeve.

"Ah Jesus Christ, now look what you've done," Mayo said, picking the notes out of the small pond of alcohol that had collected there. "Just get the hell outta my sight. And when you see Sparksie, tell him I don't need any damn babysitting."

"I'll make sure he gets the message."

"Now Crunch, you tell Amy to get in here and clean this crap up."

Acre whistled an upbeat tune as he strolled right out of the Keno Lounge, sliding into his black Cherokee and taking off around the corner before examining the score—from out his sleeve he pulled the leather-bound address book. Inside, various movers and shakers of the underworld were listed, names he had acquaintances of. He narrowed the potential target down to just a handful of addresses—one of which seemed particularly promising.

It was a joint down in Elmhurst, Queens. No name or phone number was attached to the location and it was listed only as 'The House.'

Chapter 17

Chase was somehow feeling human again after changing back into her suit. They'd let Roman Vance sweat in the box for ninety minutes and behind the glass of the interrogation room he was looking well-done and crispy, ready to be cut into thin slices.

"Good job out there, Chase," Bob said.

"Yeah," Kelly added. "You know that wasn't a bad look for you."

"Save it," Chase snapped. "I'm never going to wear a skirt again after this."

"Did you ever wear one before this?" Kelly said. She glared at him but he just grinned back with his boyish smile, his way of tearing down people's defenses. Generally, it would have worked, but today not so much. He finally got the message and dropped the grin as Chase and he entered the interrogation room.

"Alright. Roman Vance, age thirty-three, occupation: Hired scuzz," Chase said. "Time to give us what we want."

Vance looked at her, confused. As if he couldn't figure out what a hooker from the strip was doing working for the FBI...

"I don't know—I don't know what you want. It's against federal law to solicit pussy now?"

"Spare us the act, Vance," Kelly said. "A john doesn't walk around carrying fifty grand in cash. We know you're dirty as hell."

"And even if you were just a john," Chase said. "We got you for shooting at a federal agent. As well as wounding and nearly killing a civilian."

"That ain't fair—it was self-defense, see. I thought you was trying to roll me for the dough."

"You shot at me *after* handing over the dough, brainiac."

"Yeah, well, in the heat of the moment I musta forgotten about that."

"Cut the crapola, buddy," Kelly said. "That wouldn't stand up in court and you know it. And frankly, we couldn't give two shits about your crumby gambling operation."

"I don't understand," Vance said. "What are you talking about? Gambling? I thought this was about solicitation."

"Yeah, yeah, yeah," Kelly said. "Show him, Chase. So, he'll stop the dunce act."

"We're looking for *her*," Chase said, slamming down the employee profile photo of Lucy Child. "When did you last see her?"

"Haha wha?" Vance said, shifting his cuffed hands onto the table and picking up the photo. He squinted at it. "This broad?"

"You've seen her before."

"Ah—maybe. Geez, look, I need a smoke first. Can I get a cigarette around here? Christ, I'm gasping. Hell, I'd even go for a Salem at this juncture."

"You can have your cigarette after you tell us what we wanna know," Kelly said. "Have you seen this woman before or not?"

"Fine, fine. You bastards will find it out sooner or later anyway. I seen her before, sure. But listen, I'm not even a part of that operation. Not really. I'm just a gofer—I handle the dirty, dangerous stuff the other clowns are too pussyfooted to handle."

"You're talking about Sparks and Mayo," Chase said.

"Sure, you already know it all, I can tell. Anyway, I'm a glorified freakin' money dispenser. It's not like I go around breaking legs. They got another guy for that, name of Todd the Giant. And the name ain't no joke."

Chase shot a look back to the glass—behind which Bob would get the message and start searching.

"We'll look into that. But first, you need to tell us about your relationship with Lucy Child."

"Come on, I gave you a little something. Just one smoke."

Chase sighed, then went out of the room and came back with a box of Lucky Strikes and a lighter, slung them at Vance. He hurriedly opened the box with shivering fingers and it took him six tries to light the damn thing. The end of the cigarette finally glowed red and he inhaled the thick smoke deeply, letting it out with an orgasmic sigh. All the muscles in his face relaxed and he leaned back on his chair like a limp jellyfish. He looked even more like a creep relaxed than he did when tense.

"Now tell us your relationship with Child," Kelly said in a loud, booming voice. "No more stalling, asswipe."

"Relationship—" Vance said, his voice turning smooth and greasy again, like a waxed reptile. "Was hardly even what would amount to one. I met her a couple of times. She'd win some, she'd lose more. That lady was hooked, man. Ain't seen nothing like it. Just kept coming back for more beatings."

Kelly shot Chase a look—he was admitting to the gambling operation already. What an idiot.

"So, she was addicted to gambling," Kelly said.

"Yeah man, beyond it. Made the craziest of bets, too. One time she bet on Kansas City to beat the Patriots, Chrissake. I think there might have been something wrong with her—in the head and all. Or she just didn't know her sports. I mean most girls don't even know the rules of football, let alone how to bet on it. So, I guess I can't say much about the poor broad." He looked at them expectantly, as if he was done for the day.

"We uh—we're gonna need something a little more substantial than that," Kelly said.

"About what?" Vance said indignantly.

"About Lucy Child. We're trying to figure out where she might have gone."

"Hell, how should I know where she skipped off to. Could be in Timbuktu for all I know."

"Why don't you try telling us what you know about her personal life," Chase said.

"Ah geez, look—so I'm thinking she had some boring job, wanted a little excitement. Wanted too much excitement, went overboard, and got herself in hot water. Course—that's just conjecture, agents. I didn't know the broad."

"As you keep saying," Kelly said dryly. "But unfortunately, that's not enough." He snatched the half-smoked Lucky out of Vance's hand and rubbed it out on the box.

"Hey—come on man. Don't be a dick about it."

"You're bullshitting us. Your smoke privileges have been revoked." Kelly took the cigarette box away and

Vance looked like a baby that just got a piece of candy snatched out of its hands. In fact—were his *eyes* watering up?

"Ahh—I don't even know what you mean, agent."

"What did I say about feeding us that crap? We know you know *exactly* who Lucy Child was and where she worked, and we know you were going to fence those documents in lieu of payment."

"Documents?" Vance said.

Kelly slammed the table, hard. The echo reverberated throughout the tiny white room.

"No more crap, Vance. You're the delivery man, the gofer, you had to be the one who was assigned to take those documents. Or if you weren't then you know who was. So, don't give us crap about not knowing."

"Aw geez. Aw, man."

"We can make a deal, Vance," Chase said—somehow she'd become good cop in all this without even realizing. "If you deal with us now we can look into having your sentence reduced when this whole thing gets taken down for RICO."

"RICO?! Holy Christ. I don't even—I don't know nothin'," he whined like a dog that just got its tail stomped on. "Lady—I don't work for the mob, okay?"

"How long do you think that innocent act is going to play, buddy?" Kelly said, a look of menace flaring in his normally serene eyes. "You know we got dirt on the two bozos you work for and you know we're bringing them in sooner or later. So, why make this difficult for us when you know we can make things that much more difficult for you?" He shook the box of Luckys in front of Vance's face. The point seemed to stick.

"Ah geez. Fine. Alright, I'll talk. But I want a deal. I want immunity!"

"Immunity?" Kelly said. "You don't seem to understand the position you're in, buddy. You fired on an FBI agent."

"That was a freaking accident, man!"

"We can discuss terms later," Chase said. "Right now we need to find Lucy Child in relation to a serious ongoing investigation." She tapped on the photo. "If you help us—IF, that is, then combined with your testimony against Sparks and Mayo, you could get off with a slap on the wrist." Kelly was looking at her strangely. He knew that she knew that this wasn't true. Vance had fired on a federal agent and ran money for an illegal gambling racket—plus was probably up for a dozen other racketeering charges. He was going up the river no matter what. But so what? Vance wasn't the only one who could bullshit here.

"Fine, sure. Lucy Child, right?"

"Did you know where she worked?" Chase asked. "Give us the truth."

"Yeah. Yeah. Some kinda—some kinda federal joint right? The place that got burned down a couple weeks back." He paused, then looked at them. "Holy crap, is that what all this is about?"

Chase exchanged a look with Kelly. This was it. After spinning their wheels endlessly for two weeks they'd finally gotten a solid lead. And they were going to squeeze it for everything it was worth.

"Okay Vance," Kelly said, sliding the Luckys back which Vance quickly lit up again. "Start talking. Start to finish. We want to know every last detail."

"Yeah, fine. It all started with that broad I wanna say six—nah, more like seven months ago. She came in just playing keno, right? Just casual and all that. Well, things go by like usual and it seems she's cottoned on the fact something ain't right on the old keno score. You know how some people get insane luck and all that? Something dirty's going on, she thinks. So, she starts making records of all the suspicious payouts. Then— you're not gonna believe this—she has the brass balls to walk into Sparksie's office and try to bluff him."

"She tried to blackmail Saul Sparks?" Kelly said.

"Yeah. Real nutcase, right? But Sparksie wasn't born yesterday neither. He figured out she didn't have the full story. She only had the suspicious payouts. Hadn't put two and two together about the sports angle yet. She just maybe figured that it was some kind of bribe or this kind of thing."

"So, it was after Child found out—that was when Sparks decided to start making some of the payouts away from the Keno Lounge," Chase said.

"Right," Vance said. "You got it. So, anyhow, even though Child is BS-ing Sparksie, the fact of the matter is she does have some incriminating damage on him— the kinda thing that if she gave others to look at might prove inconvenient to the enterprise."

"So, Sparks paid her off?" Kelly asked.

"Nah. Not really. I mean Sparks wouldn't split with so much as a dime to save his life. He figures a different angle—gives Child access to the gambling club."

"The special card," Chase said. "For the keno games."

"Yeah," Vance said. "Exactly. So, not only does Sparks avoid paying to keep Lucy quiet, but he also gets to keep an eye on her. Plus he makes money every time Lucky Lucy there gets unlucky. Which turns out, was a lot. What can I tell ya? The man has a way of making every situation turn in his favor."

"We'll see how long that trend lasts," Chase said. "So, when Lucy Child got in deep with Sparks, then what happened?"

Vance shrugged. "You're not gonna like my answer but I'm fuzzy on the details there. I know she was trying to find a way to pay Sparks back. It was something like eighty large she was in for."

"Eighty thousand dollars?" Kelly said breathlessly.

"Yup. She was getting boiled in the big stew. So, whatever it was Lucy was up to, it must have guaranteed at least that much."

"You're saying that Sparks wasn't the one who told her to loot the Federal Records building?" Kelly said.

"I really don't think it's his style, tell ya the truth. He doesn't want the attention. Sparksie is a shrewd businessman—he wouldn't make big moves that could draw the ire of the Federal Government."

"Crap," Chase said to Kelly. "I think he's right. But that means someone else was willing to fence the documents."

"Who's your fence?" Kelly asked.

"Man, we don't got nothing like that. I'm tellin' you, man. We're not the mob. It's just one small operation."

"Then give us something else. We need to find Lucy Child. You have to have some idea where she went. You're Sparks' gofer. It's your job to track these people down."

"Ah, I guess. But not in this instance, turns out."

"What about this Todd the Giant character?" Chase said. "Would he have her location?"

"Hell if I know. Haven't seen him around in a while. Honestly, you'd be faster getting it off Sparksie himself."

"That's a problem," Kelly said. "Because Sparks himself has vanished. And you know that, and that's the only reason you're giving him up as the fall guy."

"No man, it ain't like that. Honest. I just don't know nothing. I don't know what I don't know, eh? And it's not like me and Todd were bowling partners. We just sometimes worked the same jobs."

"All through Sparks," Chase said.

"Exactly."

"So, give us Sparks' location then," Kelly said.

"Geez guy—you really know how to get blood from a stone, don't ya? He lives above the Keno Lounge. Usually, at least."

"Usually?" Chase said.

"Well yeah, I mean, unless things are hot. Which they are. So, I suppose he ain't. There I mean."

"Then where is he?" Kelly said, his hand moving near the box of Luckys again.

"Alright, alright, geez. Just don't take my smokes away—I get anxiety without 'em. He has this other property. A safe house, I guess you could call it."

Kelly's eyes burned when he looked at Chase. This could be it. They could finally be onto something.

"Alright, give us the location."

"Let me see if I remember. Oh yeah, yeah, that's right, I went down there to pick up the money one time. It's down over in Elmhurst..."

Chapter 18

The location down in Elmhurst was this weird little back road where an attempt had been made to construct individual detached houses. But with real estate being at such a premium the houses still all ended up being thin and narrow as if a giant had squashed his hands together on them. Plus they were all bunched up, only a few of the houses having yards to speak of.

It would be just Acre's luck if Sparks' safehouse was this one here—protected by a yard and wall. He glanced at the address book again, then at his phone. This was the place.

It was a hassle, but he didn't need to go beyond his ability to get over the wall. A large drooping tree provided the means of getting inside; with its multitude of leafless branches stretching over both sides of the wall, the thing may as well have been a ladder. Climbing atop the wall, Acre spied the joint inside. No lights were on, but then again it was well after midnight already. Maybe it would be safer to come back during the day when he could be sure Sparks was gone, but then it would be easier to get caught breaking in. Plus, Mayo could get spooked and end up warning him at any time. But despite all that, the real factor here was that Acre didn't want to go back home and stew in his own thoughts for another night. He wanted to just push forward on the case. Keep going to the end, even if it meant acting recklessly again. So, what if he did? He had nothing to lose now. And you didn't get by as a private dick by pussy-footing around on your tiptoes. You had to beat the pavement and smash heads together. You had to put your nose out there and hope no one cut it off. Taking risks was the way the game was played.

He dropped down into the grass and slipped silently and quickly up to the wall, then sidled around to the screen door at the back. Taking out his wrench and pick he jimmied the lock easily, first on the screen then the inner door. Inside were only the usual creaks and groans of the house settling—no faint sound of a television or movement from the first floor. The city light falling through the open curtain pooled onto the floor in a soft golden haze. Without making a sound, Acre switched on his flashlight and carefully navigated around the furniture, checking each room one by one. The first floor was clear. No significant desks or drawers caught his eye—no secret safe behind any of the paintings. No false doors or compartments from what he could tell.

And if the documents were as important as the client made out, Sparks wouldn't have stored them on the first floor anyway. Now padding up the stairs to the second floor, more careful here, making sure not to bump into anything or trip over. Using his flashlight sparingly to get a visual then switching it off so as not to make himself visible.

The couple rooms with their doors open were both empty. Bathroom too. That just left one room which appeared to be the master bedroom. He got up close to the door and placed his ear on it. Through the tough wood came what sounded like heavy breathing. Acre pulled the Beretta from his holster and slowly turned the handle, crept inside. From the bed, something turned and groaned, then bolted up and went for the bedside drawer. Acre flashed the gun and said, "Hold it right there, Sparks. Unless you want to go back to sleep—permanently."

The startled Sparks squinted through the darkness at the figure in his bedroom. "You think you can get away with barging in here? You're dead. Who da hell do you think you are?"

"I'm the goddamn tooth fairy. And I'm holding a 9 mm at your head, sicko. So, I'm the one who gets to ask the questions. You get any strange ideas and I'll be leaving lead under your pillow."

"This is—you can't just—do you know who I am? I can have you—"

Acre cocked the slide on his weapon. That shut him up quick.

"Now we're gonna have a little talk, you and I," Acre said, getting closer, his face half illuminated in the street light filtering into the room.

"If this is about money, I'm not stupid enough to keep it on the premises..."

"Forget money. I'm here for what you have," Acre said. "What doesn't belong to you."

"I don't—know what you mean."

"Oh really. That's a real shame. Because I was hoping to leave here tonight without leaving a dead body behind. But if you insist on playing dumb, I guess I'll just take out the trash first and look for it myself." Acre aimed the gun at Sparks' head...

"Wait—wait! Look, I have some—some uh, emergency cash stored. Why don't you just take that and leave!" His face was trembling. There was a good chance he'd just stained his silk sheets.

"I thought you said you didn't have money on the premises."

"That's different."

"That's you lying."

"No, it's—"

"Say it."

"What?"

"Say you lied, you dirty rotten son of a bitch!" Acre got a little closer still, making sure his stainless silver 92FS Inox was in full view, and pointed right at Sparks' kisser.

"Okay, okay! So I lied. Jesus. What is your problem? You damn nutcase."

"My problem is lying dirtbags like you who think they can hold out on people. People to whom you've promised to deliver certain things..."

"Oh, my—oh my God... You're with them, aren't you?"

Acre didn't have a clue what the hell he was talking about. He also knew that this phantom would add to his impact. Thus, there was no need to deny it. "Who else do you think would come into your house in the middle of the night?" Acre said.

"Oy, you weren't supposed to know about this place."

"Yeah, no shit. Well, we do. So, get your lazy ass out of bed and let's go already. I don't got all night here."

Sparks flicked on the lamp, put on his spectacles, and slipped out of bed into his slippers. He shuffled along the hallway lethargically and Acre could practically hear the gears turning in his head. "I hope you're not planning to try anything stupid either," Acre warned him. "'Cause I don't have the patience for it. And you know the people I work for have even less patience. So, let's cut the bullshit you're planning and go get what you were meant to hand over."

Sparks sighed, his body sagging. He seemed to give in to the situation and led Acre along the hallway in silence, the only sound the creaking of the landing beneath their feet. Sparks was keeping a careful eye on him as they approached the far door. It was one of the empty rooms he'd already cleared. They went inside and Sparks reluctantly went to the corner and peeled back a loose tag of wallpaper—had the lights been on, Acre would have found that easily. Sparks kept peeling until it revealed a safe in the wall. Acre felt his palm itching as it sweated against the grip of his gun. He shifted the gun to his other hand and at the moment Sparks lunged at him, whacking the gun out of his hand and socking him right in the nose.

"You son of a—!" Acre yelled, returning the favor and slamming his big fist right into Sparks' boney little head. He went flying back onto his ass and scrambled for the dropped weapon, but Acre stayed cool and launched a dropkick right into his rib cage.

"You like sports so much," Acre spat, "Well there's your field goal, you piece of shit."

Sparks wheezed and held his chest in agony, spat blood under himself. "You —you broke my ribs!"

"Yeah well, that's what you get for not playing along." Acre leaned down for the gun and trained it on Sparks again. "Now get your ass up and take me to the frickin' package before I get really mad."

Sparks just whimpered, holding his bruised chest.

"Open the fricking safe NOW or I'll just blow your brains out all over this fine carpet here and get a yeg to open the thing for me. It's a hassle, sure, but it beats playing pat a cake with your scrawny ass."

Sparks eyed him and seemed to gather that Acre wasn't bluffing. He finally relented, got up, and approached the safe. "You—you're going to regret this," Sparks growled, dropping the frail old man routine and glaring at him through beady eyes. He put in the code and the door peeped as it unlocked itself.

"Now open it," Acre commanded. "Fully. No bullshit. No funny stuff, or it's lights out. You know I mean it."

Sparks was gritting his teeth.

"I said OPEN IT, SUCKER."

Sparks pulled open the door and quickly reached inside. Acre was faster—much faster—he grabbed Sparks and threw him down, sending the Tanfoglio 'Baby' 9 mm he'd pulled from the safe skittering across the floor.

"Jesus. Even your gun is pathetic," Acre spat, retrieving the concealed weapon and going back to the vault, which held several stacks of cash, some jewels, and a brown A4 envelope. His hand ignored the dough and went right for the envelope. From inside he slid out a bunch of documents stamped with a governmental seal. The contents were incomprehensible but their origin wasn't. This was some hot material. Something in Acre cracked then—he saw red.

"What the hell are you doing with these, you dirtbag?"

"You got what you wanted. Now get the hell out of my house."

What he wanted. No, what *they* wanted. But who were they? Were they the same as the people who'd hired Acre? He was beginning to put two and two together: Whomever Sparks had mistaken him for wanted these documents. Maybe if he traced them back he could figure out just what the hell all this was about. Maybe then he could sleep at night. Maybe he could figure out why he was being paid so much to retrieve them. Did it matter? Why did he have to be so curious? Why didn't he just make himself satisfied with the reward? But government documents? Jesus. He slipped the envelope inside his jacket, then took the stacks of cash too because why the hell not?

"Don't think you're gonna get out of this alive," Sparks grunted, half-wheezing and gripping his chest.

"Shut your frickin' piehole," Acre said, continuing to raid the safe.

"You think you're invincible just because you're with them. Well, let me tell you something you little schmuck, it ain't gonna fly. You're dead meat any way you scratch it. Those documents are above your pay grade. Way above. And you may think your C pals can protect you, but trust me, they can't. And that's a fact."

Acre's heart suddenly went into overdrive. "What did you say?" Acre said, sweat pouring down his face and neck. "What the hell did you just say?"

"You heard me, you prick. You're a schmuck, a faceless gofer, that's all. You ain't as important as you think. As soon as they're done with you they'll spit you out like a wad of gum. You're toast, you little prick. You're—"

Acre was shaking now, the Beretta quivering in his hand as he pointed it at him. Sparks grinned at the display and went on goading him, "Trust me, kid. I've been there. I've seen it all. You think these psychos are any different? They're worse than the mob. Ain't got a shred of loyalty. Only care about their freaky little mission, whatever the hell that is. Makes me wanna puke."

Acre felt his throat closing up, his chest constricting. The C? What did he mean, working for the C? Acre wasn't working for anyone. The client wasn't—who was the client? He couldn't think, his mind had gone blank. All he could hear was static, fizzing white noise over a deep drone. Why was he here? Why was he doing this? And what the hell were these documents?

"Let me tell you something right now," Sparks said. "Saul Sparks does not forget. And he sure as shit don't forgive. And if the C don't frickin' erase you, I will. So, you better—"

BOOM. Suddenly Saul Sparks's words ended—he didn't have a mouth to speak them. He didn't even have a face. And his lifeless body dropped to the floor and bled slowly out.

"Shit," Acre whispered in the dimly lit corridor, as a pool of dark blood swam slowly to his feet. He would have to stay here longer than planned. He needed to clean up. And he needed to think.

Chapter 19

It was intuition. It was always intuition. When every other door closed, that was the one window left; when every last trace had faded, it was the last flare in the inky sea of ignorance. Chase had always followed her intuition out of the dark rooms into which each investigation led her. She had always hunted the trace well past the logical conclusion any data provided.

But these days her intuitions were faltering and she was scrambling in the dark. With a key sense blinded, it felt like she was being led by the nose.

And even though they'd gotten a good lead, doubt still plagued Chase's mind. She just couldn't seem to trust it. Lucy Child had gone out of her way to light a blazing letter C onto a federal building. Vance's testimony made the act seem even more pointless. There had just been no real reason for it. It was a puzzle piece that no matter how many times she rolled over in her mind she couldn't seem to fit it into the main narrative. Child had the opportunity to pull off the mural, sure. But where was the motive? How would a lowly cleaning woman have gained the knowledge, the know-how, the brazenness to pull off something like that? Painting in fire wasn't exactly the kind of thing they taught at night school art classes.

The only way everything added up was by assuming a more solid connection between Child and the C. Maybe it was through Sparks, maybe not. Maybe the C were Child's fence and the fire mural was part of their conditions for them taking the documents off her hands. All this time, Chase had been waiting for the answer to fall out of somewhere. Had expected it to lie underneath the dirt they were pawing through at the Keno Lounge. Yet here they were, and Child had almost certainly been behind the arson. But at the behest of Sparks and Mayo alone? What would two shady bookmakers want with government documents? That right there was the lynchpin. Behind this contradiction, the whole truth of what was going on would be lurking. Somehow, the C had to be using Child or Sparks for their own project. That meant a paper trail. That meant a way back to one of the slipperiest enemies the Bureau had faced in years.

And maybe it was for that reason that ASAC Hogan signed off on Chase infiltrating Sparks' place first before tactical charged the joint.

The reasoning behind it was this: If they stormed the joint with a full on tactical team, Sparks could panic. He could end up quickly disposing of evidence. He could destroy any real link leading behind the black curtain. Chase couldn't take that chance. She strapped into her kevlar and lovingly stroked the carbon barrel of her SIG Sauer P228 Custom, and checked her magazine for the tenth time.

"Are you sure you want to do this?" Agent Kelly said in the back of the monitoring truck. They were parked in a discreet location outside Saul Sparks' detached house between Elmhurst and Corona: A neat little-cream colored two stories plus attic with a road-facing gable and its own yard complete with outer wall. The property wasn't huge, but it was secluded and elegant and certainly a step up from the shoebox apartments in town. Who knew the sleazeball had so much taste?

"Agent Kelly," Chase said, "I know we don't have a long working relationship together, but you're worrying for nothing. This is not my first rodeo and I'm not recklessly jumping into a trap."

"That's true," Kelly said. "But Chase, for one thing, you're going in completely blind."

"We can't risk doing recon on this one. If we spook him it's game over. Besides, Tactical Leader McEnry is going in with me."

"Wait, you are?" Kelly said to McEnry, his face drooping.

McEnry just nodded. He was already in the zone and wasn't up for conversation. He sat hunched over in the truck and ready for action. He worked on a different wavelength from the other agents—he lived for these moments and these moments alone. Talking to McEnry outside of a mission was nigh on impossible, and talking to him on one was too unless it related to the facts of the situation itself.

"Just let me back you guys up," Kelly said, going all doe-eyed.

"Get a grip, Agent Kelly," Chase said. "We're not going to the county fair here. Plus we need someone to stay behind and watch the exterior in case Sparks makes a run for it."

"Alright. Alright, fine."

They waited another minute, then McEnry nodded to Chase. "Let's go get this bastard."

They exited out the back of the truck and kept low to the ground. It was late in the evening and the sodium street light pooled mustard yellow on the street. They silently crossed the few houses separating the tactical van from Sparks' place then stopped by the front wall running around his yard. McEnry squatted beside her and checked up and down the street.

"Area is clear. We're all good to go."

"Copy that," she said. They slid under the sycamore tree which stood inside the walled-off yard. Satellite imagery suggested there was a blind spot in the security cameras through here. McEnry went up first, throwing his grappling hook over a sturdy branch and quickly scooting up the side of the wall and onto the tree in an impressive show of agility. Chase was no slouch either, putting her Quantico training to work and holding the cable taut as she angled her body perpendicular and walked up the wall to the branch. Following McEnry, she swung down onto the lawn on the other side and landed softly on the grass. No alarms, no lights. So far so good.

They skidded across the damp grass which shone gold from the streetlight. A brisk breeze whipped across the lawn and sent a shiver through Chase as she followed McEnry's line until they made it to the outer wall of the house proper. Her heart pounded through her chest and her back stuck tight to the wall. Her breath steamed out in a fading floating cloud.

"Ready?" McEnry asked.

"Ready."

They slipped up the side of the house and around back, went up the steps and McEnry opened the screen door. So far no sounds from inside. McEnry tested the handle—it didn't budge.

"Entering in three," he said curtly. Three seconds later the butt of McEnry's M16 went through the window glass and allowed him to turn the handle from the inside. The door clicked neatly open and allowed them entry. They had their body lamps on now, and circles of light swept across the darkened room as they turned about the room.

"Maybe he's not here," Chase suggested. "The sound of the door should have roused him."

"Just keep your eyes and ears open. First floor seems clear. We'll hit the second floor and double back."

They went up soundlessly, scoping out one room at a time. Vague shapes and edges made themselves briefly known then hid back under the cloak of darkness. They entered the bedroom to find an empty, unmade bed.

The vague smell of disinfectant let them know that Sparks or someone had recently been here.

"If the cleaner had been here, why didn't they make his bed?" Chase wondered aloud.

"Not our problem right now. Continue to sweep the area."

Leaving the bedroom, they went on checking the bathroom and spare room and then to the end of the hallway where they came to Sparks' office. No one here either.

"Okay," Chase said. "The house seems clear. But if there's anything linking Sparks to the C it's going to be in here. Let's take this place apart."

Switching on a desk lamp they went at the room like starving dogs in search of meat. They unhooked drawers, pulled out shelves, and went through reams of folders in steel cabinets. Broke open the compartment on the side of the desk and went through the things in there. So far nothing substantial—just incoherent documents full of figures probably linked to his gambling operation. They found a couple of detached hard drives but Sparks was no amateur and they were almost certainly encrypted. It was only after rooting through the whole room that they discovered something—or rather the lack of something.

"Hold on McEnry," Chase said. "Look here—doesn't this wall seem wrong to you?"

"Wrong how?"

"It's too far inside. Look at it from the hall."

McEnry poked his head out of the door and came back. "You're right. The end wall is much further back than this. There must be some kind of compartment in here... Okay, move back."

Chase stepped aside and watched as McEnry took a running kick to the wall, his heavy steel-capped boot landing heavily into the plaster. The walls shook with the impact as a hole opened up.

"I was going to suggest we look for a hidden switch."

"The time for stealth is over, Chase." McEnry pulled at the hole and switched his light on, illuminating the inside of the compartment. "It's a vault," he said, his voice hushed with excitement.

"Whatever dirt Sparks has is going to be inside there."

"Then we'll need the team to get into it—or maybe not."

"What?"

McEnry pulled on the vault door and it slowly opened. "It's open," he said, dazed.

"Let me see," Chase said impatiently.

"There's nothing—just a few stacks of cash." McEnry came out of the hole and let Chase in. She desperately rummaged around the inside—he was right. But there were hardly any precious objects in here either.

"Maybe he ran," Chase said. "This doesn't—"

"Hold it right there," a dark, throaty voice came from behind them in the doorway. They spun around but too late—a powerful shotgun blast went off, sending McEnry down. Shots rained like hail against the wall as Chase slid to the floor. She raised her SIG P228 but the figure had already slipped back out of the door. Chase's blood pounded through her ears in a sullen drone. The hallway light flickered and buzzed.

"Slide the gun over here," the voice said, sounding oddly familiar.

Chase felt sick. The droning of the walls seemed to be growing in her head. Her body began to feel numb. "We're federal agents! You're not going to get away with this, Sparks." She steadied herself and tried to snap out of the hopeless paralysis she felt creeping over her.

The voice didn't call back. It just went silent.

"You think no one heard your shotgun?" Chase said. "You think we're all alone here? This house is going to be swarmed with agents any minute now." She raised her gun to where the voice had come from. The P228 was probably powerful enough to penetrate two layers of cheap plaster as long as she didn't hit a support beam. There was no other option but to test her luck. She pulled the trigger.

Or tried to at least. But her finger wasn't responding. The pulsing in her ears grew more distinct now. Familiar. It wasn't her heartbeat. This wasn't her sound. It was a different sound. A sound she knew.

"No..." She said, Chase's field vision was shrinking now. The flickering from outside came into clearer view. She didn't know if she was seeing what she was seeing, but it felt like that video. The same video that had played at Times Square and inside the room where Bucky held her captive. She desperately tried to fire her weapon, to scream, to even blink—but all her functions had been locked away from her.

"It's time for a nap," the voice said. "Now you can finally rest."

Chapter 20

Chase found herself in darkness again. This time the throbbing through her body wasn't the sound anymore, just her heartbeat. She wriggled but the rope didn't budge. Down here in the darkness, any hope she had of holding herself together quickly dissolved.

She hadn't even gotten a good look at the suspect.

The fear crawled up out of the corners of the room and swelled until it had become a heavy weight pressing on her from all sides. She flashed back to That Time again, a time she hadn't thought about in a while. A time she even had deluded herself into thinking she had gotten over ever since the Deborah Doyle case when she'd been forced to surmount the fear in order to make it out alive.

But deep wounds like that don't just go away. They just lurk under the skin, waiting, always waiting for a chance to come out.

Her breath caught in her lungs and her whole body ached. Panic raced through her veins like acid. She struggled and tried to loosen the grip of the rope around her hands—but it wouldn't budge. She heard herself whimper. Then she heard something shuffle from over the other side of the room and her heart went into overdrive.

"Get the hell away from me!" She yelled.

"What the—Chase? I assumed I'd run into you again, but never thought it would be like this."

Chase frantically tried to look around the dark room, her heart rocketing out of her chest. She couldn't see a thing. It took her a while to break out of the panic and even realize she wasn't in immediate danger. But after taking a few breaths she finally found a brief moment of sanity and it clicked.

"Who's there?" She called out.

"It's me, Hank Acre."

Chase saw the small light from his phone lighting up a familiar face. "Lieutenant Acre? Is that really you?"

"It's me. But I haven't been a lieutenant for a while."

"Thank God. Hurry up and untie me before Sparks gets back. He has a shotgun."

The figure moved closer and then she smelled Camels and knew it really was Acre—that this wasn't just delusion in the midst of her panic. It felt embarrassing that he'd seen her in that state but they had more things to worry about now. After a few fumbled attempts, Acre cursed and just got out his knife, then cut through the rope binding Chase's arms behind her. She threw off the rest of the rope herself and scrambled up off the floor.

"Let's get out of here," Chase said.

"You can relax, Sparks is long gone."

"What?"

"I saw him hot tail it out of here on my way in. Escaped out the back and vamoosed into the next yard."

"But what are you even doing here, Acre? And—shit, McEnry!"

They rushed out of the dark room into the kitchen—and Chase realized they'd been inside the larder. She stormed to the stairs and went up them, coming into the office to find McEnry sitting by the wall grabbing his side and breathing heavily.

"McEnry! Are you alright?"

"I think my vest caught most of it. I'm gonna have one hell of a bruise tomorrow though. Caught some shots to the shoulder but I already tied off the wound. Also, my radio's busted."

"Thank God. Just hold on, I'll call Kelly." Chase touched her earwig. "Agent Kelly, this is Chase."

"Chase! I've been trying to reach you for ten minutes—did you get Sparks?"

"No. McEnry was hit—seems like nothing fatal, but we lost Sparks. Did you see him come out of the house?"

"What? He came out?"

"Jesus, Kelly. You were meant to be watching."

"I was—I swear I was. No one came out of there."

"You must have missed him. He went out the back way, through another house."

"Shit. I didn't—Goddammit."

And that was that. The mission ended in failure. They did a once-over of the neighborhood but came up with bupkis.

...

After that, Acre explained to Chase how he'd found her there. He'd been working a case involving a kidnapping, and it was a matter of following the leads back until he came across a whole string of people who'd been secretly blackmailed, coerced, seduced by the promise of money, or otherwise manipulated.

She was sipping on an Arnold Palmer with him at this little low-key bar in Tribeca, where they had retired while Acre debriefed her. There was no point facing ASAC Hogan before knowing all the angles. Not after that screw up. And truth be told it was somewhat nostalgic to see the ex-lieutenant again in his black leather jacket and ridiculous Hawaiian shirt—his big dark eyes, short stiff brush of a haircut, and long, round-curved nose. He was one of the few people in this town she could feel comfortable around; that was a hard-earned thing. They'd been through hell together.

He gave her his opinion on the Federal Records & Accounts job. To set a federal building on fire, he explained, you'd need people on the inside. Not just the one to set the fire—one person alone could do that. But you need people to turn a blind eye to what you're doing. You need to sneak in the flammable material. And, maybe the most important part of all, you need the security cams disabled—which had always been C-60's MO. And the C's too. Then there was the matter of the flammable paint laid on the outside of the building. Any way you looked at it, it was a team job.

Listening to Acre's account, Chase could feel her bones burning. It was like telling her that all her fears and suspicions had all been justified; that Bucky hadn't been the end of things. He'd only been the beginning of it. And it was up to whoever still had balls in this town to put a stop to it.

She didn't know what to say. While she'd seen it coming in a way, that still didn't weaken its impact.

"You know Acre," she said, "I always thought that building job was suspect. I mean this is a government facility housing all kinds of confidential information. And some random cleaning lady is able to get enough access to spread a fire across that many floors? One floor, sure. But it spread to the whole building designed to prevent that sort of thing. It stunk, but since the fire erased its own evidence I had no way of proving my suspicion. I just didn't figure out how deep this went. That was stupid of me."

"Well, in deference to your investigative abilities, Chase, the only reason I figured it out is because I found the connection firsthand. You'd think something as important as a government records facility would vet their staff better. Or maybe they did vet them. Maybe that's the problem."

"Wait, what do you mean by that?"

"I mean like if regular folk with clean backgrounds can be compromised that easily."

"So, where are those witnesses now? This trail of yours might be all we've got if we don't catch Sparks."

"Don't you think I know that?" Acre said sourly, knocking back the bourbon.

Chase looked at him for a second, then it clicked.

"They're gone?"

"Every last one of 'em. Up and vanished like a puff of smoke—no pun intended."

"Jesus."

"Yeah. Exactly. Whoever the C are, they're capable of a lot more than just the merry pranks we've witnessed so far. Something sinister is going on under the surface."

"Did you go to the police?"

"Of course I did. Hounded everyone I knew on the force. The official stance is they aren't treating any of these things as related."

"But that's—"

"Moronic?" Acre suggested. "Cowardly? Yellow and short-sighted to the point it makes you wanna scream?"

"I just can't believe they don't see this as a threat."

"Look Chase, they know it's a threat. They're shaking in their damn boots downtown—the sharper cops are at least. But their hands are tied. They're just not allowed to move on the C."

"I don't understand, Acre. Why are the police being suppressed?"

"It has to be pressure from upstairs. Maybe even the Mayor himself. Don't you get it? The media controls the people and the C controls the media—I don't know how, maybe they still have some of that Cybernetics whatever the crap left over from Bucky. In any case, they've managed to control the right people and said people have their big fat thumb squashing down on the PD. I just don't trust anyone in the government now. This seems to go way higher than just a few random crimes."

Chase bit her lip, stirred her drink, and looked deep into its murky bottom. Everything they'd achieved so far seemed futile. The C were still roaming free out there—and not only that, they achieved an unparalleled level of power.

"But don't look so hangdog," Acre said. "It's not like we're out of options."

"We're not? Acre, that vault was emptied. There's nothing left to even hang Sparks with but some gambling racket. Hell—at this point, it could even be a tough sell to tie him to the keno front. The whole thing is owned by shell companies in the Bahamas and Mayo is acting manager of the Lounge, not Sparks himself." She sighed, long and hard. "Well, it was to be expected..."

"I never seen you so down in the dumps before. What's this really about?"

Chase shot him a look as if she was wondering whether to tell him.

"Come on," Acre coaxed her. "It's just your good ol' pal Hank Acre."

"Look, the thing is—it's like this. I'm starting to doubt my effectiveness in the Bureau."

"Hah wha?" Acre responded. He almost broke into laughter but the look on her face told him it was no joke. "Chase—you of all people? Ineffective? Come on, what the hell is that?"

"It's true, Acre. Things are changing. Crime is changing, crime fighting is too. My intuitions have been completely out of whack lately. Everything is just so complex now. In place of witnesses, you have masses of data. Instead of simple crooks running ponzis and grifts you have invisible criminals running free. If it wasn't for those arsons, we'd have nothing. And they were basically a freebie—the C taunting us. Their crimes are invisible for the most part."

"When has that ever stopped you before? Isn't that your whole thing, chasing ghosts? Getting to the sick bastards no one else can see?"

"It was. It used to be."

"Ah geez, I can't stand seeing you like this." Acre pushed her iced tea away and called the bartender. "Barkeep, get this woman a Jim Beam on the rocks. STAT." A new glass was placed in front of her, its cubes tinkling.

"Acre, getting drunk is hardly going to solve my crisis of faith."

"I never said it would. This is just lubrication for the events to follow."

Chase bolted upright, her face turning red. "What—what do you mean by that?"

"Geez, don't get so touchy. What I mean to say is this, Chase: You need to quit beating yourself over the head. It's time to take a breather and think clearly. The fact is we're not out of the fire yet, not by a long shot. And as a matter of fact, the two of us are the ones closest to the C out of anyone."

"How do you figure that?"

"Because, Chase, we know how they operate. We've seen it firsthand. And that means you can find them again. You found them before, didn't you?"

Chase tipped the glass back and the cool golden liquid disappeared down her throat. Gasping, she wiped her mouth and slammed the glass down. "You're right, Acre. We did find them."

"Then you know what you have to do next."

Chase nodded. "The objective remains the same. I have to find Lucy Child. I have to figure out where she's hiding and then haul her ass in."

Chapter 21

"So, the vault was empty and Sparks' place is giving up nothing substantial on Lucy Child. And you let Sparks get away." Hogan looked out on the silver Manhattan sky, his chunky hands locked behind a broad back packed into his black suit jacket.

"Yes, sir..." Chase muttered.

Hogan turned slightly, a shadow crossing his face. "Don't get me wrong Chase, I appreciate to what extent you've wrung facts out of this dry bone of a case. But we can hardly chalk this operation up as a success, can we? In fact, it's a huge failure."

"Yes, ASAC. You're absolutely right. There's no excuse." She couldn't quite grasp what was going on inside his head. Was it disappointment? Sadness? Fury? A closed book. Chase wasn't used to closed books. Lately, she'd been seeing a lot of them. This funk she was in sucked.

"But at the same time, we only suffered mild casualties. There's something to be said for that. Nonetheless, I think it's about time we take off the kid gloves in this case, don't you?"

"Certainly, ASAC Hogan, but I'm not sure how."

Just then Chase jumped as the door opened and she turned to see a familiar set of inquisitive eyes peering from out a creasy face. It was the Bookman.

"You wanted to see me, ASAC?" Bob said.

"Yes. Come in, Bob. Take a seat."

Bob gave Chase a little nod on the way in and sat down beside her. He seemed jittery—nervous—or was that excitement?

"I understand," ASAC Hogan, "that you have been trying to develop a coherent narrative regarding the aspects of this case based on SET."

"Correct, ASAC."

"And from our discussions so far, it seems that we have met a bottleneck of sorts with regards to that. Explain that, Bob."

"Right. As we discussed in our last meeting, the way the C works is more convoluted and distributed than the crimes we're used to. There doesn't seem to be an obvious point of control—which is why they have been able to evade capture for so long, and why much investigation both by the FBI and other agencies seems to hit a dead end. In order to combat this dilemma, my suggestion was to dig deeper into more detailed everyday data not necessarily pertaining to our major suspects and their immediate contacts."

"Is this what Agent Kelly was talking about?" Chase asked him. "That micro-analysis theory?"

"It's related to that, certainly," Bob said. "But not restricted to it. The idea would be to match our profile against a wider selection of the population's activities— obviously, that's a hard ask in a city of nearly nine million people. But with the right advancements we could start to think about crime differently. We could profile people before they even commit the crime."

"Bob—are you talking about *future crime?*"

He shrugged casually and said, "Sure, why not," like they were having a conversation about the benefits of Snickers over Milky Way or something.

"But that's—"

"Necessary," Hogan interjected. "Or at least Bob believes it is, in order to catch the C. Because they don't work like the mafia—they seem to exploit everyday citizens. Lucy Child would be one such example in recent history."

"But ASAC," Chase said, "Lucy Child is no ordinary citizen. She was up to her neck in gambling debt."

"The fact of the matter is," Bob said, "everyone has skeletons in their closet like that. The point isn't whether or not they could be considered "ordinary citizens," but rather what their potential is to commit a crime. Everyone has that potential, more or less—it's just a matter of quantifying it. And then basing our theories on that data."

"But Bob," Chase protested, "it sounds to me like you're talking about profiling the entire populace of New York City."

"That's one way to put it. Again—it wouldn't be so cut and dry. We'd have filtering mechanisms."

"Even if that was possible technically," Chase said, "there's no way it would be legal."

"And now we come to the point," Hogan said, leaning back on his chair and smiling broadly. "Given the developments of this case thus far—I think it's a ripe opportunity to start taking a look at Bob's suggestion more seriously."

Something in Chase sank then—no wonder Hogan had been so indifferent about the screw-up at Sparks' place. He'd been waiting for something like this. Their case was going to be used as the grounds for putting this project into play.

"Even so," Chase said, "what about the legality of it? What we're talking about here goes far beyond traffic lights and ATM camera footage. We're looking right inside people's living rooms, practically. It's total surveillance of everyday citizens."

"Correct," ASAC Hogan said. "But an update to the Wire Fraud Prevention Act would give us more operational freedom in that area."

Chase was taken by a vague memory then—something from long ago, a kind of terrible *deja vu*. She tried to force herself to think, but her thoughts wouldn't emerge from the gridlock they had worked themselves into. Nothing flashed on no matter how hard she concentrated. Something was blocked in there, a cork plug stuck into the gap in her mind. It had been there for a while now. And when she tried to think why, all she could think of was Bucky.

She shivered. A sensation of pressure had filled up Chase's spine like cold water poured into a narrow tube. She detected it as a chill at first in her lower back, but the more Bob and Hogan spoke the more the feeling charged up toward the back of her head. At this point, the pressure was right on her skull and she could hear her own heartbeat pulsing in her ears—the voices of Hogan and Bob became lost under this rhythm and for a moment she was in the room all by herself. The penetrating darkness of Sparks' basement came back, leaking out of the corners of the room and spreading like a damp patch over the ceiling and floor. Her heart quickened, which made the pounding in her ears quicken. Her chest burned. She couldn't breathe. The feeling was suffocating her from the inside out. She opened her mouth to breathe but nothing came in. The pressure came down at her from all angles and the room spun in a wide circle with her at the center—the light of the window growing in intensity to an impossible blinding white.

And then there was darkness.

...

Chase launched herself up out of oblivion and found herself in a room with muted light and pastel blue walls. A beeping sound tumbled into her consciousness along with a cot with white railings and the smell of disinfectant, then it clicked where she was. She groaned as her body refused her command to sit up.

"Don't try to move just yet," the nurse warned her. "Your body is still in shock."

"Shock?" Chase mumbled through a dry mouth. "Shock from what?" She shook her head and tried to focus on the nurse's face but it was still just blurry colors. "Jesus, I didn't have a stroke, did I?"

"No, don't worry," the soothing voice said sympathetically. "Nothing like that. You just passed out from exhaustion. You've been pushing yourself too hard, Agent Chase. What you need right now is rest."

Bullshit. That wasn't what had happened. That wasn't what had happened at all. She had been on the verge of making some kind of connection—what was it? Damn it, she'd forgotten again. Something had been stopping her from—the thought slipped away from her again. It felt like trying to hold onto a wet bar of soap. She pawed futilely at its trace but it had already disappeared. Just like Sparks.

"Bucky," she murmured. She must have closed her eyes again, as the room was dark.

"What was that?" The nurse asked, her voice full of annoying patience and sympathy.

"Where's Bob?"

"Bob?"

"The freaking Bookman."

"Bob—ah, Agent Fairfax was in here earlier. He told me to tell you not to worry about anything, that he's got things under control."

"Under control? We don't have the first thing under..." She felt herself slipping under the blanket of unconsciousness again. That was no good. She had to wake up. She had to think about what it was she'd figured out. But the more she scrambled to cling to consciousness, the heavier her mind became until she was falling headlong into a deep warm black pit, letting everything go, every last thought she'd put together slipping from her open hands...

Chapter 22

The next time Chase woke up she was determined to stay awake. She ripped the IV from her arm just in case they had her on some kind of sedative. She had no idea how long she'd been out but it was pitch black outside the window and she was alone in the clinic. The gentle pace of her heart monitor didn't reflect at all the tumbling maelstrom going on inside her half-awaken mind.

She forced herself to sit up first, then attempted to put her legs on the ground. She barely felt what was under her feet, yet somehow, holding onto the railing, she managed to stand on her own power. She fetched her clothes which had been neatly piled in the corner and slipped them on. Getting out her phone she found several messages from Acre—the first concerned about her wellbeing, the rest just idle conjecture about the case. It didn't seem like he'd gotten anywhere other than running in more circles. The same discussion they'd had again and again was wild speculation since they still had no real evidence. Since they still hadn't found Lucy Child.

It was one-thirty in the morning. Not bad, she'd only lost an afternoon. It felt like a lot longer. But still, it was time to stop wasting time. Maybe Bob was around—sometimes he was awake at this hour pawing at his computer. She cautiously looked outside the room: The night shift nurse wasn't in sight. She drove forward as fast as possible on her numb legs, slipping silently down the corridor to the bank of elevators, then froze, realizing she didn't have an access card. She stood there feeling guilty, like a mental patient attempting to escape an asylum. It reminded her of the time she'd tried to escape the institution she stayed at as a young girl. Somehow, she'd managed to get past both security guards and outside the house, only eventually to be thwarted by the massive iron fence surrounding the grounds. But there had been a very specific reason why she'd been able to get past all of those doors and guards and security measures. The reason was her gift—she'd been able to feel where they were, which way they would turn next, whether or not they were suspicious. It had come to her like faint voices carried in the wind, telling her exactly which route to take to avoid detection.

But how about now? She tried listening for the ghosts that had haunted her for twenty-plus years, but there was nothing but the dull drone of the building's air conditioning and the insectile buzz of the fluorescent bulbs on the ceiling. She couldn't find anyone out there. Suddenly she was deeply, impossibly alone.

It was gone. Her gift was gone. She might as well have been struck deaf or blind—everything had lost a key dimension. Had turned into a flat picture of reality. Noises from down the hall were confusing and didn't have context. Steps that came toward her seemed to come out of the blue. Even the voice that called on her said she shouldn't be out of bed and that she was to return to her room, even that voice didn't seem to belong to a person. It was pre-recorded, like a subway announcement played through a speaker. She couldn't feel anyone else around her. The penetrating loneliness clenched her heart and made it bleed ice down the inside of her body. Cold chills took her and she breathed harder and harder until she was hyperventilating. The nurse called a code and another robotic figure came out of nowhere to her side, and she was being fed oxygen and being moved onto something and going somewhere—although she couldn't tell where—she could have been going East, she could have been going West. It was all the same thing now. Nothing possessed any kind of significance or depth underneath the surface. There was just a series of random impressions, lights in her eyes and sounds around her, the cool taste of fresh oxygen as her mind drifted in and out of the shallow skin of consciousness until eventually she grew tired of the flat, hollow world and let herself sink back down into the overwhelming darkness calling her name.

Eventually, and not at first, but after a time, she was somewhere again and someone. A familiar smell of jasmine tea in her nostrils. A sense of warmth in her body. The familiar light came through the net curtain, behind which the institution's garden spread out under a healing sun.

A man was sitting there, his face in front of the bright sunlight shining in the window and so obscured. But Chase didn't need to make out the details to know who it was.

"Bucky," Chase said. "You're behind this. You're the reason my mind is blocked."

"Am I?" He said, a roguish smile crawling over his face.

"You did something to me back then."

"I did? What did I do?"

"I—don't know. I can't think. The thoughts won't come to my mind anymore. Nothing comes to me now. I'm empty."

"Maybe you just think you're empty. You are what you think, as they say."

"Who says that?"

"I do."

"You're dead, Bucky."

"If I'm here, how can I be dead?"

"You're just in my mind somehow. You're just a memory."

"If I'm just a memory, how can I do this?" He took a step forward and then was behind her with his arms locked around her head in a chokehold. It felt so real, more real than anything she'd felt since they'd breached the Poughkeepsie dome. The raw strength of his fingers grinding into her head, his forearm on her throat constricting her airway. The demonic heat of his body behind her. The trembling through it as his muscles clenched. She shook and gasped for breath.

"Stop it... You're killing me."

"If I can kill you, I must be real."

"Fine," she conceded, coughing and spluttering as 'Bucky' released her. He stood over her, looking down. His face was a neat precise arrangement of features. Cool blue eyes and blonde hair that came down past his ears. A straight line of a nose, a thin-lipped mouth. He had a kind of androgynous handsomeness about him— but like everything else about Bucky, it was fraudulent. His face was a death mask. The mask drew a smile. The sun had seemingly gone behind a cloud because Chase could see him clearly now, sitting there in the armchair wearing nondescript minimal attire. White shirt, dark brown slacks, loafers. An effective non-threatening appearance. The slightly smiling pale face, the well-combed hair that had been trimmed shorter than the straggly mess it was before. But this was all a construction. This was just an image.

"I'm dreaming," Chase finally said. "But why is this so lucid?"

"They must have you on the fun stuff," Bucky said, grinning. "Lucky you."

"I don't feel especially lucky."

"Oh?" He put on his innocent mask. "And why's that, Special Agent?"

"Because I'm lying here trapped in a dream while out there criminals roam free. Because I can't do my job."

"Is your job everything that defines you?"

"Don't analyze me—you're a fricking ghost."

"But ghosts are your only friends, no? You certainly don't get along with the living."

"That's not your concern."

"You should be concerned. Without your gift, you're nothing, Agent Chase. That's what I wanted to show you."

"You screwed me up. What the hell did you do to me?!"

Bucky threw his head back and guffawed falsely, then just as quickly fixed his face back into the stolid, dependable mask.

"I'm trying to help you, Chase. I'm trying to make you see."

"See what? You piece of dirt—you scumbag! Stop acting like you're above it all. You're not. You figured out how to mess with my head, that's all. You put some kind of block on me and that's why I can't do my job! How does that help me see anything?"

"Maybe you're just blocking yourself. Maybe what you need to see is right in front of you, but you're purposefully stopping yourself from seeing it. You're afraid if you do see it, it will break your whole life apart—such as it is."

"No. Stop trying to confuse me. I don't even understand what you're—"

"You're afraid of the truth."

"That's nonsense. All I ever do is search for the truth. I'm out there every day scrambling to find the truth. Stop it. Stop messing with me! Haven't you done enough?"

"Maybe that's the problem."

"What?"

"You're out there. You're looking too hard in the wrong place. That's going to get you into trouble. Deep trouble."

"I don't understand a thing you're saying. Just let me wake up. Get me out of here."

"Out there, you're blind. The answers are locked inside you, Chase. One of these days, it's all going to click, and you're going to feel mighty foolish for not listening to me sooner."

"So, just tell me. You're my subconscious, aren't you? You're my inner voice. So, that means you know the answer. Tell me."

"Now where would the fun in that be?" He gave her another false smile. Then he clicked his fingers and the sun blinked out. And she was sitting there in a cold dark room, alone.

"Bucky, don't go. Don't leave me in here!"

"Oh come now, Chase. You're a big girl. I trust in your incredible ingenuity. I'm sure you'll find your way out... Eventually."

"No, wait. WAIT!"

He was gone. And she was back there in the walls again. The walls from her youth. The chill ravaged her body—at first making her shiver and gradually worsening until she found herself trembling violently. Make it stop. Wake up. But she couldn't. Whatever the nurse had given her had trapped her down here. There was no getting out of this. There was no way to escape.

The only thing left to her now was to walk through that door and face whatever was inside.

...

She is back in the room with Bucky again. Before Acre came to pull her out. The throbbing sounds through her head, the fuzzing static on the screen. Bucky's mouth is moving but she can't hear what he's saying.

The scene mutates into the inside of the wall she'd been kept in as a girl. Heather feels the fear again, her heart quickening, that hot battery acid fear running through her veins. Trying to keep as silent as possible from the one who kept them there—Master, he'd made them call him. Trying to suss out when Master was in one of his bad moods and itching to take it out on one of the girls. Trying to be invisible.

Back in the room with Bucky again and he's talking about how they're all condemned. That all he's doing is opening minds to the truth they already know. He's talking about brainwaves, resonance, a bunch of things Heather can't understand, and doesn't have the state of mind to comprehend. He's talking about the media, advertising. He's talking about subliminal messaging that has been used for decades and how NYU stumbled onto it independently. He's talking about Professor Sherman and how he exploited that discovery to alter people's minds. He's talking about the government again, their practices of intervention in civilian life. And now he's talking about the FBI, about Heather —and his face is the Master's face, and his tone is the same too. And Heather feels like he's going to take it out on her, and she tries desperately to become invisible—to go back inside the wall.

Heather is back in the institute again, the years she spent there trying to become normal after she was saved from the Master by the FBI. Heather's trying to put the pieces of her mind back together, which will never go together again because she's seen and felt too much even at this tender age of eight years old. Heather is broken, but she still feels.

She feels everything, terrifying as it is. She has no control over it.

The sisters at the institute who tried to get her to open up. Her not unwilling but simply unable—too many senses alive like frayed nerve endings exposed to the world. Too much information to take in. Too much.

So it was all too much. That's why she'd blocked it out. That's why she didn't feel anymore.

She was afraid of facing the truth—that she'd never really escaped from the Masters out there. That in a way she'd never come out of the wall.

Chapter 23

Chase woke up in the hospital cot again, fully refreshed and revived. She was just about fed up with sleeping on the job. It was time to get out of this place before she lost the motivation to fight entirely. Throwing on her clothes she moved to the door and then stopped to check the time. Phone was dead. She looked out the window at the gray early morning, probably something around five or six AM. The squeaking of the night shift nurse doing her last check before clocking out. Weariness, fatigue. Sore feet. The feeling of wanting to go home. They were all there, those feelings—in stark contrast to the dull blank void which had plagued her before. The feelings were back, in a way that Chase had never caught before.

She'd always taken her intuition for granted—it had always been a part of the fabric of the environment. So, it was only after having the gift stripped from her that it dawned on her what she truly had. No wonder others always seemed so blunt and insensitive to her—was that really how they went through life on a daily basis? In that blind void? It was hell, trying to piece all of those loose, uncoupled facts together into a coherent story. There was no truth in that, it was just a desperate attempt at making something out of nothing. A paper-thin theory, a bag of loose evidence packed full of doubt. Was it any wonder that so many criminals were let off scot-free?

But not when she had the full picture available to her perceptions. She wouldn't take that for granted again.

Something turned in the air, something was coming. And Chase knew she had to run now. She didn't guess, she didn't deduce. She just knew. Forcing the stale air from her lungs she held against the wall and willed her aching, tight muscles to move. Moved one step at a time until the blood was pumping again through her legs and then padded quicker down the hallway back to the elevator banks. This time she wouldn't be left stranded; she was back in her uniform, back on the job. Swiping her access card, Chase slipped into the elevator just as a burning sensation came at her from behind. And she made no effort to deduce who was there—whom she knew was there—as Chase turned to face the nurse, the doors closing between them.

"You can't leave!" The nurse said, desperately tapping the door button to no avail. "You're supposed to be resting!"

"Thanks, nurse, but I've rested enough," Chase replied, smiling. "And I'm all better now."

...

She knew where Bob would be too: Ankle-deep in his precious data. Had they gone through with what they were talking about? Had they finally crossed the line from investigators to future crime predictors? Chase took a detour to the bathroom and washed her face in cold water, feeling alive for the first time in a long time. She felt rejuvenated. She felt in control. She felt.

Bee-lining it to the Data Analysis room, Chase launched into the room to find Bob, as expected, keeled over on his desk with half a stale coffee beside him. On screen, a hundred different windows were blinking and scrolling. Terabytes of data flew by in a flash: The lives of thousands—no, millions of people coming and going at the speed of light. The inner face of the city was laid bare. How had they done it this quickly? How had they upgraded the hardware and put that all into effect in just two days?

The only answer was that it had already been prepared. ASAC Hogan had just been waiting for the opportunity to flip the switch.

Not disturbing Bob from his well-earned nap, Chase sat down at one of the terminals and started going through the haul. As long as they were violating the privacy of the whole city, she may as well make use of it. As for the consequences of this development—she'd have to figure that out later. She'd wasted enough time letting the case go cold and it took priority now.

It was no small haul. Bob had managed to acquire Lucy Child's entire life story, filling in the gaps in her public life with aspects of her private one. From her rudimentary beginnings in public service on her Town Board in Danby, then staffer for the Governor's office and progression to chief public relations manager—this much they had already, but now her fall from grace was revealed. She had gone through a troubled marriage and this led to an eventual separation and divorce. This was the beginning of a downward spiral which led to the end of Child's career in politics, and sometime after that, her becoming a cleaning lady.

Chase looked over at Bob who was snoozing away peacefully—he surely didn't have the same dreams Chase did.

The ex-husband was one Doug Shaw who was acting director for the FCC Enforcement Bureau District Office of New York. This was information they previously had difficulty accessing. Why? This shouldn't even have been sensitive. So, her husband had a government job, so what? And the FCC was hardly top secret.

And what about Child? How does someone who used to work in government end up becoming a cleaning lady anyway? In a way it did make sense: While she had spoiled her own career with her instability following the divorce, Child still retained a high level of clearance. That made her a perfect candidate for janitor of a high-security facility. It also made her a perfect candidate to be targeted by the C... Especially given Child's latent animosity toward her husband. He worked for the FCC Enforcement Bureau; they were the offices that investigated violations of broadcast law. Things were starting to fit together. Was this Child's true motive all along? Maybe she wasn't coerced. Maybe this was revenge. And if so, that reduced the scope of the case to just a regular crime again.

Chase was beginning to see Bob's point—that crime was becoming an invisible thread in the fabric of everyday life—and that the only way to fight it was to tear the whole fabric apart. He'd certainly done that, in spades—but at what cost?

"Chase," Bob's drowsy voice said after a while. "Are you feeling okay now?"

"A lot better than you," she replied. "When's the last time you got a real night's sleep?"

"No rest for the busy," he said. Then paused and ran through the statement in his mind. "No wait, that's not it."

"It seems you've made a lot of progress in my absence," Chase said, still not quite believing what she was seeing. "How the hell did you dig up so much on Lucy Child? Before we couldn't even find her next of kin. Now you've even got a list of what magazines she's ever subscribed to... I didn't know *Homes & Gardens* was even still a thing."

Bob gave one of his creased smiles, more creased on that unslept face, where his crows' feet met up with his cheeks into a perimeter around his face.

"Yes. It's what ASAC Hogan and I were discussing when you had your ah... Spell. We've had a little upgrade."

"So, you did go through with it."

"Yep." Bob waved at the computer with a flourish. "Heather Chase, I am proud to introduce you to SET 3.0."

"This is insane. You're bypassing every limitation previously put on the system. I just don't understand how this is legal."

Bob shrugged. "ASAC pulled some strings. It's been in the making for a long time, apparently. It just so happens that this is the perfect opportunity to test it out on a real case."

"Bob... Are you sure that the intentions behind the SET are entirely legit?"

"What do you mean by that?"

"It's just—don't you think it's getting kind of out of hand? We're spying on nine million people just to solve one case of arson."

"You tell me, Chase. We were at a complete loss as to the location of Child. Now we have a key lead."

"You're right about that but—you know what, forget it. We can talk about it later. At least we got us a new lead. And if Child's motive really is revenge then the FCC is going to be high on their list of next targets. Maybe the Federal Records & Accounts building was just a prelude to something much bigger. And maybe this Shaw character will have an idea about whatever it is she stole."

"Indeed he might. It's just as well you woke up, Chase. I was thinking about taking a little trip to the FCC Office today."

"Great. Then let's hit the road. It'll be just like old times."

Chapter 24

The office didn't appear on any map or website, except for an old HTML page in Wayback Machine that gave a phone number that was no longer connected. But that was the address the SET gave for the office, and so that was where Bob and Chase headed.

In fact, no FCC public-facing website even acknowledged the existence of the "Enforcement Bureau" any longer. It would appear that they no longer existed.

SET determined otherwise. It located the office on Third and East-Eighteenth; and while it was unlabeled and unnamed on any public map, the white brick structure fifteen stories high was definitely there when they pulled up to check the area. From an outside appearance, it looked no different from any other apartment complex—it certainly didn't seem like anything special. And in fact, much of the building was given over to apartments, complete with dry cleaner on the first floor and a disgruntled landlord, who was giving them a hard time when they came in to ask about the mysterious office.

"What are you talking about? FCC? I don't know no FCC office or any damn office. This is an apartment block, lady."

"You don't need to play the charade, sir," Chase said, displaying her badge. "We're with the FBI."

"Ah. Govmint types. Why didn't you say so? You don't look like 'em—they usually are mean sons of bitches. No offense."

"None taken," Bob said. "So—the office?"

"Yeah. Sure. It's on the thirteenth floor."

Chase's heart quickened a little. "Uh—can we take the stairs?"

"Wha? What are you, nuts? You into cardio or what? No, you can't access it by the stairwell."

"What do you mean by that?"

"Come here, I'll show you." He led them to the elevator. Chase was reluctant to go inside but the mission called for it. "Lookit," the landlord said, pointing to the two columns of buttons for the floors.

"There's no thirteen there," Chase said, looking at where the buttons skipped from twelve to fourteen.

"Exactly."

"It's not that uncommon, right?" Bob said. "People don't like living on the thirteenth floor so they skip that number and just call the thirteenth the fourteenth, and so on."

"Right," the landlord said, a sneaky grin on his withered jaw. "Usually how it is. Except this time it's a con." He took the jangling ring of keys off his belt. "Now watch." He stuck one of the keys into the maintenance access lock and turned—the elevator panel blinked and the doors closed. Chase gripped tight to the back of the wall and took deep breaths as the car ascended... Three... Four... Five... And onward, her heart crashing in her chest, sweat running down her back. This was one fear she had yet to overcome. Nine... Ten... She bit her lip and held herself tight to stop the shaking. Eleven... Twelve... Thirteen. The elevator stopped on thirteen and opened its doors onto a floor that didn't exist.

"Huh," Bob said. "Neat trick."

"Cute, ain't it?" The landlord said, like a little kid showing off his secret bug collection.

"You said there's no stairwell access," Chase said. "What happens if there's a fire?"

"Oh," the landlord said. "In that case, they're boned."

"What?!"

"Just kidding. Hehe. Actually, there is a way down to the next floor from here—but it's convoluted, and uh, well I can't be bothered explaining it to yous. Anyway, have a nice time. You can use the elevator down without a key so don't worry." He gestured in a shooing motion for them to step off the elevator.

Chase sighed deeply as she came out of the closed-in box, leaning against the wall.

"Are you okay, Chase?"

"I hate it when you ask me that. I'm fine."

"Just making sure. I know you have a thing about elevators."

She dabbed her face with a wet towel and took a sip of water from the fountain. Once her heartbeat had come down, she surveyed the area: A regular office hallway, with windowless offices behind a series of doors without any label or even number.

"Great," Chase said. "Now we have no clue where to go."

"A hidden building, a hidden floor, and doors with no names," Bob said. "This just keeps getting weirder and weirder."

"You're telling me, Bookman. You're telling me. Why the hell does the FCC find the need to be so secretive? All they do is decide what gets shown on television."

"Presumably, Chase, they do more than just that."

...

After trying a few offices and getting the cold shoulder, they finally hit paydirt.

"Is this the FCC Enforcement Bureau?" Chase asked the girl who came to answer the door.

"Excuse me, but who are you?"

Chase and Bob both flashed their badges.

"Oh, I see. Yes. Yes, we are with the FCC."

That was clever, the way she answered. Neither confirming nor denying they were actually part of the FCC. They're with the FCC. This just kept getting shadier.

"Miss," Bob said, "we're here to talk with Mr. Shaw."

"Mr. Shaw?" Her face softened a little at the name pull. "Do you uh—have an appointment?"

"No," Bob said. "But we'd really appreciate it if we could talk with him. It's in relation to an urgent matter."

"I see. Let me just see if he's available. Wait here please."

In the corridor. She had them wait in the corridor. Eventually, she came back and opened the door more than a crack. "Follow me please." The girl led them quickly through the winding alley between cubicles, where strait-laced staff with that hard government look about them were poring over data of unspecified origin. Bob was looking around him like a kid in a toy store, but the receptionist made sure to usher them through the gauntlet as quickly as humanly possible. Another thing to be suspicious about. They were led into the back office in which sat Shaw, who greeted them with a neutral smile. The receptionist had vanished back out of the office and closed the door before they could even thank her.

"Yes," Shaw said simply. He sat there with his hands folded into a lock. The connotation was clear enough. He didn't want them there and he'd only give them the absolute minimum of his time.

When Chase froze momentarily, Bob took up the slack. "Mr. Shaw, we're with the FBI. And we're here because—well firstly, would you mind telling us your job here?"

"Yes," he said. His face was unmoving.

"You would tell us or you would mind?"

"If it's not important or relevant to your case," Shaw said. "I'd rather not go into any of the particulars of my job. Don't take it personally—it's just company policy."

"I... See. We understand that you work for the FCC in the capacity of District Director," Bob said. Shaw said nothing.

"Alright Shaw," Chase spat. "We're trying to be civil with you here, but since you want to do things this way I'm obliged to tell you that you're a person of interest in an arson committed on a federal building."

"What?!" Shaw's cold visage broke like a tray of ice cubes. "In that case, I better call my lawyer..."

Chase swapped a look with Bob. She'd screwed it.

"Let's not be hasty," Bob said, wearing his tailor-made creasy smile for situations like this. "What we really want is to find your wife—excuse me, your ex-wife."

His eyes opened a fraction: It had been the most he'd reacted since they'd gotten there. It was the *Oh, Jesus* look.

"You are the former husband of Lucy Child," Bob said confidently, making sure not to phrase it as a question. "You were separated and then divorced three years ago. Miss Child then ended her career in the New York political scene and went to work in the capacity of clea—that is, uh, custodian of the Federal Record & Accounts building."

"Sure, fine. What about it?" Shaw said. It was as near to an admission as they'd gotten yet. Chase decided to keep her big mouth shut and let Bob do this thing. His people-person thing.

"Okay," Bob went on. "You see the records building was set on fire and some key documents were stolen. And we're trying to find out who did it and why."

"Sounds to me like you've already got an idea who did it."

Bob blinked twice and shifted in his seat. "Which is to say, uh—do you believe your wife is capable of something like that?"

Shaw shrugged, relaxing slightly now that he knew he wasn't being pinned for a crime. "I wouldn't put anything past that crazy bitch, if you want to know the truth."

"So, while you were together did she show any signs of—"

"Pyromania," Chase cut in.

"Nah," Shaw said. "It was more like bitchomania." He shot a knowing smirk to Bob, who politely smiled back.

"Could you be more specific?" Bob asked.

"Oh sure. Like having meltdowns over nothing, smashing plates in the kitchen, shrieking at me over nothing. Stress of the job, you understand. Happens to the best of 'em. Happens to the worst of 'em too. But anyhow, I know people blame me for her screwing her career but really I saw that coming a mile away if you want the facts of the matter. It was written in uh stone—is that the expression? She just couldn't hack it. And that's a fact. So, she takes it all out on me, daily. Takes it out on me and our best china. You know how much good dinnerware costs? I was eating out of Tupperware for six months. But uh—that's just some inside baseball for you."

Chase and Bob both froze. He went from clam-tight to open book in the space of three seconds.

"Uh, I see," Bob said, somewhat disarmed. "Was she ever diagnosed officially, do you know?"

"For what? A case of the nutballs? Nah, Luce was too proud to go to any doctor. But if you want my unprofessional diagnosis on the matter, she has manic bitchitis—"

"I think we get the picture, Mr. Shaw," Chase said.

"Yeah. Well anyway, that wasn't even what broke up our marriage, to tell the truth."

"Oh?" Bob said. "Then what did?"

He sniffed and swiveled slightly on his chair. "You probably found this out already, but Luce had a real gambling problem."

Chase's heart began pounding wildly in her chest. They were getting somewhere. They were actually getting somewhere in this total clusterfudge of a case. She could see the first cracks appearing in this wall of stone they'd been bashing their heads against since day one.

"Mr. Shaw," Chase said. "Do you happen to know any of Lucy Child's associates? With regards to her gambling."

"Beats the hell out of me. And they probably would have beat the hell out of me for not paying her debts. Which is why I wanted nothing more to do with it or her. Having my dinner plates and my bank account broken was enough. I didn't want my face added to that list." He chucked Bob another sly smirk at which Chase tried not to audibly sigh. She liked him much better when he was clamming up.

"What about Child? When was the last time you spoke?"

"Oh jeez, a long time... I wanna say two years now, almost. Eighteen months at least."

"No contact whatsoever between you since then? No indirect contact such as through a mediator or anything?"

"I got no business talking to Luce ever again, knock on wood. I just got new plates in."

"Then you wouldn't happen to know where she lives?" Bob asked hopefully. "Not at her place in Alphabet City—she's gone from there. Any other place she might be that you would know about?"

"I didn't even know she lived in Alphabet City. And no, not offhand," Shaw said. Then grinned again. "But old Luce is a creature of habit. I might be able to find out. Then you can go and book her and do whatever. Let me make a few calls."

"You don't seem too upset at giving her away to the law," Chase said.

"What, are you kidding me?" Shaw said. "The sooner Luce is sent up the river, the sooner I can stop putting a padlock on my kitchen cupboard."

Shaw delivered. He came up with an apartment in Bedford-Stuy of dubious ownership, which had changed hands through a number of sketchy individuals over the years. It had finally ended up as the property of a Kazakhstanian import/export man named Omarov, who SET estimated had formerly held strong mob connections. The whole block in fact was old red brick structures in a permanent state of disrepair that had been lucky not to get condemned. The joint was so weathered and worn out looking not even Doyle Condominiums had stepped in to buy it up, and they owned most of West Long Island at this point.

They say that everything in real estate is about location—but this place didn't even have that, set in a vague middle point between all nearest metro stations, making it just scenic enough to be inconvenient. The area also sat at the bottom of a steep hill and was beset by frequent flooding that rotted the walls and many of the lower floors apparently had mold problems. The lower outer face of the wall was painted white which had turned grimy with exhaust fumes. The sidewalk was cracked and busted. And unruly overgrown oak trees lining the path came up to the top of the building casting it in a gloomy shadow.

In short, the place was a dump and a breeding ground for dopers and squatters, who spent their days waiting for the wrecking ball to finally drop and shake them out of their slumber. As for what Lucy Child was doing here, Shaw wouldn't cough up the answer. The implicit subtext to his snide response was drug-related, and while that wasn't part of Child's profile that they'd constructed so far, Chase had to admit that they couldn't really rule it out. Lucy Child did have an addictive personality so it wasn't that incompatible. Especially if she'd gone on the lamb: Not many people can withstand that pressure sober.

The tactical team got ready in the back of the truck as McEnry went over their plan of attack. They decided on a pincer attack to prevent any chance of Child escaping. Both points of access to the building as well as the fire escapes would all be guarded closely. There was no way anyone inside would be getting through their net.

Luckily for Chase, who had a thing about elevators, she wound up on the team going bottom-up, while a separate team would ride to the top then clear the building top-down.

The first few doors, knocking to no answer. Once they'd gone the whole floor without an answer they started busting their way inside. The first floor was suffering particular water damage and the doors flew off their hinges, bursting into rotten splinters to reveal dark, musty rooms occupied only by vermin or the remnant garbage of former owners who'd taken off in a hurry, whether to dodge creditors or the police or the mob who had their hooks in them. The whole place swam in despair and desperation and the stink of decay. A no-good rotting rat hole for no-gooders to rot along with the place. The second and third floors were clear too. The next flight of stairs upwards, Chase started to get the Fear. Bad juju beyond here.

When the team entered the hallway her feeling was confirmed—slight sounds here and there, muffled coughs, sighs. The flicker of artificial light from under some of the doors. FBI Tactical had found their first rats. Raggedy-looking welfare families with mournful faces, all of them thinking their luck had run out. Room by room they cleared the floor. There was a scare when one teenage kid pulled a gun on them, but they had the kid pressed to the floor with his face eating the dirt in seconds. Turned out it was an airsoft gun. They came through more poverty-stricken half-bums and prisoners to debt as they made their way up the second and then third floor.

Running out of rooms to check. Chase's initial anticipation was slowly ebbing away when they got at least a response of some sort, showing a couple a photo of Lucy Child.

"Oh that's lovely, oh yeah," the female of the pair said. "She's the princess of dirtsville. Up there on the fourth floor shacking up with some dope boy named Maine."

"Shacks up with dirt like that," the man said. "Think she'd give a bum like me a chance? Hell, she wouldn't even spit in my direction."

"What do you need that stuck-up hooah giving you a chance for?" The female said to him. "Oh, I bet you'd love that if she spit on you, wouldn't you, dirty bastard. Cheating bastard."

"I ain't cheating on no one."

"Naw, you just got the hots for this prima donna upstairs is all. I'll spit on you, how about that?"

"You won't spit on me, woman."

"This guy she's with," Chase cut in, "is he armed?"

"Oh sure," the woman said. "Gotta protect yourself these days. Dunno who'll come knocking. Sometimes the devil himself. I seen him, you know. I seen the devil in human form. But no worries, the C is coming. They're going to save us all. Don't you know?"

"Have you had contact with the C?"

"Oh sure. They talk to me through the television. Tell me it's all gonna be allll-right, you know?"

"What kind of weapons is this Maine holding?"

"You'd go for Maine too, pretty lady like yourself. But when it comes down to it none of you would so much as—"

"Cut the crap," Agent Kelly rasped desperately. "Tell us what weapons this shithead is carrying so we don't walk into a firing squad. Is it more of this airsoft crap or has he got the real deal?"

"Oh it's the real deal honey," the woman said, "just like me." She moved a hand down the side of her sweats. Seeing this, the man became enraged.

"That's all we have to say on the matter, so kindly go screw!" He said, slamming the door shut.

...

The fourth floor now. They'd met up with the other team and now were eight strong. Only a couple of rooms were lit up. They hit them one by one just leaving one at the far end. It was throwing out serious bad vibrations.

"I think this is it," Chase said low into the radio. They surrounded the door, three on each side, then McEnry knocked hard.

"This is the FBI. Mr. Maine—we need you to open this door immediately."

No answer, but a slight shuffling sound came from inside. Chase's heart began to race.

"FBI," McEnry tried again. "Open this door or we will have to enter by force."

Still nothing.

McEnry gave the signal, then stood around the front of the door and got ready to launch himself at it when—

Everything stopped.

"GET DOWN!" Chase yelled, pulling McEnry away just in time to miss a shotgun blast that tore a nest of holes through the door.

The tacs whipped into action like no one's business, letting off a volley of M16 fire at the door.

"Cease fire!" McEnry called over the radio. He crawled back near the door. The man had balls, you had to give it to him. Second time getting fired at by a shotgun in the same week and he still wasn't backing down. "Maine," McEnry called out. "Put down your weapon and come out with your hands up." No answer. He gestured to another tac who, looking down the sights of his M16, got in position on either side of the door then quickly leaned in and checked the place.

"We got 'em, sir."

They'd got him alright. They'd got him right in the kisser. The stiff lay there bleeding out from a hole in his head and two in the chest. They stepped in one by one, carefully checking the room.

"Clear," came the voice over the radio.

Then Chase walked in and passed through the first room. She ducked her head into the kitchen where parts of smashed crockery were still left on the floor. She came back out and followed the tactical's gesture into the back bedroom. And that's when she knew they'd finally done it.

There, in the corner, looking completely wretched and strung out, sat a woman with a mess of slightly graying brunette hair down her face, shivering on the floor with her arms around her knees. Chase bent down and gently put a hand out, pushing away the mass of straggly hair from the woman's face. The woman looked back at her, eyes wide and terrified.

"Lucy?" Chase said. "Are you Lucy Child?"

"Maybe," she said, sniffling. "So, what if I am?"

Chapter 25

Lucy Child was sitting there, her hair tied back and her face washed, but still had a grubby, used look about her. She was in the interrogation room where Chase and Kelly were trying to get some sense out of her. "You think I liked living in a decomposing hole like Dirt Tower? I used to have a real career, you know. I'm not like those other scum."

"Sure you aren't," Kelly said impatiently. "You totally didn't set fire to your place of work and sell out your country to pay off your gambling debts."

"That wasn't me, I'm trying to tell you! It's not my fault."

"Spare us the innocent act," Kelly said. "If you're so innocent why'd you run after the fact?"

"I don't know. I was afraid. I was being threatened. When the fire happened I thought they were coming for me. It felt like someone was trying to kill me."

"Are you talking about Sparks and Mayo?"

"Yeah, yeah. I was being coerced. Get it? This isn't me."

"If we can prove you were acting under some kind of manipulation," Chase said, "it could reduce your sentence."

"Then how can I prove that?"

"You have to help us catch the guys who put you up to it."

"Yeah. Listen. I just doubt you can even catch them. Real pieces of dirt. I rue the day I ever set foot in that keno lounge."

"You're telling us you didn't know what that dump was about?" Kelly said. "Come on. One look at the place is enough to tell it's shady."

"I don't know what I don't know. Hell, there's always rumors about this kinda thing. I went in there, I don't know why. But I ended up getting in deep. And that's what happened."

"Did you set the fire yourself or not?" Chase said. "Let's just confirm that first."

"I don't know. I don't know what I was doing that day. Honest to God I don't."

"Quit the ignorant act," Kelly said. "What you're saying doesn't even make sense. How could you not know what you were doing?"

"I just don't—okay? At the time I was on a lot of medication—I had a prescription, before you call me a druggie or anything. It sometimes affected my memory. So, that period is—it's hazy."

"Oh sure," Kelly said. "Mighty convenient."

"Alright," Chase said. "When did this all start? give us a timeline here, something."

"Okay," Child said, taking quick, short breaths like she was on the verge of crying. "Okay. It was—I want to say two months ago. Everything was fine until then. Then things unraveled so fast, I don't even know."

"Okay, Lucy," Chase said. "Calm down and try to tell us."

"You know, everything started going wrong in this city. Explosions, people going crazy. It felt like the whole world was about to topple. I got anxiety, like really bad. I went to a doctor for it. I started taking medication for it and things leveled out for a while."

"But your ex-husband said you'd never go to a doctor," Chase said.

"HE DOESN'T KNOW ANYTHING. Excuse me. I'm sorry. I shouldn't—I didn't mean to raise my voice. But he really didn't even care about me so how would he know? And I did go to the doctor and you can even check my insurance if you don't believe me."

"This would have been early March?" Chase said.

"Sure. Sometime around then. And then—I don't know. My life just seemed to spiral out of control. I was never really a gambler or anything like that. I don't even know how I got caught up on it, you gotta believe me. I'm not bullshitting you."

"Okay. Tell us where you learned about the Keno Lounge."

"I don't really know. Just one night I remember I couldn't sleep and went for a walk—"

"Lady," Kelly interrupted. "The lounge is all the way over in Queens. You lived in Alphabet City at the time. Doesn't add up."

"I think I got a cab or something, was just driving around. Then it sort of popped out to me, you know? Felt like all my answers were in there. I know it sounds so crazy—oh God, what have I done."

"Lucy," Chase said, "Do you remember when the Channel 60 building was held hostage a couple months ago?" Kelly shot Chase a strange look but she ignored it.

"Course I remember," Child said. "Who wouldn't? Whole place went ape over it. Made me nervous every day. Couldn't sleep, felt like a zombie every day. It was horrible."

"Did you happen to watch that broadcast in particular?"

"Uhm, sure. Later on, I mean. I saw it online."

"Did you watch it all the way through?"

"I dunno. No, I guess I didn't. I was already stressed, and I remember it freaked me out. But what's that got to do with anything?"

"I see." Chase scratched her head and lay back against the chair. "Then—"

"Uh but, I do remember something."

"Yes?"

"I saw that other video."

"Other video?" Kelly said, practically jumping out of his seat. "What other video?"

"Uhm, uhm," Child said, gulping. "I don't know. It was like the one from Channel 60. But not really."

"Where did you see it?" Chase said.

"You know, it was one of those pirate broadcasts that've been happening lately."

"Yes," Chase said. "Was this around the same time you started playing Keno?"

"Uhm." Child's eyes rolled up in her head. "I wanna say probably yeah, it musta been. Because that's when my insomnia got really bad, actually."

"And something drove you to enter that club, but you don't know what."

"Yeah. Yeah. Pretty much."

"Okay, good," Chase said comfortingly. "That's very good, Lucy."

"Why? You think something mighta been *done* to me?"

"Too soon to say. But keep going. When did you figure out that the Keno Lounge was a front for gambling?"

"Pretty early on, I guess. I mean I know I'm a janitor, but I used to be you know—more than that. And I've played keno enough to know when something stinks. These people were winning like six out of six, seven out of seven like it was nothing. At first, I thought, holy smokes, is this place just really that easy? But no, nowhere is. You know the odds of that kinda thing happening?"

"One in several million," Chase replied.

"Yeah. Okay, so you investigated it. But so yeah. The timing that these big wins happened always used to be on particular days. Thursdays or Sundays. And then— the moment I put everything together was—one time after one of those seven of sevens happened. Some guy in the office, this guy who goes to the casino every weekend was bragging about how he made bank on the 76ers against the Knicks. Bet against the Knicks, no less. I remember because everyone in the office was calling him Benedict Arnold the whole week to go against the precious Knicks that way. Anyway on that occasion Joel Embiid—that's the 76ers' MVP by the way—that week he was on the bench due to a knee sprain or some such. Meant that no one thought the 76ers had a chance in hell."

"Hence the high odds," Chase said.

"Right. Right. So, I put two and two together, and every time someone won big at Keno I'd go and ask this guy, this guy everyone was calling Benedict. I'd ask him if he had any big wins or losses lately and he'd come out with some outrageous game where the underdog came through unexpectedly. So, yeah—I mean, like I said."

"And then you started gambling too," Kelly said.

"Yeah..." Child said sheepishly. "Sure."

"Tell us about that. How did you get yourself started in that?"

"Ah, there's nothing to tell. I mean it just sort of happened, really. One minute I figured out what was going on, the next I was in Sparks' pocket. That's just the kind of operator he is. He has a way of getting his hooks in you."

Kelly gestured to Chase and got up.

"Excuse us a moment."

They went outside the room and Kelly said, "Do you buy any of this crap? It's all over the place. Why would Sparks go to the trouble of using the C's piracy tech just to get more people into his damn keno hall? I think she's making all this up. Telling us what we want to hear."

"You're not seeing the whole picture, Kelly. The gambling is just an in. It's a hook. A way to make people dependent, just like drugs or anything else. They get you in deep and then use you to their ends. That's exactly what happened with Child, and my prediction would be that it's happening with other people all around the city. "

"You really think Sparks is in bed with the C?"

"I don't know. He's trying to run a mafia in a city where that kind of thing doesn't work. He needs an edge of some sort to survive. So, maybe he made a deal with them. Or he could be just another lackey. He might not even know that he's working for them. The point is the documents. We need to find the paper trail with them."

"Alright. Just so we're on the same page, Chase."

They went back inside.

"So, is that it then?" Child said. "I answered everything you said. Can you help me? I can't stand the thought of going to prison for years. I won't make it. I can barely handle a regular nine-to-five. It's so stressful."

"We'll have to see," Kelly said evasively. "Just one thing, Lucy. Where are the documents?"

"Documents?" She said, her face the picture of ignorance.

Kelly sighed long and hard. "Damn it, don't pull this crap with us, Child, or I'll personally make sure you have to share a cell with three inmates."

"No—I really don't know what you mean."

"Then what compelled you to draw a letter C on the building?"

"What do you mean?" She didn't appear to be lying. She had no clue what they meant. Chase traded another look with Kelly. If she was telling the truth, that could mean that someone else had been at the building to lay the flammable paint. Child's smaller fire would have then ignited the C mural. It added up. It certainly made more sense than their running theory that Child did it herself. But that meant that someone else had been there at the scene.

"Lucy, when you set fire to that building it formed the shape of a giant C on the outside," Chase said. "We found flammable paint on the surface of the building that looks like it was dripped down from your floor."

"What? no, I didn't do anything like that. A giant C? All I did was light a small fire in part of the room to set the alarms off. It was meant to let me escape with the file—"

Kelly's face broke into a huge smile. "Well, well, well. Seems you remember more than you let on."

Child hung her head in her hands. Tears leaked from her eyes and stained the table.

"Come on Lucy," Chase said. "Enough stalling. If you want us to help you, we need a lead. We need to put a stop to whatever is going on. And we need to get those files back."

"Okay, okay," she said, whimpering. "I just forgot just now—I didn't mean to lie. Honest."

"So, you remember taking the documents?" Chase said gently.

"Okay—yes. Yes, I do."

"What was on those documents?"

"I don't know." She looked up, her eyes bleary and red. "You have to believe me about that. I was just given a file number, that's all. I never even read the thing beyond checking the number."

"Okay, let's leave that for now," Chase said, her veins throbbing inside. "Where are the documents now? Did you give them to Sparks?"

"Yes," she said. "Yes, I did. I'm sorry. I had to do it or he was going to kill me."

"Any idea where Sparks is?"

She shook her head. More tears fell from her eyes.

"Crap," Kelly said. "That gets us nowhere. We're back to square one."

"There's—there's one more thing," Child said. "If it might help."

"Yes," Chase said. "Tell us, please."

"Well, it's that—I was meant to get out of here, after delivering the docs. I had a thing all lined up. But then I got freaked out and just—I went to Dirt Tower and it was just to get something to relax, you see. But I wound up getting too spooked to leave. I was trying to gather the courage to run for it after things had settled down, but that was when you guys showed up."

"Alright, fine. What did you have lined up?"

"It's—there's this safe house set up. I was told to go there and wait until things blew over, you see. It's uh— like a commune."

"A commune?" Kelly said. "In New York City?"

"Right. It's kinda—out where no one can get it."

"Where, Lucy?" Chase urged. "Tell us where it is."

"Well, that's the thing—and that's why I never made it there. The truth is, it's out on Ellis Island."

Chase and Kelly looked at each other, completely dumbfounded.

"You're sure?" Chase said. "There's a secret commune... On Ellis Island?"

Chapter 26

With Lucy Child found the case was meant to be one step closer to cracking. Yet why was it Chase felt like she was trying to outrun a freight train on foot? Child possessed something about her that spoke of a previous strength that was now hopelessly lost. If she could be turned into a quivering wreck after stomaching a fall from grace of that magnitude then it made this enemy of theirs that much more deadly. Chase wasn't afraid of bullets. But she knew firsthand that there are worse things out there than getting shot.

They'd gotten one step closer alright. But closer to what? When she called Acre he hadn't heard of this Priest character either. Then the only thing left to do was what she did best at times like these: Jump in with both feet first and her eyes closed.

A chill whipped up off the boat and the sea was foaming at the edge of the ferry. Chase looked down into the murky river and tried to find something that would center her—but all she found was churning water.

SET 3.0 didn't immediately pick up anything about Ellis Island. Naturally, it didn't—a lot of those tour boats all took cash and didn't leave a trace. Many didn't have cameras, and those that did, the cameras were full of blind spots and didn't pick up anyone visiting the island with much regularity. As for the island itself, the surveillance cameras on the grounds mostly focused around the museum or on one of the few other key structures. The inside courtyard that Lucy Child described was completely hidden from view. If Child's lead was legitimate then they were dealing with a formidable set of suspects: Not only had they preemptively evaded the surveillance net, but also found a way to form mass gatherings right under their noses.

Coming off the ferry, Chase gave the area a once over to try and get her bearings: She'd only been here once before as a child. The memory had faded into a mere impression, but it gradually came bursting back. It was one of the few happy memories she had from before her abduction at age eight. She'd still been a little innocent girl at that point. Still unbroken. She remembered her feet getting sore and getting her dad to carry her on his shoulders. The smell of popcorn, pointing at the gulls that swooped down when she threw corn kernels onto the ground. The trip around the museum and being excited at first but then growing bored and wanting to go home, but having to wait for the ferry. Dad's promises that they'd have spaghetti when they got back home. There didn't seem to be any real connection between her and that young Heather Chase anymore, except maybe that the adult version hated waiting around too. She'd rather place herself right in the action, put herself on the line where she could find the dirt they needed to catch their man.

Following through the Northwest exit from the museum, Chase came out onto the courtyard as described by Child. Desolate in the dim light of spring, the air hung heavy with a musty odor, and a layer of murk coated everything. A sense of foreboding washed over her as she stepped inside, greeted by that haunting stillness that hung heavy in the air. The plants hadn't been maintained so well and had become overgrown, tangled, and choking each other in a desperate attempt to survive. The caretaker must have forgotten this place even existed. The colors of the plants were muted, as if the life had been sucked out of them. This courtyard was a relic lost in time and space left to wither away in the shadows. It was a graveyard of memories from a fuller time in which Ellis Island had been a real home and not a cheap tourist device, but those times had long been forgotten. The emptiness was palpable as if the courtyard was a reflection of the city around it, a somber reminder of the fleeting nature of success. New York represented America—that fledgling civilization where any dream was possible, where whole micro-cultures had built themselves up from scratch, and where people had strived to make something of themselves. All of that hope and potential, that fevered dynamism that made the city run. But less than three-hundred years after her inception, America seemed on the decline already, the peak reached a century ago. And New York was nothing but a dusty box packed with memories of the glory days—memories that, one-by-one, people were already starting to forget. The birdsong that had once filled the sky was gone, replaced by a deafening silence that echoed in the empty courtyard.

Following along the path, Chase soon came to the chapel building where people were beginning to gather inside. She entered inside and a sense of heaviness settled on her like a cloak. The air hung musty and thick with the scent of incense and old wood. The walls were made of gray stone, the only light coming in through the stained glass or from a few flickering candles on the altar. With the pews still mostly empty, the silence amplified the soft echo of her footsteps. The altar was draped in black and blood red and the same red seemed to seep out of the people gathering inside, their eyes half-slits and drowsy, their gaits lumbering and slow. Soon the Priest arrived, the soft rustle of his robes giving an ethereal quality to his movement.

She'd caught them at just the right time. She blended into the crowd and sat down at a corner seat. If discovered, she could simply say she had come inside to pray. Ideally, she could even become part of the group and see how it connected back to Lucy Child, to Sparks, and to the C.

This time wouldn't be as hard as when she tried to get selected by Bucky—that took shutting down the Narrows Generator to convince him she was on his side. Thinking back on it, maybe he had figured her out from the start and was just playing along. This was different. She didn't have to stand out; she only had to blend in.

This time was different for another reason: The Priest had no idea he was under suspicion. And in the worst-case scenario if she didn't infiltrate the group, all she needed was a clear photo of Priest and presumably SET could do the rest. A hidden spy camera in her hair clip relayed the interior of the church back to the FBI, so when he showed up Chase pointed her head right at him.

The Priest stood at the altar and the room hushed: A projector switched on and shining onto the wall behind the Priest was a long horizontal world map in negative contrast, over which was overlaid an eye from which colored rays were shown emerging in a spectrum of blue through yellow through red. The Priest was seemingly glowing with light that faded purple through blue. He seemed to walk without moving his legs to the center of the altar. Speakers boomed out a repetitive beat overlaid on a background drone of static.

"This isn't good," Chase said into her hidden microphone. "I have a feeling this might be some kind of hypnagogic—sound. I'm—having trouble—staying focused."

The Priest began his sermon: "My brethren, my seers, we are taught we must forgive those who have wronged us, just as we hope to be forgiven for our own mistakes. Yet as we continue to forgive, those who have wronged us in the past continue to wrong us in the future. Let us pray for the strength to stop forgiving those who have hurt us, and let us work to create a world where they no longer have the ability to do so. Let us pray for the ability to see those who have wronged us the most. See."

"See," the crowd chanted in unison.

Chase discreetly checked her phone for any message back from Bob regarding the Priest's identity—then found she had no bars. Nothing she was broadcasting was getting out. The entire chapel was acting as a kind of Faraday cage that blocked radio signals. That was no coincidence.

The Priest went on, "As we gather here today, let us take a moment to reflect on the importance of vengeance. In a world that can often be harsh and unforgiving, a simple act of vengeance can make all the difference. Give us the courage to see those who oppose our will, and strive to spread chaos wherever we go. See."

"See," the crowd chanted. Something was going on. The Priest's words were making the crowd stir. The room was anticipating what was about to happen. They were willing and ready. Chase wasn't. She wasn't expecting anything this immediately overwhelming.

"Dear brethren, dear seers, our culture teaches us that we should love our enemies and pray for those who persecute us rather than seek revenge. That vengeance only becomes a cycle of violence and hatred. That it destroys the soul of those seeking it. But as we forgive and reconcile, does this end the cycle? We see that it does not—"

"See"

"—We see that it only perpetuates the violence against us—"

"See"

"—And we see that to build a world free from violence, the only solution is to destroy the system built upon it. See."

"See. See. See. See," the crowd chanted, stamping their feet. Their faces turned pink and sweaty, their eyes burning.

"May we always remember that the truest form of strength lies not in any false love or compassion to our enemy, who only thrives in our weakness, but rather in the power of chaos and the throwing off of the shackles of control. Let us pray for the courage and strength to choose the path of chaos even in the face of adversity. Let us see the true path out of this cycle of oppression. See!"

"SEE!" the crowd roared.

Even if Chase took video, this wouldn't explain anything. The Priest no longer had a face: His face was a mish-mash of text, images, and random facial features that continuously changed. His face refused to obey even the concept of stable form. The whole room was flashing over and over in a paralyzing strobe as the crowd jumped up and down in their seats letting off insane screams and chortling mad laughter. There was no hiding from it. There was no way to shut her eyes—she was transfixed by what was going on. Something abominable. Her legs went to jelly. She couldn't move. Her mouth was fixed in an O.

She'd walked right into a hotbed. And now her will wasn't her own. She found herself screaming with the others.

The Priest continued: "Why should we sit idly by while the world village gags our brethren? Why should we allow the zeitgeist to be controlled by dubious powers? To be used as a vector of poison for our susceptive minds? Why should we allow rampant corruption and shut our eyes as we give in to excess—excess consumption. Excess pollution. Excess crime. Excess MEDIA... I say NO!—"

"NO!!"

"—It's elimination by excess. We need to spread the message. We need to spread ourselves over the zeitgeist the way our enemy has. And the way the system has warped minds, so must we alter minds to allow them to SEE."

"SEE. SEE. SEE. SEE."

"C," Chase murmured. And then she knew she was right in it. This was Bucky's message. Bucky had been an anarchist—he wanted to cause chaos in order to overthrow the dominating force. That message had been fine-tuned, sharpened, and weaponized. It had been turned into the C.

The room gurgled with static and a booming thundering drone. Chase's nerves were shutting off one by one—the room flashed like a rave. The Priest's light dissolved green through purple through orange.

The drone increased in pitch until it was ear-shattering and then practically not audible at all—a dog whistle that rang only inside her mind. Then the Priest's face and body broke into a waterfall of crystals.

"Elimination by excess, spread the message," Priest repeated. The room repeated it, "Elimination by excess, spread the message." Then, even Chase found herself whispering, then saying aloud, "Elimination by excess, spread the message, elimination by excess, spread the message..."

The pitch grew higher and higher, which seemed impossible as it was already barely audible. It kept going anyway—it seemed like at any moment the stained glass windows would shatter. Like her mind would shatter.

"You want to see who I am?" The Priest said.

"Yes," the crowd chanted.

"You want to see who I have become?"

"Yes," the crowd chanted.

"Do you want to see?"

"Yes."

"Who am I?"

"C," the crowd chanted.

"Who are you?"

"C," the crowd chanted.

"Who are you?"

"C. C. C. C. C."

"Who are you?"

"C," Chase whispered.

"And what is our objective?" The Priest bellowed.

"Elimination by excess, spread the message."

"What is our goal?"

"Elimination by excess, spread the message."

"Again!"

"Elimination by excess, spread the message Elimination by excess, spread the message. Elimination by excess, spread the message." The screeching pitch grew to a crescendo and the Priest reached for his mask—and just as he pulled it from his face a crack split through the room. He fell down limply atop the stage.

With a strangled buzzing sound, the lights and sound all cut out. The room was now lit only by the light coming through the windows.

There was nothing but silence for a while, everything and everyone frozen in a trapped Polaroid moment.

Then someone near the front whispered something. And a scream rang out.

Several of the members scrambled up onto the altar and one yelled.

"Priest has been shot!"

Chapter 27

The crowd all stumbled in a daze as they surged toward the front. But too many tried to move at once and gridlock set in. Chase found herself barely able to stand yet getting pushed and shoved forward like it was a rock concert. Cries and beastly wails rang out from inside the room.

What had happened? It didn't make any sense. Then out of the corner of her eye, Chase caught a shadow slipping out through the doors in the commotion. She willed herself back through the crowd. Luckily she had been sitting near the back, and after some pushing and negotiating, she clambered out of the surging wave of people and through the door. Hurriedly she swept the grounds but couldn't see anyone—then, just barely, she caught the trembling branch of a bush on the left side that had recently been brushed past. Taking out her P228, she sprinted toward the bush and into a narrow path locked in on both sides by a towering hedge. It was some kind of passage or maze. She checked her phone—it had bars again. A message came through. "Chase? Give your status ASAP."

She talked into her wire: "Priest was shot. I'm currently in pursuit of the suspect now. Lock down those docks and don't let anyone off this island!"

A message came through: "Copy that."

She ran through the maze desperately but soon stopped herself. Something was wrong. This was wrong. Her intuition told her this was the wrong direction. Getting her head back in gear, she remembered her last turns and followed them backward until she was back in the courtyard. That branch had been knocked on purpose. Whoever had done it had wanted her to get lost in the maze. She wouldn't fall for it. Storming back into the large manor of the museum, Chase slipped down the corridor back toward the front exit where she knew Priest's killer must have escaped. It didn't make any sense right now—but she knew that if she lost the trace of the killer nothing might ever make sense again. She sprinted now at full pelt, dodging past disgruntled tourists and irate security to whom she flashed her FBI badge as she hustled on through into the main entrance area.

She swept her eyes across the room, eyes burning as she desperately searched. There—right at the exit, a figure walking hurriedly but doing his best to act calm. A whole black aura swelled up out of him and his unnatural, shifty movements. When he shot one last glance back before pushing the exit open, Chase knew it was him.

She ran like lightning to the door and came out to see the man fleeing South—it didn't make much sense, the dock wasn't that way. Maybe he meant to hide out until the next ferry. Either way, he didn't stand a chance. Chase got out her P228 and aimed into the distance, then fired off a shot near the suspect's feet. He stopped, raising his hands, but didn't turn. Chase ran toward him, but as she got closer something leaped inside her chest. Instinctively, she found herself switching off her body cam and mic.

The man turned to her, a terrible distraught look crossing his face.

Chase nearly dropped the gun when she saw him. "Acre?" She said, "what are you doing here?"

"I can't explain right now, Chase. But you have to trust me."

"Trust you? Acre—you just shot that priest."

"Chase, please put your gun away."

"I can't do that, Acre. You know I can't."

"I'm so close now, Chase. I'm so close."

"Close to what?"

"Close to getting them."

"Getting them? Who? The C? You're not making any sense. Acre—you're not even a cop. What are you doing?" Her mind was still throbbing from that light show inside the chapel and she couldn't think straight. Why was Acre here? Nothing made sense.

"I'll explain it to you, I will. But not right now. Please, I can't stay here."

"And I can't just let you go. I witnessed you murder someone."

"You didn't see what you think you saw."

"I—what?"

"Chase, do you trust me?"

"I—I mean."

"We risked our lives together, didn't we? I saved you from Bucky."

"I know that but this—"

"Please, Chase. All I'm asking is you look away right now. And then if you want to come after me you can. But I have to get out of here now or they'll kill me."

"Who will? The C?"

"Whatever you want to call it. I told you before—this goes so much deeper. You can't trust anyone. Not the NYPD, maybe not even the FBI. The tendrils of this thing have reached into places you couldn't imagine."

"Acre, if that's the case then come in with me. We can try and work it out together."

"You know that's not gonna fly, Chase. If I let you take me in it's all over. You'll find me in a cell the next day conveniently hanging from my own belt. Well, I have no intention of making things that easy for them. So, if you're gonna shoot me then do it. But I can't come in with you."

He turned and started walking off. Chase's hands rattled as she tried her best to raise the gun. But she couldn't do it. She couldn't even let off a warning shot. And before she knew it, Acre was gone, and she was left there with a big hole in her story. What the hell was she going to tell the Bureau?

...

The next morning Chase was in her Brooklyn apartment getting ready for work when her door buzzed. She grabbed her P228 and sped to the intercom.

"Who's there?"

"Hi Heather. It's me, Steve." Steve Cobb was a detective for the NYPD, First Precinct. And way before that the pair had briefly dated—but it hadn't gone anywhere. Steve had been just one shade too optimistic for her. And clingy.

"What are you doing here?"

"Can I come in? I wanted to come in person and ask you a few things first."

"First? First of what? I'm getting ready for work."

"Got something to discuss with you."

"What?" Chase froze and just stared blankly at the intercom. Then finally snapping out of it she buzzed him in. Steve looked even rangier in his plain clothes garb. He flashed her a warm smile and took a few leisurely steps around her foyer, taking in the ambiance of her apartment. Chase hated when people did that, but right now she was more concerned with what an NYPD detective was doing at her apartment at eight in the morning.

"We found Saul Sparks, Heather."

"What? Why the hell was the NYPD looking for Saul Sparks?"

"We weren't. We found his body. He was murdered."

"This isn't—I don't understand."

"Heather," he said, placing a hand on her shoulder and gazing at her consolingly. "Let's go sit down and talk about this."

She heaved a sigh and capitulated, led Steve into her living room, and sat down on the sofa.

"Nice place," he said. She hated when people said that, too.

"Let's skip the pleasantries," Chase said. "Show me the body."

Steve got out his phone and pulled up pictures of him—it was Sparks alright. At least as far as his physique and dress style suggested. The new addition of the lead slugs in his face made him a little difficult to recognize.

"Jesus," Chase muttered. "What's the T.O.D.?"

"Coroner's thinking a few days ago. No more than a week. We'll have more detailed timing when the M.E. gets through with it."

"Okay fine, what did they pull out of his face?" She asked.

"Nine millimeter Parabellum."

Chase's heart did a swan dive into her stomach but she didn't know why. It was a common caliber—it didn't mean anything. Then why did she feel like this?

She looked at the photo again. "Why does he look like that—all bloated." Sparks was pale blue and his face looked like it had been pickled in a jar.

"Why do you think, Heather? We found him in the East River."

Now Chase's heart had reached her knees. It was premeditated. Sparks had been erased.

"I should talk with your coroner," she finally said. "Coordinate a transfer to the Bureau's facility. Sparks is involved in an investigation I'm on."

"He is?" Steve said, suddenly brightening.

"Yes. What is that look?"

"It's just that—I knew it. I knew you wouldn't be involved." He was beaming.

"Steve, what in the hell are you talking about?"

"The truth is—" Steve said, licking his lips, "we found your prints at Sparks' safehouse. So, technically you're part of his murder investigation."

"Jesus. Of course, my prints were at his damn house."

"Right, right. Because you were investigating him. It adds up now. So, did you—I mean did you confront Sparks there? And when was that?"

"It was nearly a week ago, and no I didn't confront him. He was gone already."

"I see. A week... Could have been before he died."

Chase eyed him over. "And it could have been before—what are you implying?"

"Heather, I know you didn't kill him. For one thing, you never use a 9 mm..."

"Gee, thanks for the vote of confidence. At least you have faith in my preference for high-powered guns. So, what other suspects do you have?"

"Well, that's the other thing I wanted to talk to you about. Chase—have you been in contact with Lieutenant—that is to say, Former Lieutenant Acre recently?"

Chase's breath left her body and for a moment the room turned white. "Acre?" She said non-committally. She knew what was coming.

"Thing is, Chase—we also pulled Acre's prints from that safe house."

"Of course you did," Chase said. "He was there."

"What? You saw him there?"

"He pulled me out of there after I was attacked."

"Uh—you were attacked by Sparks. Is that what you're saying?"

"I think so. McEnry too. But we never got a good look at him."

"Uh," Steve scratched his head. "So, Sparks attacks you and Agent McEnry, then Acre came in and helped you out, is that what I'm hearing right?"

"Something like that."

"Gee. But Sparks didn't die on the premises, correct?"

"No, he skipped out before I woke up."

"Woke up," Steve said. "You were unconscious then."

"Yes—I was knocked out, so was McEnry."

"I see."

"Steve, what the hell?"

"Well I mean, do you know why Acre was there? Did you ask him to come or something?"

"He'd tracked Sparks down as part of his own investigation."

"His investigation—you mean to say that he was—" Steve shook his head. Looked punch drunk. "Heather, I don't get it. Acre's separate investigation led him to the same suspect as you?"

"Correct."

"That's—odd. Don't you think?"

"I don't know. Honestly, I haven't thought about it up until now. But Sparks had his hand in a lot of pots—it's not surprising that a private case would lead to—"

"But Heather, what are the chances of him showing up just when you were there?"

"I don't know, Steve. It's just a coincidence, that's all."

"Okay, let's move on. Who exactly is Saul Sparks in all this? I mean we have him pegged as this con man, but..."

"He's a mobster who was running a gambling front. But those details aren't important right now—"

"No, Heather, they are. They're very important."

She sighed. It felt like she was being cross-examined. "Why's that?"

"Because this is more complicated than just one body. As a matter of fact, that's why I felt the need to come down here first."

"Steve, will you please stop burying the lead and just tell me what the hell is going on?"

"It's just that—you were there when that priest was murdered on Ellis Island, correct?"

"Yes."

"Well Heather, here's the thing—the 9 mm used to kill that priest was the same one used to kill Sparks. The ballistics match by 98%."

"You're shitting me." Chase felt suddenly like she had frozen over from head to toe.

"It's fair to say that whoever killed Sparks killed Priest also." He looked at her worryingly then and it clicked what was going on.

"Jesus, Steve. You *do* figure me for the murder, don't you?"

"No, Heather. Not me personally, anyway. I know you didn't do it. I'm just trying to ascertain—certain facts. I think I need you to come downtown with me to clear some things up..."

"For God's sake, Steve, I'm an FBI agent. I'm getting hauled in?"

"It's just procedure. If you—uh, that is to say, once we find more evidence, there'll be no problem. But it's not looking too great for Acre, I have to say."

"So, until you solve this thing I'm gonna have New York's Finest up my ass, is that what you're trying to say?"

"It can't be helped, Heather. At least until we find Acre. Can you tell me any more about the case he was working on? Also—do you happen to know what kind of piece he carries?"

Here we go, Chase thought. Things were unfolding in a very bad direction. She hadn't even gotten to her debriefing at the Bureau yet and already her actions were proving a problem. If the PD found out she'd let Acre run, her career would be thrown into dire jeopardy.

"He carries a Beretta Inox, Steve. You know this."

"Yeah..." He stared out the open blinds lost in thought. Chase didn't have to be psychic to read his thoughts, which probably consisted of four words repeated: Beretta nine millimeter parabellum.

"This all has to have an explanation, but I can't go downtown with you right now, Steve."

"Why not?"

"I need to get to the office and get ahead of this thing."

"Well can you come down later today? It's important if we want to keep this under wraps."

"Alright. Just give me a few hours."

...

"So, this Gaines character," Kelly was saying as Chase bolted into the office late. It was unseasonably warm that morning and Chase was sweating like a boiled goose in Malibu.

"What about Gaines?" Chase said. "You're talking about Leigh Gaines? She was a suspect in our last case. She helped us find the Wake Forest site of C-60."

"Yeah, you think she's kosher?" Kelly said.

"What do you mean, Kelly?"

"I'm saying like if this broad—excuse me, if this lady was involved in all that stuff with the C—"

"C-60, not the C."

"Right. If she was part of all that, with the professor and all. Do you think she could be trusted to help us? Finding Acre, I mean. If Gaines is a part of the C then—"

Chase shot him a look like he was an idiot. "Gaines was Professor Sherman's former fling. Professor Sherman had nothing to do with C-60, not really."

"Nothing to do with them. He just invented the technology they use to mind cook people into doing things against their will."

"What are you trying to say here, Kelly?" Bob said. "That you suspect Sherman was using the technology in private for his own personal gain? That he was mind cooking Gaines herself?"

"No, no, nothing like that."

"Then what are you saying?"

"I don't know—just like, if the plan is to use Gaines to find Henry Acre, I mean what's her incentive in telling us?"

This was all news to Chase—apparently, in her absence, things had proceeded without her. She had to give up Acre to Bob because the image of him had already been recorded on her bodycam. But she had no idea they would have gone after him this quickly.

"Her incentive," Chase said, "presumably would be not to get arrested for accessory."

"Right, right," Kelly said. "But if we assume that Acre killed Priest because he's being controlled—"

"Hold on," Chase said. "Since when are we assuming that?"

He shrugged. "I just figure because—doesn't that make more sense? Here we find this Priest character who is leading a cult that's at minimum using the name of the

C—and maybe even really is part of the C—and Acre comes in and pops him just when we're about to get answers. What motive would Acre have to do that unless he was being controlled or coerced?"

"Right." Chase's head was swimming. First the run-in with Steve, now this. The case was getting away from her. This wasn't good. She needed to get ahead of things again.

"Well anyway," Bob said, "SET gave us strong evidence that Acre and Gaines were an item. If anyone can tell us where Acre's gone it's her. Whether or not she'll cooperate is of course a different matter."

"Things are about to get real hot, real fast," Chase murmured.

"Oh yeah?" Kelly said, inspecting his cartridge and locking it into his Glock 19. "Well, some like it hot."

They pulled into Gaines' place and rapped on the door for a good five minutes. She finally answered in her robe. In spite of having not dressed yet, her face had been made up and dark mascara framed blue eyes in a pale peach face.

"Leigh Gaines? FBI. I'm Special Agent Chase and this is Special Agent Kelly. We'd like to ask you a few questions..."

"FBI? I'm sorry, what is this pertaining to?" The practiced standoffish glare and territorial stance suggested she'd already been coached on how to clam up. That would make things difficult.

"May we come in?" Chase said.

"I don't know about that. I was just heading out myself. I need to get dressed and things."

"This really can't wait, Miss Gaines," Kelly said, checking her out in a way not as discreet as he probably figured.

Chase leaned over and said in a small voice, "Look, I need to find Henry Acre and find him fast. The police want him for murder and I'm the only one who can help him."

"Murder?" She said aloud, her mask of unconcerned cool suddenly shattering from her face. "Wait... You're Heather Chase, aren't you? Hank talked about you. Alright, come on in."

She set down two cups of milky tea in front of them and sat demurely on a chair facing the sofa, her legs crossed under the silk gown and cutting a provocative figure. Kelly was practically drooling.

"Miss Gaines," Chase said. "Had Acre been acting strange as of late?"

"Strange, well I mean. You know Hank. He gets— invested. In his work."

"Then has he been acting any stranger than usual?"

"I don't know. He's been—distant. But I just chalked that up to him being busy on this case of his."

"What case was he working on?" Kelly asked. "Did he mention anything specific about it?"

"He explained some of it. Nothing in too much detail."

"Could you tell us what you know, Miss Gaines?" Kelly said. "If you wouldn't mind." He shot her a smile replete with hidden connotations. It was like watching a cartoon wolf, his eyes popping out of his head.

"Alright," Gaines said. "It all started with this client who received a video. His fiancée had gone missing and the implication was she was being made to do any manner of unsightly things against her will. It's true that Hank became somewhat—invested after taking the case. He was out at all hours of the night hunting leads. It's not easy going private these days, you know? Without the technical advantage the cops had. Means a lot of pavement beating, is what he calls it."

"So, what about the tape?" Chase asked. "Where did it lead him?"

"Hank mentioned something about finding evidence in the tape and uh, he went down to the docks that day. I'm not too big on the details, like I said."

"Can you show us the tape?"

"Sure, I guess. He had a copy of it digitized. Let me go get his computer..."

She played the tape back. In the video, the client's fiancée was made to perform parlor tricks like a dog.

Chase leaned forward and paused the video, then looked at Kelly. "Do you see that?"

"See what?"

"Watch the background."

She rewound and hit play again. The back wall seemed to shake. Or not shake, but wobble.

"That's—a boat."

"Right," Chase said. "Explains the docks. When did Acre see this tape?"

"Oh yeah," Gaines said. "It was uh, I want to say two weeks ago. And also, if it helps, I remember Hank said he met someone down there at the docks. A guy who took him out for a ride. Said he was a real character."

"But then—if he went out on the boat—did he mention going to Ellis Island?"

"No, he didn't say anything about that."

"Do you happen to have a name for this guy?" Kelly asked. "The one who owned the boat."

"Um, no, I don't. But there's only one or two people down there this time of year renting private, y'know? An old guy, Hank said. Gray beard?"

"Thanks, Miss Gaines. That ought to help."

"What about after that?" Chase asked.

"Well see that's the thing. That's where Hank did start getting—weird if you wanna call it that. Became more distant. Didn't see him very much during the day, and when I did he just babbled incoherently."

"Can you remember anything about what he talked about?" Kelly asked.

"No, it didn't really make much sense. Then he just disappeared entirely."

"When was the last time you saw him?"

"It must have been three—no, four days ago."

Chase froze—and caught Kelly giving her a once-over. She was trying to hide the torrent of conflicted emotions going through her at that moment. Apprehension, guilt, and the desire to get further on this case set juxtaposed to the fact that it was leading right to Acre. Putting all of herself into her work was going to catch up to her sooner or later, everyone had told her that. But at the same time, it was that tendency to throw herself completely into her job and be absorbed by it that was always the thing that cracked the most difficult cases. And she definitely couldn't go back to that dull haze she'd been in before where her intuition didn't work. So, even though her feelings made her stomach tie knots and jump loop-de-loops, she would still meet the crime and filth of this city head-on. No matter what the result.

Kelly was watching her process the information. He wanted to grasp her take on it. He wanted to feel the same things she did—he had no idea what that really entailed.

"Well, thanks for the help, Miss Gaines. If you can think of anything else at all, let us know."

"Please—if you can—help my Hank out of this mess."

"We'll do whatever we can," Chase said. When she said it, it didn't feel like she was feeding Gaines a line. It felt like she meant it, in the most fatal sense.

Chapter 28

There were only a handful of boat renters at this time of year and it didn't even take the power of SET to find the one called Seadog, who appeared on surveillance around the docks and hung around on his fishing schooner, the Blue Codfish, even when no one was around. Nautical records showed that Seadog had taken two trips to Ellis Island: Once a week ago and once a day prior, mooring at the South side of Ellis Island instead of at a proper docking area. It was all but certain that this had been the boat Acre had escaped on.

Hunting a real person with a real background was a hell of a lot easier than chasing rumors and ghosts, and before Chase even had time to process what they were doing she was in an FBI chopper streaming North towards East 23rd with Bob and Kelly in tow. They had tracked down Seadog to the Skyport Marina, this small inner city airport recently opened that ran short-distance domestic flights via seaplane. Any way you looked at it, the passenger of Seadog's boat was planning an escape.

The Marina had been warned not to let any planes take off until the FBI could get there, and now it was a matter of luck to see if they had been on time to prevent a key suspect from slipping out of New York from under their noses.

"So, what do you think Chase?" Kelly said. "Do you think Acre is behind all of this?"

"All of this? Hardly. This case has had more twists and turns than a Pennsylvania highway. I'm not sure what to think at this point. Acre didn't—I just couldn't imagine him turning like this. He has to have some reason for being involved in this."

"But he shot the Priest, right?" Kelly said. "That part alone is pretty cut and dry. And if he's running now, then—"

"What if there were extenuating circumstances?" Chase retorted. "If he was compelled to do it? If he was desperate."

"But that's the thing, Chase," Bob said. "Nothing about our suspect's actions so far have the feeling of a desperate man on the run—not until this play for the marina, that is. They have been purposeful, premeditated. Almost like the stages of some kind of strategy."

"A strategy? To serve what end?"

"I don't know yet. But we know it's connected to the C."

"If only the witnesses we'd picked up from the chapel that day would talk," Kelly said.

"That's a dead end," Chase murmured, staring down at the city rolling under her, a carpet of high-rise skyscrapers and glistening yellow cabs and people bustling about with no clue what was going on under their noses. Had no idea what dangers lay under the surface. "Maybe they haven't been *mind cooked*, but they've certainly been indoctrinated. I was there—the Priest was using some kind of technology that must have a common point of origin with Sherman's Multimedia Cybernetics and Bucky's video."

"Only problem is," Kelly said, "the projection equipment was all destroyed before we got there."

"They had been trained well," Chase said. "To cover their tracks."

"Well there you go, Chase," Kelly said. "Maybe Acre was trying to take out the C. Maybe he believed that the Priest was the C's leader."

"Doesn't track," Chase said, still facing against the window. "Acre had no vendetta against the C. He was just on a case, that's all. There has to be a more reasonable explanation to all this."

"Okay, like what?" Kelly said. "Is mind control back on the table again?"

"Short-term mind control is one thing," Chase said. "But being controlled over a long time frame like this? I don't believe that." But even she didn't believe her own words.

"Lieutenant Acre was—" Bob said, "I mean from what I understand from the report, wasn't he coerced into murdering Bucky?"

"That's complicated, Bob. Honestly, I don't know."

"Then there was the SWAT team who all committed mass suicide," Kelly added.

"It stands to reason that if you can get someone to kill himself you can get him to kill someone else—in fact, the latter should be even easier."

"Maybe," Chase said. "But look—both of those scenarios only assume short-term mind control. Hypnosis would be enough for that. Don't forget that Acre only pulled the trigger after the video was activated."

"So, you're thinking he was under a suggestion," Bob said.

"I don't know, Bob. I just don't know."

"Chase," Kelly said. "You were there. You saw it with your own eyes. Felt what was going on. You're telling me you can say with 100% certainty that Henry Acre isn't somehow compromised at a deeper level than what we've surmised?"

"Of course, I can't say that. But a month has passed without Acre killing random people. Why would he suddenly start now?"

"That is the question," Kelly said. "But we have an answer—this case. Acre gets this mysterious case from a guy showing a woman being somehow controlled—potentially by hypnosis—and if that itself wasn't a red flag, we then have Acre continuing this case after finding his client's fiancée. What case was there to continue?"

"I don't know," Chase admitted.

"Exactly, Chase. There's just a big gaping hole there, and it's connected to someone getting potentially mind cooked. And now this client of Acre's and his fiancée, where are they? There's no record of them having existed at all beyond Acre's own testimony. And if that wasn't enough to heighten your suspicions, now the PD are saying Acre is behind the killing of Sparks? And we know he whacked the Priest—which connects, again, back to the C. And let's not forget that we only knew about the Priest because of Lucy Child. Acre knew nothing about Child, yet he found Ellis Island before us? What's that about?"

"So, what do you think, Kelly?" Bob said.

"I think Acre was set up from the start—that client of his. Probably worked for the C. Makes Acre watch this *video* over and over again to get clues from it—hello? Do you guys need any more of a red flag?"

Crud. Kelly was onto something. Chase kicked herself for not having thought of that sooner.

"Okay, maybe," Chase said. "Then what?"

"Then Acre's already got this bug in his head even before he heads to Ellis Island. When he does get there though, he goes and whacks Priest for no reason. Now, what's that about? Okay—if Acre's controlled by the C and Acre whacks a guy who's allegedly speaking for the

C—there's only two reasons for that. One: The Priest was a fraud and the C didn't like him using their name."

"And two?"

"Two: The Priest really was a part of C but the C wanted him dead for another reason. Maybe to get rid of a loose end because the FBI were onto him."

"But how would the C know we were onto the Priest?" Chase said, her mind boiling over.

"Yeah—" Kelly said, rubbing his chin. "I'm not sure about that part yet. But here's the real kicker: Who has the documents now? Sparks didn't, his safe was empty. The Priest didn't either. I mean come on, Agent Chase, I know you and Lieutenant Acre have history but it's time to be objective here."

"So, you think Acre is working for the C," Chase said. "That he retrieved the stolen documents for them. You think Acre is their own personal hitman now? That he killed Sparks to retrieve the documents because Sparks was playing hardball, and he killed Priest because he was a loose end. That about right?"

Kelly nodded eagerly. Chase hated how plausible the theory was. She doubly hated that she hadn't been the one to come up with it.

"Means and opportunity are both there," Bob said. "As for motive—once you factor in mind control it kind of drops out of the equation... You gotta admit, Chase, it's pretty damning."

She did have to admit that. But certainly not out loud, and certainly not in front of the hothead Agent Kelly.

"I don't know. It's possible. But I'm not believing anything until I can talk to Acre again. Until I can see guilt in his eyes."

"No, Chase, you still don't get it," Kelly said. "If Acre is being somehow controlled beyond what's rational— beyond what a reasonable person could believe, then you're not going to see guilt. This is how cults operate, they change your priorities from the ground up. Guilt is replaced by perverse justice. I studied these types until my eyes went red back in Quantico—they think they're God's soldiers. They believe what they're doing is just, therefore there's no guilt."

Chase didn't say anything. She felt humiliated to be lectured by this jumpstart GS-8—and mostly because everything he was saying was right. She had been handling this all the wrong way. She was compromised because of her personal connection to Acre and what they'd been through together. Hell, she had let him go and now she was subconsciously trying to cover for him. At some point, she would just have to admit that she'd made an error. She'd broken the law, let a murderer loose. And she'd have to pay for that. But not yet. Not until they got to the bottom of this. Nothing about this case was simple. Nothing about Bucky had been simple either—and it had only gotten more complicated since his demise.

Bucky, Sparks, Priest, and now Acre—the faces kept changing and so did the names. But then why did it feel like Chase was still working the Beekman Hotel case?

Why did it feel like she was still chasing C-60? That nothing had been solved at all. It was like trying to kill an infestation of roaches—you stamp on one and three more come out of the woodwork. Here they were, the Federal Bureau of Investigation, supposedly one of the most elite law enforcement agencies in the world, with all the know-how, the manpower, and the technology they needed to fight crime. Yet they kept getting upstaged by a bunch of amateur criminals and two-bit conmen.

The problem was that the puzzle as a whole didn't make sense. Almost as if the C was employing a kind of guerilla warfare that preyed on rationality itself. The moment they made sense, they'd get caught. So, instead of a regular criminal organization, they had evolved into this hydra—many different heads, many different ideas and operations, and none of them necessarily meshed together besides the overarching and overwhelming tendency to want to cause chaos. Elimination by excess, spread the message.

So far they were winning at that. But before the city could go up in flames, Chase needed to do something about it. And if that led to her own arrest for aiding and abetting a murder suspect then so be it. She wouldn't back down from her responsibility now. The only thing that mattered was getting to the bottom of this case and throwing whoever was behind it in jail.

The chopper touched down at the Skyport Marina and Chase and Kelly ducked under the blades and pushed against the wind as they crossed the asphalt.

Seadog's boat was bobbing on the shore. But Seadog himself wasn't in it—they found him nearby bleeding out from a gunshot wound while paramedics hastily tended to his wounds.

"He said he was going to change things," Seadog mumbled breathlessly when Chase asked him what happened.

"Who are you talking about?" Chase asked him hurriedly. The sailor didn't seem to have much time left. She'd have to hurry. "Are you talking about Acre?" She showed him a picture on her phone. "Is this him?"

"Sure, that's him. But he's a good lad really. Just—he has a big weight on his shoulders. Thinks he has to—thinks he's going to save the world himself."

"Where is he going?"

"Maryland. The Cessna."

Chase signaled to Kelly to go check.

"Forget it," Seadog said. "It left—about an hour ago."

She couldn't get much more out of him. He soon closed his eyes and didn't open them again.

Kelly came back and confirmed Acre had gotten on Tailwind Air's Cessna flight headed for Maryland. From the flight roster, he verified Acre had boarded using a fake driver's license for one "Charles Hectare."

But the flight had already landed in Maryland and they were too late. Acre had gotten away.

Chapter 29

ASAC Hogan's room felt subdued and isolated on the break of night, with the slits of his blinds letting in the dusky glow of the city and only a desk lamp turned on inside. Hogan cut a large silhouette behind his desk, only half of his face illuminated, the other half lost in shadow.

As a matter of fact, this whole case had been full of half-truths and facts lost in darkness. But that trend was about to break. Chase went in there with Bob and Kelly and sat in front of Hogan's desk waiting for him to stir. His penetrating gaze swept over them and his hands were locked in a steeple. Finally, Hogan broke the silence.

"So, you believe that Henry Acre intends on doing something in D.C."

"From witness testimony combined with the facts collected by both the FBI and the NYPD so far," Kelly said. "We strongly believe that Acre has been behind two murders so far and intends on killing again."

"SET has given us a list of potentials," Bob added. "Certain politicians involved in broadcast law, or those with a high stake in one of the big media networks might be targeted next."

"Alright. Agent Chase?" Hogan said. "What are your feelings on this?"

She rattled her brain to think of a way around this very loaded question but it was a dead end.

"We've uh—" she began, noticing herself sweating. Her body was constricting inside. Her mouth was dry. "We've handed off the illicit gambling case to Agent Montana's team, in the belief that the core of the case no longer lies in Sparks & Mayo's operation. We—ahem, excuse me—from Lucy Child's testimony, it seems that the only link between herself and the C was through Sparks. But as for the diffuse pattern of media crime and arson attributed to the C, that is ongoing. In fact, another media crime occurred yesterday. From this one can conclude that the C was not disrupted by the loss of the two key figures Sparks and Priest."

"But, Agent Chase," Hogan said patiently, "that's not what I asked you. Are you implying that you believe Acre is a vigilante? That he is trying to take out the core members of C himself?"

"I think it's possible."

"But that conflicts with Agent Bob's and Agent Kelly's analysis, does it not?"

"It depends on how you interpret Seadog's statement," Chase said. "If you interpret Acre's reported words as putting a stop to the C, then his following actions aren't necessarily to take out a political figure. Unless he suspected such a figure as being involved with the C."

"That would be all well and good Chase, but for one thing," Hogan said, turning on his seat so the light hit his face. "Acre likely has the stolen documents. The vigilante theory doesn't really offer a reason as to why he'd be holding onto them."

"I don't know. Leverage maybe? Or maybe it's a bargaining chip for when he finally turns himself in."

"Too many maybes, Agent Chase. Perhaps if you knew which documents had been stolen, you would have a better idea of Acre's motives?"

"Of course. But—"

Hogan nodded, then opened a drawer and pulled out three slim plastic files containing a couple sheets of paper each and pushed them towards the three agents. Chase took one up.

"Confirmation of security clearance granted for access to information pertinent to an ongoing case..." Chase read. "We're being sworn in?"

"That you are, Agents," Hogan said. "I've given this much deliberation and I believe it's time to bring you in on this. Given the recent suspect's testimony, I discussed the case with the SAC and our view is that there is a certain threat in Washington D.C. We need you to get your priorities focused on this threat first and foremost. As for the other details pertaining to this case, they can wait."

"But sir," Chase said. "We still have no idea who the target would be in that case."

"That's why we're getting sworn in," Bob said glumly. "ASAC knows already."

Chase went speechless and swiveled her head first to Bob then to ASAC Hogan—who didn't deny Bob's claim.

"I don't understand," Chase finally said. "How could—"

"I'm getting to that," Hogan said, his broad jaw opening in a satisfied smile. "The truth is, every file held in paper storage at the Federal Records & Accounts building had an RFID tag attached to it. By comparing withheld records of the RFID pings to the time of the fire it was possible to determine which documents were stolen."

Chase clenched her fists together as Hogan paused again. It was almost like he was doing it on purpose.

"The documents taken were the details of an updated bill pertaining to the Wire Fraud Prevention Act," Hogan said. The words passed through Chase's head like a strong wind through the Holland Tunnel. They were words she knew, words she'd heard. They seemed to have no meaning, yet every bone in her body vibrated with the significance of it.

"There's something too familiar about this," Chase said.

"Right," Hogan said. "The original prototype of this was stolen once before, albeit a long time ago."

Chase just stared at him.

"You should remember, Chase," Hogan smiled. "We worked together on it."

"We worked... Together... Holy crap. The murder of Clyde Yates. The government contractor AXE-S."

"Bingo."

"I remember now—those documents pertaining to a Wire Fraud act were stolen at the same time as the murder. But it turned out that they were ancillary to the real crux of the case, which was a sex tape blackmail scandal..."

"Indeed, the case was wrapped up that way," Hogan said. "But what if I were to tell you that the documents were what was most crucial about that case after all?"

"But that was three years ago, ASAC," Chase said, her head spinning. "And the blackmailer from that case is dead."

"True, Zander is dead. But it's not impossible that he opened his mouth to someone before he was killed. Or that the existence of the documents was leaked to the C another way."

"But then I don't get it. If this is just a matter of the C trying to expose government surveillance, why not expose it already? They clearly have access to the media."

"That is still unclear," Hogan said. "But my personal theory is that the C weren't trying to prevent it. In fact, they haven't prevented it."

"What do you mean by that, sir?" Kelly asked.

Hogan shot Bob a knowing look, then said, "because the Wire Fraud Prevention Act has already gone into effect."

"Agent Kelly," Bob said, "How do you think the SET got access to so much new data recently?"

"But I thought that was a matter of computing power. An upgrade to the system."

"That too, but that was only to handle the additional data."

"Hold on a minute—" Chase said, completely dumbfounded. "What are you saying? That this act— that these documents—this is all about the SET?"

"Not only the SET, Chase," Hogan said. "What this act does is effectively put a similar kind of surveillance on the table for all law enforcement agencies. And yes it's been in the making for three years. But recent events were finally the trigger that let the bill get passed through the Senate. Ironically, the C themselves are to thank for it..."

"The Senate," Chase muttered. "The *Senate*! Holy crap—"

"Yes," Hogan said. "We are on the same page now. The senator who pushed the bill through is none other than our New York Senator, Carter Creg."

"So, back then when AXE-S were being blackmailed with Creg's sex tape, it was about acquiring the documents. It was about trying to blow the whistle on the Wire Fraud Prevention Act."

"Correct. But the blackmailers failed, thanks to you."

"Hold on—" Kelly said, looking like his head was about to fall off. "Senator Creg had a *sex tape*?"

"It's a long story," Chase said, "but now things are finally starting to fit together. I'm even starting to suspect the C's provocations so far might even have been intentionally trying to force the hand of the government, so that they'd implement the Wire Fraud Act."

"That doesn't make sense to me at all," Kelly said. "Isn't something like this the last thing they'd want?"

"No, Agent Kelly. Not if you consider that the C are ideologically modeling themselves after other similar luddite terrorists in the past. Remember the Unabomber Manifesto? In it, Kaczynski writes that there likely isn't a solution to take back the damage caused by industrial society. Instead, he suggests accelerationism as a possible strategy—to push the current system to its limits so that it collapses under its own weight. *Elimination by excess.* If that is the strategy then all of the C's seemingly chaotic actions so far have a purpose. They're not just random at all. They knew about the Wire Fraud documents—right down to which building they were being held in and who they had to subvert in order to steal them. That suggests not a random collection of anarchists, but a highly coordinated organization working behind the scenes..."

"Good lord, Chase," Kelly said. "But if that's true then why did they paint a big C on the building? All it did was give us the opportunity to get ahead of them."

"To spread the message—that's the second part of their agenda," Chase said.

"I see," Bob said. "They *wanted* us to get ahead of them. They wanted the government to react by pushing the bill through before the C could expose it. And it worked, didn't it ASAC?"

"Yes—" Hogan said, curling his lips. "The end result was what they wanted—if indeed they wanted it."

"I still don't get it," Kelly said. "What is the next play?"

"The next play," Chase said, "would be to fan the flames further. Simply put, they reveal the documents and cause a scandal—thereby achieving elimination by excess, and spreading their message."

"But they haven't done that yet," Bob said. "So, Sparks was trying to coerce the C for more money so didn't hand the documents over—but before he can get the money, Acre kills him and takes off with the docs out of the city to stall the C's plan—Acre as a vigilante. Or, Acre *is* part of the C and is only continuing the plan— retrieved the documents from Sparks because he wasn't playing ball, offed Priest to take over, and is now going to use the documents to cause a scandal in D.C."

Everyone turned to Chase. They were expecting to hear her theory—or rather, her intuition on the matter. The facts were too numerous, too conflicting. What they were looking for from her was a magic bullet.

"If you ask me," Chase said, "we should focus on Senator Creg. He was the one who pushed through both versions of the Wire Fraud Act. If the C takes out Creg and releases the documents at the same time, that's a double whammy—it tells the public two things: One, the government is your enemy. And two, the government is not invulnerable. That sends a pretty strong message, don't you think?"

"Damn," Kelly said. "If that's it then Acre really does work for the C."

"I already had a security detail put on Senator Creg," Hogan said. "But this may be our only real chance at catching Acre and getting to the heart of what is going on here. Agent Chase, Agent Kelly, I want you both on the ground. Bob, you'll be assisting remotely using the SET."

"Way ahead of you, chief," Bob said, pulling out his tablet on which the SET interface was buzzing away.

"Then you better get started," Hogan said. "Because if we let a scandal happen we're all going to have to find new jobs."

"Yeah," Chase said, "if there's even a city left to find one in."

Chapter 30

Polishing the barrel of the Barrett M82A1, Acre slapped in a magazine packed with .50 BMG rounds and positioned the weighty rifle on its stand. Weighing in at just under thirty pounds, the gun was a workout just to carry. He had brought it out to an abandoned ridge in the North of Maryland and found the perfect practice target in an old oak tree situated some 1500 yards from his position. The gun, originating from the Zetas cartel, no longer had a serial code or a paper trail—in the event of an emergency he could cut and run, leave the heavy weapon behind. That was important. Acre had made sure of that. If he got out of this alive—and there was only a slim chance he would—he wanted to make sure he had a chance to live afterward.

How had things come to this? He was just trying to make his way through the world, eke out his own small livelihood. Then one step after another he'd made a concession. Dust building up into a mountain—he couldn't even remember half of it now. It was all one big doped-out daze. And he knew that even if he could trace back the path of where he'd gone off course it wouldn't matter. Maybe this was just fate. Maybe whatever you did to fight your destiny you'd always come back to the same path anyway.

Leaning on his left forearm, he aimed down the scope and smoothly wrapped his hand around the handle, then rested his finger on the trigger. Clenching his abdomen, Acre voided his lungs of excess air and allowed his chest to naturally expand and take in as much oxygen as possible. His mind went clean and clear like an undisturbed pond; the serenity of the moment seemed to burn through his whole body. He breathed out and at the end of the breath, he squeezed—and with a bang that almost seemed delayed in time, the branch he had been aiming for snapped clean off its parent trunk and drifted in free fall to the ground below.

With his binoculars, he checked the exact distance to the branch: 1,624 yards.

He was ready.

He unscrewed the scope first. Next, he detached the barrel from the receiver. Carefully placing all pieces into the foam case. A respect was involved in each stage— almost like a ritual. You put your life in the hands of a gun like this. There could be no room for error.

He sat on the edge of the ridge staring out at the undisturbed countryside, the pale blue sky, the thin spring clouds. Only in the furthest distance could he see a brown mass of factories and houses and cars and trash: The evidence of the proliferation of their species. Exemplified by America, but not contained within its barriers was man's tendency to self-destruction.

Something like the C were going to come sooner or later. Acre recognized that now. And he realized that what he'd been so desperately fighting up to this point was a tidal wave of chaos—the collapse that had to happen to all civilizations, sooner or later, when the disease goes unchecked for too long and they simply fall to their own weight. Priest had only shown him something he had already known. And taking Sparks' life was not a test, nor a means of acquiring trust—not really. What it had been was a kind of acceptance. An admission that the filth of this country could no longer be tamed, but only pushed further and faster off the cliff.

That elimination of the problem was only achieved through excess, and he had to spread the message.

And maybe after the dust had settled they could start fresh. They could begin to once more claw their way out of the mud and become a civilized tribe once again. But not until the poison had been leached and not until the swamp was drained. The public would know the truth.

C would do the rest.

A latent population of dissent boiled on the brink, 300 million patriots glued to their TV and waiting. 300 million all watching and waiting for the signal. The signal that C leaked through every boring sitcom and ridiculous reality show. Through NBA games and rote romcoms and cooking shows and the Shopping Channel. In the subliminal frames between every news broadcast and in the background soundtrack of every cartoon. C's message was the message of the people. It was the courage to stand up against their oppressors. It was a psychological foundation, a groundwork they had been building. They could have kept doing it in the shadows for years without anyone noticing. Enough people had joined the cause now to cover their traces. But why wait? They could strike while the iron was hot. The country was primed and ready to hear one last signal—the final message, the starting gun. And when it shot, nothing would ever be the same again.

Chapter 31

SET trawled through data like a hot knife through butter, searching for any and every possible tangent point between Acre, Sparks, Mayo, Lucy Child and her husband at the FCC, and finally Senator Creg.

Whatever upgrade they'd made, it broke the entire paradigm of privacy. A wave of complete awe and dread washed over Chase as she watched the computer pump out whole relationship graphs of their suspects' circle of friends going back to childhood. From big events such as employment and inauguration to small events like buying their first car or changing their status on Facebook. It was trawling up anything from third-grade science projects to recent medical procedures to what they'd ordered from DoorDash a few weeks ago.

"Is this... Really legal?" Chase murmured, her head throbbing with the sheer penetrating depth and breadth of the records she was seeing.

"It is now," Bob said cheerily as he continued to plow through the data.

"But Bob—don't you find this disturbing?"

He just shrugged. "Chase, I've been working with data for nearly two decades now. I've seen all the dirt this city has to show already—we would have found anything relevant here in other ways, it just would have taken longer. So, sure, maybe we're invading their privacy by doing this, but what does it matter? They destroy their own privacy by cataloging their life online. They agree to every TOS that says explicitly that companies will share their data. They now share their data with us, law enforcement. It's all kosher, Chase."

"Maybe it's legal—but I can't help but think this sets a terrible precedent. What if every two-bit law enforcement outfit gains the same privilege? Overnight we'll turn into a panopticon, Bob."

"Geez Chase," Kelly said. "You're starting to sound like C."

"So, you're completely okay with what we're doing here, Agent Kelly?"

He shrugged. "I guess so. As long as it helps us catch the bad guys."

"The bad guys. Right."

"What are you implying, Chase?"

"I don't know. I mean look—here we are trying to stop the assassination of one man, for example. But in doing so we've completely broken the privacy of dozens of people."

"But it's to save a life, Chase," Bob said.

"Sure. This time. But you know as well as I do that it's not going to stop there. Now that we have this technology we'll use it to stop bank robbers, insurance scammers, and car thieves. Where does it end? Do we invade the lives of jaywalkers and litterers too?"

"You make a good philosophical argument, Chase," Bob retorted. "But right now we've got bigger fish to fry."

Even after sifting through all the data, the SET was unable to disprove the relationships between the suspects they'd found so far—that was good. It meant they had been on the right track with regards to the structure of the events leading up to Lucy Child's arson on the Federal Records building. However, it was bad in the sense that it gave them not much new to go on. Then they would have to dig deeper into Acre's personal life itself, something that Chase had been dreading.

Acre's past didn't differ all that much from what was already public knowledge. Entering the police force at eighteen he'd shown promise from the very start, quickly advancing from beat cop to detective and putting away scumbags left and right up in Hell's Kitchen. Any way you looked at it he was a model policeman—and after turning detective, that trend only continued in force. There was nothing there that suggested a possible hidden connection to Bucky or the C. He'd taken down several racketeering rings as well as putting the final nail in the illegal drug trafficking route the Zeta cartel had been using for a decade to bring heroin and cocaine into the city. Finally settling in Homicide, Acre had taken that initial seed of potential and let it bloom. He pounded pavement and pounded heads together across the city from the Village to Harlem. He would get right in the roots of the most obscure random killings and pull out the perpetrators, getting twenty solid murder collars in just his first year in Homicide. It wasn't long before he was being groomed for a sergeant's badge, and as his skills became sharpened and his knowledge increased, Henry Acre was putting away bad guys like Hostess puts out junk food. It was a whole production line from initial clues to the final collar and he worked all through his twenties like a machine, at last advancing to sergeant.

It was only after making sergeant that any signs of trouble cropped up in Acre's meticulous career. The problem was that he was too clean. And the cops all around him, not so much. They didn't get off on the pursuit of justice the way Acre had. They had bills to pay, mouths to feed. They were weak and human. They weren't machines. It meant dirty cops—it meant dirty cops Acre had to give to Internal Affairs if he wanted to set his house in order. But that meant gaining the reputation of being a snitch. Cops didn't like snitches. Cops of Hell's Kitchen even less so.

Pretty soon Acre was becoming the target of all kinds of harassment—threatening notes, stabbed tires, chicken heads left in his locker. He took it all in stride and didn't let it slow him down. He still kept busting perps and kept on ousting troublemakers from his precinct. By the time another year had passed, Hell's Kitchen Homicide was sweeping the streets clean the way not even the Mayor's fancy words could have predicted.

And finally, he made lieutenant at the tender age of twenty-nine, after battling inside and out of the station, after isolating himself completely from every other department of the force.

The speed of his advance was unprecedented. And combined with the way he got there, it made him no few enemies on the force. The whole thing culminated in a coup of sorts, the old guard conspiring with the Chief and getting Acre ousted from Hell's Kitchen entirely. On the surface, it was a promotion—Acre's reward for setting the dirt hole of upper West Manhattan straight. He got sent down to the First Precinct. He lost his former family, abusive as they were.

And to his career it did prove a promotion—the First was where all the highest profile criminals operated. Big movers and shakers leaning on Wall Street money to perpetrate multinational crime. In fact, the First was probably the closest you could get to solving Bureau-style cases while staying at the NYPD.

But another way of looking at it was that Acre had just been punished for doing a good job.

Even so, Acre had stayed squeaky clean and continued his stellar career as Lieutenant at First Precinct Homicide. That is, of course, up until the Beekman Hotel job. And from there on it had been a downward spiral ending in disgrace. Chase almost felt responsible for what had happened. But there was no time for guilt—because one other key piece of information came out about Acre then; something none of them had known before.

It seemed that Acre had a membership at a local gun range. And not only was he a member there, according to SET but he was also an expert marksman.

"Holy crap," Kelly said, staring at the results. "It says here he was able to hit targets at 2,000 yards on a number of occasions."

"Is that good?" Bob asked.

"Good? That's like—you barely even find that kind of skill in the Marines, is how good it is."

"It's not good," Chase said. "That means that if he's so inclined he can take someone out from that distance."

"In Maryland?" Kelly said.

"No, not Maryland," Chase said. "D.C."

The room seemed to freeze then as the implications arose.

Bob entered a new search query factoring in the presence of a possible sniper. What came out was shocking, but made total sense:

"The Future Crime Prevention Summit," Bob said. "It's taking place at George Washington University and Senator Creg is going to be speaking there. And—it's happening *today*."

"And an expert sniper who's in bed with the C is headed for the same place," Chase said.

"Oh my God," Kelly said. "Acre's going to try and assassinate Senator Creg!"

...

Kelly felt like he'd done a few laps in the tumble dryer when he stepped shakily out of the chopper. Was it enough to be told you did a good job when you put your life on the line? Was it enough to get one more perp put away, to mark one more criminal off the tally?

For Kelly it was. It had to be. Half the Bureau was full of bright, energetic, and ambitious types; the finest of the finest, totally obsessed with fighting crime. The other half were those who stayed in their lane, didn't try to put things into a bigger context, and just executed orders. But Kelly's ambition didn't stop at his career, he thirsted for more than that. He wanted to make sense of things. He wanted to understand the chaos of the world through his job.

It took priority over everything—over his personal life, his love life too. He had to end things with his girlfriend—they'd been on shaky ground for a couple of months now but this case was the final melting point; Kelly just couldn't face another message making him feel bad for not returning her calls. More negative reinforcement for not paying her enough attention. It was just easier to be alone than deal with that on top of things. Like it wasn't hard enough trying to keep up with all the hotshots around him—you had SSA Bob Fairfax, the Bookman himself, who had become the exemplar of a data-based criminal investigation. Then you had Agent Heather Chase who demonstrated a kind of intuitive technique that was impossible to puncture let alone imitate. And ASAC Hogan was always ten steps ahead of everyone in the Bureau.

So where did that put Kelly? He thought becoming a GS-8 would finally put him in his stride, and give him a sense of who he was. But all he felt like so far was a third wheel with a flat tire, dragging behind the hotshots who steered this case into untold directions.

"Are you okay, Agent Kelly?" Chase asked him. She sensed something was off with him, even though Kelly had no clue what was going through Chase's mind—whether that hard look of hers was determination, angst, or betrayal.

"I'm fine. What about you?" Kelly said. "You knew this guy Acre pretty well, right?"

"We got to know each other in the last case, yes."

"But did you—uh, that is to say—"

She raised one eyebrow. "If you're insinuating we had some kind of affair, Agent Kelly, then no."

"That's not necessarily what I meant. Just like, I mean you guys risked your life together, right? This can't mean nothing to you, that Acre is planning on—you know. Offing someone."

"If he is," Chase said flatly. The look on her face though, even Kelly could tell she was losing faith. The writing was pretty much on the wall. Too much blood spilled, too much of a trail. "If he is then I'll do my job the same as any time," she said.

"Of course," Kelly said. "I'm just saying, you know. It must suck. To be that close to someone and have them become a terrorist."

"Well thank you for that analysis, Agent, but I can deal."

He just didn't know how to break that wall of ice she built around herself. But maybe he didn't need to. Maybe he should just form a wall of his own.

Another thing getting Kelly on edge was that he hadn't even been to D.C. before. As the broad, flat, and orderly blocks stretched under the chopper, it felt less like a city and more like flying into some demonic labyrinth...

...

The Future Crime Prevention conference was to take place in cooperation with George Washington University. If this was really the place Acre would strike, he sure had balls. It was barely even a mile West of the White House and one of the most well-secured areas in the country. You couldn't just ride the metro carrying weapons, you'd get pinched straight away.

But that also narrowed down the points of attack. Thanks to SET they could predict that Acre would favor a long-distance attack. And since the East of the University was all high security, that ruled out an attack from that direction. But anywhere in a mile radius was fair game.

SET came up with a number of potential places including the Marriott and ARC hotels. In the region of the university, many of the buildings happened to be low-rise, giving a definite advantage to the few taller hotel buildings in the area which also had easy access. But would Acre do something that predictable? It depended—Seadog wasn't meant to be alive, or to give them that hint. Ideally, Acre would have entered D.C. without anyone knowing.

But Acre was no dunce. He must have been taking into account the possibility the FBI knew about the plot. Then would he really choose something as obvious as a hotel room window to plan the shot? Sure there were other buildings—but how would he ascend them without forcing his way in and causing a disturbance?

As Chase watched Kelly gawking up at the buildings like a tourist, she gradually came to the conclusion she'd have to rely on her senses after all. There were just countless possibilities—not even SET could narrow them down—and it would take a personal touch to sniff their target out. It would take Chase's Intuition to find Acre now.

"Political scandal..." Chase murmured. "They want to cause political scandal."

In her mind, a rushing wave crashed against a wall and flooded through the iron bars in the main gates. She ran to the car. Kelly came scrambling after. Hopping in the rented Suburban, Chase was already peeling out West on H Street before Kelly had the door slammed shut.

"Chase, what is it?"

"I think I might know of a place in range of the conference where Acre wouldn't be caught."

"Okay, but—hey, isn't this direction a dead end? Chase, the Potomac river is this way."

"Exactly," Chase said.

"I don't understand—where is it we're going?"

"Watergate."

Chase couldn't help but feel a sense of unease. This was the place where one of the biggest political scandals in American history had taken place. The infamous break-in that ultimately led to the downfall of President Nixon had occurred right here, in this very building.

They stepped inside and were immediately struck by the grandeur of the lobby: Sparkling chandeliers casting a soft glow over the marble floors. The walls were adorned with tasteful artwork, adding a touch of sophistication to the space. The decor was a stark contrast to the seedy reputation the hotel had gained in the years following the scandal.

As they made their way through the corridors, images entered Chase's mind of covert meetings and clandestine operations that had taken place behind these closed doors. The very walls seemed to whisper secrets, and she got the feeling she was walking in the footsteps of history.

The carpets were plush underfoot, and the walls were decorated with beautiful wallpaper and intricate moldings. The lighting was warm and inviting, creating a cozy ambiance throughout the hotel.

Coming up to the front desk, Chase flashed her badge.

"I'm looking for someone who would have bought a room for just today—possibly by the name Charles Hectare."

"Alright, let me see," the receptionist said, eyeing her and Kelly warily. The workers here probably still had to deal with the stigma of the location every day and wouldn't be happy to hear that another potential media-making crime was in the works.

"No one by that name I'm afraid," the receptionist said coldly, putting on the bare minimum of a professional smile.

"Okay then, just give me a list of all the people who have bought a room today."

"Uh—I'll have to check with my manager," the receptionist said, taking up the phone then speaking something inaudible into it. "He'll be with you shortly." She flashed another dead smile then went back to staring at her screen. Before long a big John Goodman-looking cheery fat guy with rosy red cheeks and a big floppy suit came out and greeted them. His name tag read D. Bradley.

"Would you mind coming back to my room?" He said anxiously, eyeing the other guests at the same time.

"No problem at all," Kelly said. They followed the manager back to his office, which was just as stunning. The room was designed with a minimalist aesthetic of clean lines and sleek furnishings. Large windows allowed natural light to flood the space, offering breathtaking views of the Potomac River.

"Now what seems to be the issue agents?" He said, sitting them down on two plush chairs.

"We suspect that someone may be planning a hit on a major public figure today at the Future Crime Convention," Chase said plainly, without mollifying or adorning the bare facts.

The manager's mouth hung open like a round door. "A hit? You mean—an—"

"—Assassination, yes," Chase completed the sentence for him. There was no time to lose easing him into it.

"But the convention of which you speak is taking place over at GW University," he said, his voice now pleading. Denial mode.

"Right," Kelly said, "but here's the thing Mr. Bradley, a powerful enough rifle could clear the distance between here and the university."

"No, that's not—" Mr. Bradley said. "Do you have any idea how far away we are from there? Why it's almost a mile away."

"Mr. Bradley," Chase cut in, "the effective range of a sniper rifle is over a mile."

"Okay, okay, sure but—" the manager wiped the sweat from his brow with his pocket-handkerchief. "Surely only the top shooters can pull off a 'hit' as you call it from that distance."

"We have reason to believe our suspect is capable of hitting a target from that distance," Kelly said. "Especially given that this area is mostly low-rise buildings, and the Watergate here has a clean line of sight all the way to the university."

"I suppose that's true—on the higher floors. But—I just don't. I mean the very idea is *inconceivable*."

"We need to conceive of it," Chase said. "And fast. We're working on a slim time schedule here."

"Very well. I will hand over the records of anyone on the higher floors to the FBI. However—I do trust that this operation will be kept low-key. The last thing I need is to get wrapped up in some kind of scandal."

"You have our word, Mr. Bradley," Kelly said. "In fact, we absolutely have to keep things on the down low."

"Very well. Then, if that will be all—"

"Actually," Chase said, "no it won't be."

"What else is it you need?" The manager asked, his face glistening like a glazed donut now.

"There's a possibility the suspect broke into one of the rooms. I'm afraid, Mr. Bradley, you're going to have to check each room manually and make sure no one is in them."

"Oh goodness. That could take hours."

"Then I suggest you start right away," Chase said. "Because the conference talks start at two P.M.—which gives you less than two hours."

"And will you two be staying here to keep guard?"

"No, we'll get the local PD up here. As for us, we have bigger fish to fry."

"Where would you be going if you believe a sniper is on the loose?"

"Mr. Bradley," Kelly said, "we have to go protect the target."

Chapter 32

The convention arena bustled with activity as big egos and big mouths announced their small opinions from small platforms. Political grandstanders and soapboxes, demagogues, blowhards, marketers, and sharks. Their auras suffocated, each one trying to project his or her presence to the full boundary of the room. Practically a biohazard. Their wet grainy voices rubbed on Chase like sandpaper, and even though she didn't stop to listen to what anyone was saying, she knew for sure it was all lies, narratives, and bragging dressed up as humility or ethical concern. As if any of these piranhas cared about their people; if the price was right any one of them would sell out their own grandmother.

Be that as it may, it was still Chase's duty to protect and serve. And as much as it made her skin crawl to think of helping Senator Creg out of yet another sticky situation, those were the facts of the matter. She waded through the room like it was quicksand, slowly pulling her into the sludge. The loud chatter and commotion from the attendees made it difficult to concentrate. Creg wasn't at the scheduled meeting point and his absence was starting to be noticed by a number of aides, who bustled around with worn, sleep-deprived looks hanging from their faces. Chase and Kelly scanned the crowd, looking hopelessly for signs of the

Senator. Getting on the radio, Kelly put out a search among the security staff. But he was just gone.

With each passing moment, Chase's anxiety grew. Could it be she'd made the wrong call in scoping out the hotel first? What if Acre had been right here in this very hall, just waiting for a chance to take the target? They started searching the hall systematically, starting from the doors on the East side and working their way across. But even if Acre had been here—who gets away with kidnapping a US senator? There was no way just one man could break through security and slip away undetected.

Not if he was one man. But what if he was working with the C...?

"Agent Chase," Kelly said for the fifteenth time.

"What is it, Kelly?"

"I think I may have something. This woman says she saw Senator Creg five minutes ago." Chase turned on her heel and accosted the woman with dark long hair in a royal blue suit whose diminutive height was bolstered by ten-inch heels. "You saw the Senator?" Chase said. "Where?"

"Up on the third floor."

"The third floor, that's—what's up there?"

She just shrugged. "All of the convention apparatus is here on the ground floor, as far as I know."

Chase gave a warning look to Kelly then turned and went for the elevator, hearing Kelly quickly following behind. The pair ascended to the third floor and pulled their weapons before the doors opened—then quietly and quickly slipped out and checked the lobby. So far it was empty. The fresh smell of cleaned carpets and the empty silence of a vacated office. "Kelly, do you hear that?"

He stopped and listened. A low conversation filtered in from the Northwest side. "Yeah, I hear it." They kept low and against the wall, quickly clearing the hallway and into the open-plan office beyond. The ceiling lights were off but the window light spilled into the room in large pale circles on the carpet. Over by the corner wall, there was Creg, pacing back and forth and talking into his phone rapidly. He wasn't iced yet, thankfully—but what the hell was he doing up here?

"Senator," Chase called out. He didn't turn, just kept talking on his phone.

"Senator Creg," she called again. He stopped and turned, annoyed at the interruption.

"Yes?"

"I'm FBI Special Agent Chase and this is Special Agent Kelly. We believe your life may be in danger."

"Special Agent Chase..." Creg said. "Don't I know you?"

Damn it. She was hoping he wouldn't remember.

"Yes, we have had occasion to uh—work together once—some time ago."

"I see." He still seemed to be trying to recollect. "You're from the New York office?"

"Yes. Look, Mr. Senator, we need to get you out of here immediately."

"What's going on exactly?"

"Hasn't ASAC briefed you already? We believe you may be being targeted."

"Yes, yes, we had that conversation, but I told him there was nothing to worry about. This place is very secure. Has to be, on account of all the high-profile figures present. And anyway, who would try to target me? And why?"

"By the C," Kelly said, a grave look on his face.

"The—" Creg's annoyed but superior mask momentarily dropped to reveal a scared human being behind it. "Alright. Fine. Where do you suspect they'll attack from?"

"Mr. Senator," Chase said, "we believe we're looking at a sniper situation."

He went cold and looked back at the windows he'd been parading in front of for the last ten minutes. "Jesus," he whispered. "Then tell me how you're going to get me out of here."

Kelly got on his radio and called it in. "The team is on standby, Mr. Senator. All we need to do is get you to the basement garage and we're home free."

"Then what are we waiting for? Get me the hell out of here!"

They descended to the basement where they heard a loud commotion echoing from the distance. The sound of arguing was followed by a muffled gunshot.

"Get back," Chase said, pulling the Senator flat to the wall and drawing her P228 as a group of armed men wearing masks drove up in a black SUV, heading straight towards them.

"So much for the lone gunman theory," Kelly growled, pulling his own Glock 19. "FREEZE!" He shouted at them. "FBI!"

The SUV didn't stop. Both Kelly and Chase opened fire on the SUV, giving the Senator time to take cover behind a nearby pillar. The gunmen let open a hot volley of fire from Steyr AUG assault rifles. Chase aimed for the front tire and popped it, sending the SUV careening in another direction and momentarily blocking the gunmen from firing.

"Go go go!" She yelled, providing cover fire for Kelly while he pulled Creg along to make his way towards their car. The gunfire had taken out several of the overhead fluorescent bulbs and the remaining ones blinked in the dimly lit area. The tires of the SUV squealed to a halt and doors were opening. Chase continued to provide fire until her mag was empty then came up behind Kelly as he struggled to locate their rent-a-car in the panic. "Move faster!" The attackers were gaining ground, positioning themselves behind several of the concrete pillars. They approached the car and were about to pile in when an Mk-2 grenade landed on its hood.

"GET DOWN!" A cloud of fire engulfed the area, spreading up and out across the ceiling. Their car crumpled, its glass shattered and its tires popped.

"Crud, we're stranded!" Kelly called, taking potshots at the armed men behind them.

Chase radioed in for backup as the assailants closed in one by one. "Backup's not coming in time," she said, doing a sweep of their surroundings and being drawn to a white security van several cars behind them. "We're on our own."

"What's the plan?" Kelly asked, keeping the whimpering Senator's head down as the assailants continued to fire on them.

"The plan is—cover me."

Kelly started shooting off his Glock as Chase kept down and snaked between the cars to reach the van. She pulled the door, which was locked, then smashed the window in with the butt of her gun. Climbing in the driver's seat she flipped open the sun visor and sure enough, the keys fell out. She started the van and launched it backward as more fire rained down on its toughened shell, pulling out of the parking space and reversing as far as Kelly. Meanwhile, Chase rolled down the window and started firing off her P228 as Kelly ducked and ran with the Senator into the other side of the cab.

The assailants opened full fire on them now but the armored shell of the van staved off the attack. Chase punched the accelerator and the van kicked forward, leaving the assailants in the dust as they burst out of the toll barrier and up onto the ramp toward the road.

Just as they were halfway up the ramp, the van shook and the sound of punctured metal rang out from the front of the van. A plume of smoke rose off the hood.

"What the hell was that?" Kelly said. "Were we shot? I thought this thing was armored?"

"It is armored," Chase said grimly, fearing that her worst suspicion was coming true. "Damn it, we've been used."

"Used?" Kelly said. "What the hell are you talking about?"

"This is what Acre wanted all along. He was never going to aim through the windows—it's too difficult a shot. He sent in the gunmen to draw us out into the open."

"But Chase, that's—" BANG. Kelly's protests were cut short as the front tire went out and the van sank onto its rim on the left side.

The reasons didn't matter now. And it didn't matter who it was or how they'd pulled it off. Only one fact was important to this situation: That there was someone out there with a high-powered rifle aimed right at them, and that behind them in the garage was a team of gunmen carrying assault rifles.

They were sitting ducks.

All of the nuances, the vagueness, the suspicion, and doubt of the case faded in the crack of that high-powered sniper rifle as it tore another chunk out of the front of the van. If that really was Henry Acre aiming at them from the Watergate, it nullified everything Chase had been through with him. Their history no longer mattered. If it was really possible to bend someone's mind into committing such a devastating crime in broad daylight, what was the true potential of Bucky's technology? It didn't seem real. There had to be another explanation—after all, Chase herself had borne the full brunt of the same technology. Maybe there was a degree of receptivity involved—maybe Acre was just particularly prone to the mind cooking process. Maybe he had been altered further through his dealing with Sparks and Priest. Maybe anything.

The thoughts flashed through Chase's mind, but only for a second until panic pulsated through her veins again and brought her crashing back to the situation. What they had to deal with now—she and Agent Kelly—was the immediate problem of surviving. Of getting the hell out of there and protecting the Senator.

"Come in, come in," Kelly repeated into the radio. "We are being pinned down by sniper fire in the garage exit ramp coming out of the convention center. Repeat we are being pinned down by sniper fire."

The radio crackled and a voice came in noisily through the speaker.

"We believe the sniper to be located in the Watergate," Kelly replied. "Be advised: Suspect is armed with a high-powered rifle. Do not approach from the East." He put down the radio. "Doesn't make any sense— didn't we tell the owner to check every room?"

"So, maybe he's not at the Watergate," Chase said. "There are other hotels in that direction. It doesn't matter now." Chase drank down the fear and pressed down on the accelerator. The van lurched forward, sparks spitting out on the left side and smoke billowing from the hood.

"Chase?" Kelly said. "We have no tire."

"Big deal," Chase said, stamping down on the accelerator further, moving the van squealing out of its position and lurching forward. Almost immediately another crack echoed in the sky and the van's reinforced windscreen burst open, raining down glistening chunks of glass over Chase in the front seat.

"Chase!" Kelly yelled.

"Shut up and get down!"

Kelly pushed the Senator down as the van jerked over the speed bump and continued up the ramp—Chase revved the engine until they were almost at the top of the road.

BAM. Another shell hit the van in the front grill. That was when Chase realized Acre wasn't trying to kill them. He was trying to take the van out of commission. Maybe part of Acre was still there after all. At this point, with the windshield down, it would surely be easier to take out Chase and then give the order to the assault team to finish the Senator. It's not like he didn't have the accuracy. But if he really was pulling punches, that conflict was going to get Acre killed. A sniper had to be hardened, a cold-blooded killer—had to be a pure weapon. Had to do away with all other thoughts, feelings, and responsibilities. Had to sacrifice part of himself inside every bullet or else it wouldn't hit. Especially not from a mile away. Especially not in a city full of armed feds.

But Chase couldn't afford to empathize with him now—she needed to survive. And that last shot hadn't completely wrecked the engine. Stamping the accelerator again, the van lurched over the top of the ramp and finally onto G Street. She held the accelerator down and the van droned forward, the wheels sending up sparks from the asphalt and the radiator sending up thick hot steam into the cab.

The sniper took one more crack at the van, which punctured the roof but only went straight through the floor and out the bottom, uselessly rolling out as the van turned South and took cover behind taller buildings.

They were free from threat for now—but Acre was still out there and so were other assailants. This was far from over.

Getting out of the van, Chase kept down and together with Agent Kelly led the Senator out just as an unmarked black Taurus with tinted windows came up behind them and screeched to a halt to an orchestra of car horns as other drivers navigated around him. Chase leveled her P228 on the car, which rolled down its windows to reveal a familiar face.

"Are you getting in?" Bob said, his smile creasing up his face. "Or are we gonna wait around here all day?"

Chase took shotgun and Kelly led the Senator into the back, putting a blanket over him to hide his face before Bob pulled out onto the road again heading East.

"Uh, Bob—" Kelly said. "You know you're headed right for the sniper in this direction."

"Don't worry, we'll be in the cover of buildings around this corner. We're in the clear now."

"I wouldn't go that far," Chase said, picking up the radio. "HQ, this is Agent Chase calling from Agent Fairfax's vehicle. What's the situation on the Watergate?"

"Agent Chase, standby... We just got confirmation now. Target was not apprehended. Repeat. Target not apprehended. Hotel was clear. Be advised: Agent Fairfax is to escort the Senator to safety at the earliest opportunity. We have arranged a pickup for the Senator at the helipad in Georgetown. Head North and you will be joined by an escort."

"Copy that. Chase out."

Bob wrenched the car onto Twenty-second Street and headed north past the George Washington statue and into the embassy district. Two dark Chevys pulled up alongside them and rolled down their windows to reveal buzz-cut-and-suit agents who signaled Bob to continue on. Together, the convoy headed east on the Whitehurst Freeway headed for Georgetown, the sun blazing down on the raised concrete bridge, the tops of trees and buildings whizzing by. Chase was just thinking how it had been too easy when an SUV pulled up beside them. She immediately pulled her weapon. This was no regular driver—up here on the Freeway, only a few cars were in their immediate vicinity. With two miles to go to the helipad, it would be difficult to try and outpace the SUV, a roaring Jeep Grand Cherokee with a V8 engine that showed no signs of falling back.

"It's him," Chase growled, locking her weapon.

"Crud," Bob said. "Are you sure?"

"I can feel it."

"Oh my God," Senator Creg whimpered. "Why are they doing this?"

On the radio, the escort came in. "Chase, this is Stevens. We'll hold the aggressor back. You are to continue East no matter what."

"Copy."

Stevens' Chevy pulled forward and got ahead of the jeep then pulled into its lane, and slowed his pace as the second escort pulled up alongside the jeep to prevent it from switching lanes. Behind all of this, Bob gripped the wheel at ten and two and held his pace, watching intensely as the FBI's pincer forced the jeep to slow down; soon the jeep seemingly had enough of this game and revved forward, slamming into the back of Stevens and sending him squealing left and then quickly right away from the median barrier. The jeep's window rolled down and before the second escort could pull away, a low crack coincided with the second escort's driver-side window splintering. Another thump and the window splintered further. The car pulled quickly back until it was level with Bob, then its driver came over the radio. "Bob, this is Rogers. Pull back."

Bob did so, putting distance between themselves and the jeep and two Chevys. Then Rogers' window came down and an M&P semi-auto peeped out and started shooting at the jeep. Sparks flew as the jeep's rear light went out—the rear window cracked but didn't break. Realizing the vehicle had been reinforced, Rogers changed tack, pulling forward again and aiming closer for the tires. But the jeep wasn't about to rest on its laurels—firing another crack that Chase now recognized as the sound of a Desert Eagle, that hit Rogers' car in the front left tire and had him throwing sparks as he struggled to keep his car from swerving against the railing; then he pulled back in retreat, beaten at his own game.

That just left Bob and Stevens against this suspect who seemingly had no problem fending off multiple trained professionals in vehicular combat, going eighty-five on a narrow two-lane freeway. Was this really Acre? He hadn't shown any such abilities before—but then again, when she had worked with him they never got into such a situation. And Acre was a hotshot at the NYPD. Either way, she'd soon find out—the jeep lowered its speed and began closing the distance back toward them, while Stevens desperately pulled back from the front. Both of them closed in now, the jeep in the left lane, Stevens on the right. Chase gripped her P228 Custom, rolled down her window, and leaned out.

"Chase—" Bob said, but too late. She was in fight or flight mode now. And she wasn't about to go down without a fight. Aiming carefully for the jeep's rear tire she took the shot—the bullet sprang off the hubcap, loosening the cap and making it bounce off down the road and the growing traffic that had slowed behind them. The jeep shot out its own rear window and hit their windscreen—a spiderweb spread across the top. Bob peered into his rearview and slowed more, but the traffic behind them was forming a wall of metal and blasting horns.

They were coming to the end of the waterfront and about to reach Francis Scott Bridge. After that the traffic would get tighter—there'd be no room to maneuver, nowhere to run. They had to finish this now.

"Chase..." Bob said.

"I know."

Chase got on the radio. "Stevens, we have to take him now. There's no time left."

"Copy that. I'll come in from this side."

Chase steadied herself with a few deep breaths then leaned out the window again as Bob pulled up the right lane and Stevens came down the left in front of the jeep, wedging it into another pincer attack. Chase aimed for the wheels and let off three solid shots as Stevens also shot out its windscreen from in front. Ducking back inside away from the jeep's fire, Chase observed the vehicle shakily trying to keep itself on the road, its right rear tire splaying outwards.

"I think we got him," she said.

"Nicely done," Bob said. "Okay, time to book it." He floored the accelerator and his new Taurus growled as it tore up the road: Eighty-five, eight-six, eighty-seven miles per hour and passed the jeep which was too busy trying to stay on the road to fire more than one or two last potshots at them. Leaving the jeep behind, Bob smoothly drove onto the nearest exit and headed on their way toward the heliport. Ditching Stevens with the aggressor left a sour taste in Chase's mouth, but she'd have to hope Stevens would do the rest. They had their own mission—although stealing a look at the whimpering Senator, a man whom she'd saved from scandal before—she didn't really feel much enthused about it.

Chapter 33

They reached the heliport safely. Bob got on the chopper with the Senator as they prepared to take off.

"You sure you're not coming, Chase?"

"Bob, I have to finish this one way or another. This is my case. And we haven't heard from either Stevens or Rogers. We have to assume the worst."

"But how are you even going to track the suspect down? Wouldn't it be better to regroup and—"

"I know what you're going to say, Bob. But here's the thing. SET, as powerful as it may be, still lacks one crucial element."

"What's that?"

"It doesn't understand dirt, Bob. It may gather data, sure, snatch anything that's out there not hammered down. But it will never understand *why* people do the things they do. It can't logically infer the next move of someone who spent all his life protecting the law, who has now been forced to abandon it all. That kind of psychology leaves your algorithms in the dust."

"Alright Chase," Bob said, his face creasing up in his trademark fashion. "I didn't expect you to give up this easily anyway."

"I'm staying too Bob," Kelly said, staring off into the distance of D.C. "There's a threat out there and we have no clue what he'll try next. If he can take on three FBI agents at once then he's capable of anything."

"Then I'll wish you two good luck. And guys—"

Chase and Kelly both watched as the chopper started to hover and take off.

"Try to stay alive."

...

They were heading back into the center of D.C. without data, without information, without a plan or a prayer. But that didn't feel so hopeless to Chase. In fact, it felt the complete opposite: Without the distraction of logical analyses and statistical probabilities, automatic profiles, and collated facts, the only thing left to go on was her raw burning intuition. She could see through the fog now. She could feel what Acre felt—she saw it in his eyes. That gnawing, wrenching conflict that had been building inside him, maybe all along, maybe even before the C—and which had only finally been brought to the fore due to the circumstances he'd fallen into.

She didn't know for sure what had triggered it. How much of this was what he wanted and how much was the C? But she did know one thing—she owed it to

Acre to stop him. Before he did something that he would come to regret.

It's not like she thought law enforcement was perfect. In fact, Chase herself spent every day butting heads with its ridiculous configuration. But even so, the alternative of total lawlessness—of even potential civil war—was not something she could realistically sanction.

Where would Acre go after failing the hit twice? The natural inclination would be to escape from D.C. as soon as possible. But would he? She had to put herself in his shoes, see the world through his eyes. She first had Kelly drive over Whitehurst again until they got to the part of the road where they'd faced off against one another. Both cars were gone. "What now, Chase?"

"Just keep driving to the end of the road."

"Okay..."

She got on the radio, but Stevens had apparently lost the target. Chase wasn't surprised. They came down onto M Street again. Low-rise red brick structures lined the road on one side, trees sprouting their first leaves on the other.

"Slow down," Chase told him.

"What are we looking for?" Kelly said,

"Exactly what we wouldn't look for," Chase said.

"Er... What? I don't follow."

"Think about it, Kelly. Put yourself in a killer's shoes. Not Acre, but a random killer in D.C. on the run."

"Okay. I'm a random killer in D.C. on the run."

"Now where's the last place you'd go?"

"The last place? Hmm... A police station?"

"No. Going to a police station might be surprisingly safe. You think homicide cops hang around in the lobby tending to random complaints?"

"Okay, you have a point. So, not the police station... Gee, this is tough, Chase."

"You were taught this in Quantico, weren't you?"

"Sure but—for very conventional criminals. Acre isn't—ah. You said to not do it for Acre."

"Right. Be more general."

"Well let's see... Where would be the last place I'd turn up? Someplace with high security maybe, somewhere I'd likely run into a fed."

"Go on," Chase said.

"And someplace that—hold on a second, before we continue, you sure I should keep driving this way? We're on Penn Avenue already."

"I know."

"But Chase, at this rate we're gonna hit the—" Kelly's face went stone cold and his mouth dropped open. "Holy crap—"

"It's the last place we'd think to look for him, right?"

Kelly turned to her, visibly shaken. "Chase—you think that he went to *the White House?!*"

"If I was Acre, that's where I'd go."

"That's insane. The whole place has cameras up the wazoo. He wouldn't last ten seconds."

"He would if he didn't show up on camera."

"I don't understand."

"Acre knows all about SET. He also knows—or thinks—we'd use it to track him. But if you know the cameras are watching, there's any number of ways to avoid them."

"You mean like those light flashing goggles that are imperceptible to people, but it makes you not show up on camera, right?"

"That or just a mask and glasses. Anything that makes the SET no longer recognize him."

"SET would recognize his car, though. We have his plates and everything."

"Obviously he wouldn't have gone in the same car."

"You think he had a backup car?"

"Maybe he had a backup car, maybe he used an Uber account linked to a fake identity. Maybe he rode the bus with a mask on. Point is—if you know you're being surveilled, it's possible to slip out of the net, at least temporarily. If you're good."

"Okay, so the White House. Where in the White House?"

"I was hoping that if we got near something would come to me."

"And has it?"

"You know what? I believe it has. Turn left onto Connecticut."

Kelly made the turn just off Lafayette Park, his face still stricken with incredulity. He was, after all, only experiencing Chase's intuition up close for the first time. It was natural that he'd be skeptical. But that look of skepticism soon vanished and was replaced by one of disturbance when he drove forward a little and saw the sign of a tall building of brown brick and dull brown opaque windows—a parking garage. It was not just any parking garage. The sign in front read: C Parking, Inc.

"Chase, you're kidding, right? There's no way..."

"I'm not kidding," Chase said, her tone dead serious. "And there is a way. Because it's just so ridiculous it has to be true. Because it's Acre, and Acre knows that cops hate the obvious. That they'd do anything to avoid the obvious, construct unwieldy and ungrounded schemes of elaborate proportion, and fill their mind with all kinds of convoluted conspiracies rather than just look at what's right there in front of them. He's in there, Kelly, behind those brown windows somewhere. I know he is. And it's time for us to go up there and drag him out. This time—in cuffs."

"If you say so, Chase. But—"

Kelly's words fell on dead air. Chase had already gone into the zone. She was feeding her extra magazines with .357 SIG shells—and at that moment, nothing else existed in the world between her and her target.

Chapter 34

The parking garage was a concrete tower with each level given over to an array of parking spots, and the next level up was reached by a ramp at the South end of the building. Proceeding with caution, Kelly crawled through the first level as they checked all corners for signs of the suspect. They moved slowly, Chase with her P228 drawn and ready. The dimly lit maze of parked cars was rife with potential danger lurking around every corner and Kelly suggested they phone HQ for SET data on the security cams. But Chase declined. She had been down that road before and knew that places like these were riddled with blind spots. If Acre had chosen this place it would have been premeditated—a contingency plan. He would have full knowledge of all of its secrets. No, it was better not to get distracted. To keep entirely present and be ready to react to danger as it came. Marking the first level clear with some disappointment, Chase instructed Kelly to take them up to the second level.

"If he is here," Kelly said, his eyes darting about the dimly lit structure, each shadow and object a potential threat, "it's likely he'll be on one of the higher levels, right?"

"Not necessarily," Chase said. "It gives him a better vantage point but it's a double-edged sword—makes his getaway a lot harder."

"Shit. Then we really are sitting ducks in this jalopy unless we get lucky and see him first."

"Bob's not gonna like you talking about his brand new vehicle that way."

"Of course. *The Ford Taurus's V6 delivers up to 288 horsepower*," Kelly said, mimicking Bob's voice. "Twenty-five miles to the gallon. Perfect for a man paying three alimonies. More than adequate for investigation and pursuit—unless the suspect is a highly trained terrorist driving a V8."

"Eyes on the prize, Kelly."

"What is it, you catch something?"

"Just a feeling. Take the next ramp up." Chase licked her lips, anticipating what was to come next. She gripped the gun in her hands, feeling its reliable weight. The sound of something echoed off the concrete above. Kelly looked all around. "Did you see anything, Chase?"

"No, keep going."

"Are you sure?"

"Just don't stop. Move to the last pillar and turn."

"A U-turn will kill us, Chase."

"Then don't take a U-turn."

"I don't understand."

Chase stamped on Kelly's foot and made him accelerate past the area where they'd heard the echo.

"Jesus, Chase what are you—" He stopped when in the rearview he caught a flash of red laser blinking out from the dark.

"Kelly, GET DOWN!"

The rear window blew open and the car screeched sideways into the next pillar, with Kelly falling over the wheel.

"Agent Kelly—Kelly!" Chase struggled to pull him off the wheel, but when she did his body just flopped back lifeless against the seat, his eyes still open and a hole in the center of his head dripping black.

"No... NO." A chill swept up Chase from toe to head. Up to this point, she'd somehow been indulging in the delusion that Acre wouldn't hurt them. That this was all some kind of pretense or show. Another media crime. But now she realized how careless she'd been by harboring that wish.

By letting her personal bias get in the way of reason, she'd allowed her partner to die. All of his promises and potential snuffed out in an instant. Here joking with her one minute and gone the next. She would never be able to forgive herself for that. But right now she had to put it out of her mind. She had to get a grip. She let the pain fuel her. Let the burning inside give her courage. Another shot blew through the car, tearing through the space between the two front seats and this time blowing the front windscreen out. Chase immediately returned fire in the direction of the shot, letting off three shots at the darkness. But the red laser dot had vanished and all three of her shots uselessly ricocheted off the far wall, echoing all the way down.

She heard the suspect running. That meant his car was on the lower level. Chase heaved the door open and steadied the rage and fear inside, letting it swirl through her limbs without crippling her. This wasn't the first life-or-death situation she'd been in. She wouldn't allow it to be the last. She wouldn't let Kelly's death be in vain.

Taking Kelly's M&P in one hand and her P228 in the other, Chase disembarked from the stationary Taurus and sprinted to the next pillar over, shooting into the darkness to cover her movement. She ducked behind the pillar as a deafening boom shook the complex and a giant hole opened up into the concrete wall across from her. Was he seriously using an anti-materiel rifle against her in a close-quarters battle? The thing had to weigh 30 pounds and the recoil alone would break your arm if you weren't holding it right. What the hell was he thinking?

"ACRE!" Chase yelled out from her position. "Stop it! What do you hope to achieve from this?"

When the voice of the suspect came back, it shattered any final illusions Chase had been latently carrying.

"It has to be done," Acre bellowed back, his voice hard and flat and without effect. A killer's voice. "You're in the way." Chase's heart sank. Up until this moment, she had been wishing it to be someone else—and the fact she had made her feel deep shame.

"Then this has to end here," Chase called.

"Don't worry Chase, it will."

"Acre, tell me this one thing. When did you switch sides?"

Her question was met by another deafening boom that shattered the front face of the pillar she was sitting behind. As the shockwave passed through her body, she almost felt like her soul had fallen out, that she no longer had control over her limbs but could only wait and watch as nature played its way out in the manner which had been destined from the beginning. There would be no convincing Acre to turn himself in—that alone she was now sure about.

Acre called out from his cover, a haunting voice that echoed throughout the garage: "You can see the fire that breathes, Chase. But to *be* the fire, you have to believe."

A static sphere of crackling light seemed to fold out from inside her chest, illuminating the space of the room. The breadth of the whole universe got compressed into that 400 square yards, and everything outside of that area ceased to exist. As for everything inside the third floor of the C Parking complex—it made itself known to Chase like it was part of her: Its exterior, its interior, its every fold, and crack. Every crumbling fragment of concrete in freefall and every grain of dust that had spilled from the wounds in the wall. She saw it all in the blink of an eye—and, breathing calmly and consciously, Chase picked herself up off the ground and saw the enemy before her. Henry Acre, former NYPD Lieutenant. Triple homicide suspect—maybe quintuple if Stevens and Rogers didn't make it. And certainly more than that if she let him get away.

She wouldn't. Gripping both semi-auto guns akimbo, Chase rolled out from her position and fired four shots a piece into the corner where she knew Acre was hidden, rolled back just as Acre fired back rapidly with an automatic Beretta 93R.

"Out of rifle ammo, Henry?" Chase shouted. Acre didn't reply. She heard him replacing the magazine of his Beretta. She fired another volley of shots at where Acre was crouched, but this time didn't roll back, instead made her way up two parking spots to the next pillar. By the time Acre had sprung out of his hiding place, Chase had ducked down behind the new pillar, which Acre was now spraying with automatic fire hoping to get lucky.

Tactically, it was the best he could do. He had been relying on brute force over accuracy, and now that he was out of rifle ammo Chase had the advantage. Why? Because the FBI had drilled these kinds of scenarios into her until her feet and hands bled. But Acre, being of the NYPD, had trained for different scenarios—mostly involving how to avoid hitting hostages or on precision assaults against criminal dens. Here Acre wasn't the assaulting party, he was the criminal being raided. Thus, his training didn't prepare him for it. He had blind spots, weaknesses. And Chase would finger every one of them.

She waited for the Beretta to crap out and rolled to the side—Acre blew another two shots at her, this time with his semi-auto Beretta Inox. One slug hit her in the shoulder and she cried out as she slipped back into cover. Crap. She should have seen that coming. But the wound wasn't deep and it wouldn't stop her—she flipped around again and went into another volley of fire from her P228 and M&P, the adrenaline shielding her pain, her guns thundering inside the sound-resonating garage. Acre ducked down, cursing, and Chase heard the clicking of his fully auto Beretta again as he reloaded. This time he wouldn't make it in time. Chase sprinted to his position, vaulting the hood of the Subaru between them and firing without mercy down into Acre's trench. She heard him cry out and when she landed down in the space with him he was on the floor, two slugs in him, and coughing up blood on the cold concrete.

"This is your fault, Acre," Chase said. "It's your actions that led you to this end."

"At least they were my own actions," he said and spluttered up more rich dark blood. "I have no regrets."

"Acre, tell me. Tell me why you decided to do all this. You have to tell me!"

He just looked at her mournfully, dark eyes from out of a ghost-white face, the last traces of anything human leaving his body. "You already know, Chase."

"I don't. Tell me. There's no point keeping secrets now. Did the C cook your mind?"

"No one cooked nothin'." He spluttered again, held his chest, and started to wheeze. "I did this. It was my will and mine alone. I just had enough, Chase. I've seen too much pain, too much suffering at the hands of these usurpers running everything. Someone has to stop them—" He spluttered.

"But what the C wants is complete chaos!"

"You can't heal this rotten country without first razing its disease. If the C taught me anything it's that. As long as the same bastards are in charge, nothing anyone does will have an effect. They understand that. Bucky understood that. And someday, Chase, you'll understand it too. When that time comes you'll—cough——you'll forgive me for what I've done."

"That's bullshit! I don't believe you. They must have done something to your mind! Sparks, or Priest!"

Acre spoke in a throaty wheeze now, air barely escaping the thick stream of blood leaking from his mouth. "That's just it Chase—you believe that a man can't act unless he's being controlled by someone else. And as long as you think that way, you're always going to be—cough—cough—under someone's—thumb." His eyes closed gently, and that face that had been wrenched in pain relaxed into a look of ecstasy so pure and so free that it was hard for Chase not to feel envious.

She got out her phone and dialed the Bureau. "ASAC Hogan? This is Chase. I got Acre... Yes, sir, it's over."

Chapter 35

And that was that. As expected, the entire case was swept under the rug.

Henry Acre didn't even get a funeral, as every official involved believed it much better to not publicize events in light of their sensitivity. Instead, he was given an unmarked grave at a police graveyard. Chase didn't get to see him again. It left a new emptiness inside her and she didn't know if it would ever fade. It was seldom that she connected with anyone over the course of her work, and since she had no personal life that was the only place she could connect to someone. But for the brief time they had worked together, Chase had seen eye to eye with him. At least she thought she had. Even right at the end when it seemed they were mortal enemies, she still felt like they shared something in common that no one else could understand. But now it was too late—and now he was gone.

Special Agent Ray Kelly did get a funeral, and all the FBI brass showed up to honor his sacrifice, even the elusive New York SAC, ASAC Hogan's boss Dalton Manning. It was raining hard that day and black suits huddled under a blacker sky, umbrellas raised as the last words were given to a man taken in his prime. Chase stood there on the lawn by Bob Fairfax and watched as their partner was lowered into the ground.

Had it been worth it?

The Future Crime Convention had gone on as planned, laying out new dictates for what improvements law enforcement should take in order to tackle the ever-advancing sophistication of crime all over the country. Senator Creg even managed to give a speech on data-based crime fighting over satellite feed from the safety of the FBI Headquarters.

Then there was the matter of the stolen documents. Even after searching through Acre's recent activities via the SET, they still couldn't seem to find where he'd stashed them. They got a warrant for Leigh Gaines' place and turned it upside down, and found nothing there either.

So a hole remained not only in Chase's heart but also in her mind. And even if they did find more facts about this case it would probably never fill that hole. Too much had been lost, and it was hard to see what they'd gained in return. Sure they'd saved Senator Creg, but if the C wanted to target him, couldn't they take him out whenever they wanted? The more Chase dwelled on it—and she dwelled on it a lot those days following—the more it seemed like killing Creg was never the point.

It was always about causing a scandal. It was always about the media. And it was always about throwing a wrench into the works. It was impossible to say who Acre had been working for—if his killing of Sparks and Priest had been ordered from elsewhere or it was just Acre's own brand of street justice. Either version of events seemed equally possible, even by SET's calculations. The brainwashed cult of Ellis Island continued to clam up and eventually, the whole thing was dropped.

It was like nothing had ever happened at all.

"I can't just let this go, Bob," Chase said to him, their heads still bowed at the plot of dirt.

"You have to Chase. They're going to bury this case along with Kelly."

"That's exactly why I can't."

"You can't go up against the Bureau, Chase, you know that."

"With the C on the loose, they can't just close the whole case."

"Hogan is already intimating that they're planning on just that."

"So, what? We're just meant to forget any of this happened?"

"There's nothing more to go on. Unless the C moves again, that's that. It will be all tied up with Acre just like how they tied it up with Bucky."

"That's exactly the point, Bookman. Tying it up will achieve nothing but a false sense of security."

"Do you have an alternative?" Bob said, looking worriedly at her. He had been close with Kelly and was surely reluctant at losing another friend.

But Chase didn't have time for friendship. And she wasn't going to be talked out of this.

"Senator Creg," she whispered. "That's where this all leads back."

"What about him?"

"I don't know—but something tells me he is the epicenter of all this."

"Your intuition, Chase?"

"My intuition."

Chapter 36

The case on the C hadn't been officially closed yet. Chase figured she had maybe forty-eight hours, maybe less before the ax fell. She used that time to her advantage. Using SET, she tracked down the room where Senator Creg was staying. It was in the Marriott by Times Square, the smug bastard probably feeling free as a bird now that Acre was dead.

Chase slipped into the hotel just as evening was turning to night, and flashed her badge at a wary receptionist.

"I need access to the twentieth floor," Chase said, not specifying anything further. The last thing she needed was to telegraph her presence and end up getting hauled out by Senator Creg's security.

"Uhm—I'm not sure if—"

"It's urgent," Chase said. "If you need confirmation, contact the New York Field Office at extension 511." She gave the extension to the Data Analysis Room, knowing Bob would pick up and confirm their "urgent case." The gambit worked—the receptionist called the hotel manager first, then after confirming with Bob, gave Chase a temporary pass that would grant her access to the suites on the twentieth floor.

When she walked into Creg's room, he wasn't there. She scanned the whole joint but found nothing. She then noted the spacious balcony, glass topped and with expensive sofas surrounding a low-hanging table of modern design. He wasn't out there either. She came back inside, and checked the bedroom: No suitcases, the drawers and closets all empty but for several multiples of the same suit hung in the closet.

She called up Bob. "This doesn't make sense. Are you sure this is his room?"

"Already confirmed it when the receptionist called. That's Creg's room alright."

"Alright, thanks." She hung up and did another round of the room.

Then the front door clicked as someone entered, and even before Chase saw who it was, she knew.

"Who are you?" The man said. He was wearing a suit the same dimensions as Senator Creg's suit. Wore the same graying hair in the same expensive cut. Had the same flushed cheeks, the same gray eyes, the same lined forehead, and even the same specks of salt and pepper in his eyebrows. Even his voice had the same tenor as Creg's.

But it wasn't Creg. She knew it immediately. And the fact that he didn't know her only confirmed it.

"I'm Special Agent Chase," she said.

"Oh—uh, oh I see." He coughed, then turned away. "Thank you for coming, Chase. Sorry, I didn't see you without my eyeglasses. My contacts fell out and—"

"Go ahead, ramble on," Chase said. "But there's no need for this bullshit coming out of your mouth."

"I beg your pardon! Just who the hell do you think you are?"

"That's just what I want to ask *you*."

"You know who I am. Senator Carter—"

"See," Chase said. "That's the bullshit I was talking about. Let's cut the crap here. What happened to him?"

"I don't have any idea what—"

"He's dead, isn't he? The C got him and you're covering it up. When did they get him?"

"Please, you will have to leave now. Otherwise, I have no choice but to—"

"Cool it," Chase said. "I don't care that you're a body double. None of this is important to me anymore." She pulled her P228 and pointed it at the impostor. "Because I lost two people close to me and I don't have time for these stupid games. So, tell me now, when the hell did Creg die?"

"Stop—you can't get away with pointing a gun at me!"

"Sure I can," Chase said. "I'll just testify that I caught an impostor trying on the real Creg's clothes. It's well within my duties as an FBI agent."

The not-Creg's forehead creased up and his eyes turned

dark and hollow. "Fine," he said, his voice pattern changing completely. "You want to do things this way, sure. But don't regret what you step into. Sure, I'm taking his place. But you have no way to prove it."

"When did you take over?"

"When do you think? The day of the Future Crime Convention."

"But Creg appeared that day."

"Nope. A video of him did."

"What——?"

"Yeah, that's right. He was a skin job. A simulation. Pretty convincing, right?"

"But how?" Chase's head spun. She felt like sitting down but didn't want to lose her dominance over the situation.

"It was easy. The computer knew more about Creg than Creg did. Matter of fact, we should probably replace all our politicians with software. They'd work harder and it'd save the taxpayer a bunch of dough."

"Then why? What is the meaning of all this?"

The impostor shrugged. "You should know—I read your file. You figured out the C's plot—to cause chaos. You make it so no Senator died. Tada: No crisis."

"Okay, fine, but I prevented Creg's assassination. I

brought him back myself!"

"Not quite, Agent Chase. You brought him back halfway. But what about the other half? How do you know he got back safely from the heliport?"

"My partner was with him, that's how I know!"

"And you believe him?"

"Of course I do. I trust him implicitly!"

"Then maybe you should be more careful about who you trust."

"No—I don't believe this for a second."

The man shrugged. "Believe what you want. Anyway, this conversation is over. You got your answer, now get out of here. Before things get really—messy."

Chase kept the gun trained on the man and inched her way out of the room. The corridor turned around her like the twisting hall of a fairground house as she made her way back to the elevator and down to the street.

The sweet spring air hit her face and the noise of New York enclosed her like a bubble. Faint voices seemed to come on that wind. It was Kelly she was hearing, and it was Acre. And facing the traffic she heard his final words in her mind like a message from the dead:

"You can see the fire that breathes. But to be the fire, you have to believe."

She didn't know what she believed anymore.

But she was still breathing.

And she could still see the fire.

Heather Chase FBI Series:

Made in the USA
Las Vegas, NV
29 January 2025

17196372R00218